# No Longer Yours

*Sara LaFontain*

26 Trees Press, Tucson, Arizona

Copyright © 2018 by Sara LaFontain

All rights reserved. No part of this publication may be reproduced, distributed or transmitted in any form or by any means, without prior written permission.

26 Trees Press
3661 N. Campbell Ave #379
Tucson, Arizona 85719
www.saralafontain.com

Publisher's Note: This is a work of fiction. With the exception of Bowling Green State University and its surroundings, all names, characters, places, and incidents are a product of the author's imagination. Locales and public names are sometimes used for atmospheric purposes. Any resemblance to actual people, living or dead, or to businesses, companies, events, institutions, or locales is completely coincidental.

Book Layout © 2017 BookDesignTemplates.com
Cover Design: Leigh McDonald
Editor: Amanda Slaybaugh

No Longer Yours/ Sara LaFontain -- 1st ed.
ISBN 978-1-7326857-4-1

To Rowan and Willow,
Even though you aren't old enough to read it.
Seriously, put it down now.

# *Chapter One*

*Six months earlier: Parsons, Ohio, February 2014*

Cherry Dryden's dreams are about to come true: she is ovulating. The test confirmed it this morning, giving her a smiley face in the little plastic window. The next forty-eight hours will be the optimum time to finally conceive a baby. What a shame that Gary had to coach his team's early practice this morning, she reflects as she stares at the stick. *We could've gotten started now. I could be pregnant by breakfast.*

She texts Gary before work: *It's a happy face! Baby time!*

He responds: *Girl, Imma knock you up!*

This is exciting, she thinks, as she floats her way through the school day. They've talked about children for so long, and now, finally, it's time. Just two months ago, at Christmas, he gifted her a box of digital ovulation tests.

"Does this mean what I think it does?" she asked, heart in her throat.

"We've been together over thirteen years. That's long enough to be sure, isn't it?" he responded, and that night she threw away her birth control pills.

After having The Talk, the rest of holiday break was full of research as they studied conception methods. She started taking folic acid and hard-to-swallow prenatal vitamins. She choked down fish oil capsules, even though the smell made her gag. She made a chart, took her temperature daily, and began using the ovulation tests, and now, finally, they can move forward with their plans.

This really is the best of all possible times to have a baby. They are in excellent shape financially, they've paid off the last of their student loans (early, too!), they own a comfortable house in a good neighborhood, and depending on when the baby is born, she could maybe take a whole semester off to stay at home with it. They are ready!

Gary sends her messages throughout the day. He has to judge projects at the elementary school science fair, but he'll be home as quickly as he can. He is just as excited as she is. He texts again: *Sex + Wine + Sex + Dessert + Sex?*

*Last alcohol for nine months, I'll get an expensive bottle*, she responds, adding a winky emoji for good measure.

Finally, school lets out, and after taking about an hour to finish grading papers and to stop in the theatre and assist with the drama club's rehearsal, she is ready to head home. There will be time to swing by the store and pick up wine, and something fancy for dinner. Steak? Gary always likes that.

As she walks out to her car, she notices a man leaning on the vehicle parked next to hers. She doesn't know much about cars, but she can identify that one. It's a Jaguar XF, Gary's dream car. He has fantasized about getting one for a long time, but that's way out of their price range. He'll be jealous she saw one at the school. The man looks up, directly at her, and straightens. Oh, darn it. That means he's waiting for her. He must be a parent.

"Cherry Dryden?" he asks as she gets close. Using her first name, that's unusual. She tries to think of whose father he might be. "Cherry, I don't know if you remember me, my name is Tyler Rivera. I'm Megan Rivera's husband."

"Oh, yes, of course. I met you at the holiday party," Cherry replies. She should have recognized him from his television commercials as well—Tyler Rivera, owner of every car dealership in town. No wonder he has a Jaguar. They had chatted briefly while waiting in line at the buffet. She stands a bit awkwardly, balancing her cardigan and a stack of papers in one hand while trying to get her keychain out of her purse with the other.

To be polite, she asks, "How are things going?" The elementary and middle schools share a staff parking lot; he must be waiting for his wife.

"Well, not great. Megan and I are getting a divorce." He seems nervous, shifting from foot to foot and looking at her as if he's anticipating a reaction.

"Oh, I'm so sorry to hear that," she says. She has no idea why he's telling her this. She doesn't know him or his wife very well. Megan teaches second grade, like Gary. She finds her keys and holds them in her hand, ready to go, hoping he hurries up.

"Yes, it's a terrible shame," he says, and she fears he's about to launch into a story. For as long as she can remember, complete strangers have liked to confide in her. Gary complains every time they go shopping because she can't make it out the door without a cashier or fellow shopper

*No Longer Yours*

wanting to share all their problems with her. But she doesn't want to listen to Tyler's tragic tale of divorce, she wants to buy wine and go home and take her shoes off and make love to her husband in a position beneficial to conception. She uses the key fob to unlock her door, hoping that the sound will signal to him that it's time to go.

But Tyler ignores the hint and continues. "The worst part is that Megan has decided to ruin two marriages. I've got some photos here that my attorney is going to use as exhibits in court. They're not pretty. I brought you copies though, because I thought you might want them."

"That's sweet of you to think of me, but we don't cover civics in the sixth grade, so I don't really have a use for legal exhibits." She forces a friendly smile, but this is rapidly becoming awkward. She had talked to him for what, ten minutes, over two months ago? She didn't think they were establishing a friendship, and he knows she's married. Did he think she was flirting before?

She suddenly understands. That's what this is. He's telling her about his divorce because he's going to ask her out. Oh, Gary is going to laugh about this later.

"You're misunderstanding me. These photos aren't appropriate for your classroom." He slips his finger under the flap of the large envelope in his hands.

"Look, Tyler, I'm sorry," she is about to let him down gently, to apologize and politely state that she hadn't meant to lead him on, but then she catches her first glimpse of the photos he is showing her. She drops everything that was in her arms. There is a roaring sound in her ears and her vision starts to blacken. She reaches out to steady herself. Tyler grabs her and stands there uncomfortably for a minute, with one hand supporting her and the other holding a color photo of her husband, her Gary, laying back in a bed naked. It's not an obscene picture though—Megan's head makes sure of that.

## Chapter Two

*Present Day: Ferry's Landing, Minnesota, August 2014*

"Long-term parking," Cherry read the sign out loud. She'd been talking to herself for most of the journey in a desperate attempt to combat the loneliness. When she left her parents' home in Madrid, Ohio yesterday morning, she told herself she was full of hope and optimism as if saying it enough times would make it true. She was starting over and she was doing it on her own. This was a sign of independence. She didn't need Gary, she didn't need anyone. Her new life started now. The mantras all rang hollow.

On the first night of the drive, she stopped in the Wisconsin Dells and stayed in a resort. Some of her former colleagues had told her the vacation town would be a good stopping point, since she 'deserved to have a little fun.' But as she sat in the resort bar sipping an overly sweet cocktail and looking at the children playing in the indoor waterpark, she couldn't help but feel resentful. Happy families everywhere, and she was completely alone. She was supposed to be pregnant by now, she was supposed to be preparing for her own family, and it wasn't fair that her entire planned future had been ripped away. When she finally went back to her room, she laid down on the far-too-empty queen bed and cried.

But she was improving now, right? She'd eaten a big breakfast, and driven the rest of the way, with her music cranked up and singing as loudly and tunelessly as she could. Well, the tuneless part was unintentional. But loud?

Heck yes. Gary always used to tease her about her singing, saying what a shame it was that someone who loved to sing so much had such a flat voice.

"Lucky you, Gary. You don't have to listen to me anymore," she told his invisible presence. And she rolled down her window and sang along to the songs she knew and made up words for the ones she didn't. It made her feel better, or at least chased some of the sadness away.

And now here she was, in the small town of Ferry's Landing, gateway to the Piney Islands. They liked their descriptive names in this part of the country, apparently. As she drove down to the lakefront, she tried to keep an eye out for stores she might need but hadn't spied much that would be of use to her before she reached her destination. The docks were lively, filled with larger crowds than she would have expected, but then she remembered it was still tourist season.

She followed the signs and found her reserved space. "Here I am, C-22," she announced to herself. She pulled in next to a van with *The Inn at Whispering Pines* painted on the side.

"Hello van, I guess we're neighbors now." As soon as the words left her mouth, she felt silly. She'd progressed from talking to herself to talking to inanimate objects; she needed to stop before she embarrassed herself.

There wasn't much to unload from her trunk. Very few things had come out of the marriage with her. She'd made Gary buy out her share of all their furniture and household goods. Better to walk away with a check than to have to sanitize everything Megan's naked body may have touched, and Megan had been everywhere. They had even done it in her home, turning the house she and Gary had bought and

*No Longer Yours*

decorated and loved into a tawdry lover's nest while she was on a girls' weekend in Windsor with Katie. How could Gary betray her so completely? And worse, why did he let her find out such details from the local news?

No, she had wanted nothing from their broken home. She took her clothes, and her personal items, those few things that were untainted in her memories. She ordered brand new sheets and towels, untouched by her husband's lover, and shipped them all directly to her new address, which was a furnished apartment. She wasn't ready to deal with the hassle of trying to buy furniture and decorate and make friends and learn a new town and start a new job and ... she was too overwhelmed for a moment to move. Her future weighed down upon her, heavy and lonely and harsh.

When she was ready, when she managed to breathe again, and clear the tears that threatened to overflow from her eyes, she took her two suitcases and purse and dragged them to the ferry's ticket office. She took a deep breath to prepare herself and got a nose full of the rather unappealing scents of diesel fumes and fish. These were the smells of her home now, she supposed. At least it smelled better than sex and betrayal.

"You look familiar," the woman behind the ticket window said.

"Oh, no, this is my first time here. I just took a job teaching on Whispering Pines Island," Cherry explained.

"Ah, that's why! You've changed your hair. I'm Vivian Ryan, from the village council."

"Yes! I recognize you from my video interview! I'm so excited to be here and start working." She tried to sound much more cheerful than she felt as she put a hand to her head, slightly embarrassed. Her hair was starting to grow back from her spontaneous and misguided attempt at a pixie cut. Gary preferred long hair, so somehow she thought chopping hers off would show him that she was moving on. Unfortunately, short hair did not flatter her face, and she didn't like what she saw when she looked in the mirror. But she wouldn't have liked her reflection anyway, even without the terrible haircut. All she could see when she looked at herself was a broken woman.

"Welcome, we're so glad you took the job. All four of my boys attended that school, and my granddaughter is there now. I help out by teaching a course on island history in the spring. You'll find a lot of us volunteer there, it keeps us busy." Vivian's weathered face cracked into a friendly, open smile. "We were expecting you yesterday. I hope you didn't have any problems on the trip."

The effusive greeting lifted her spirits, at least a little bit. She smiled in relief. "I decided to break the drive into two days. I'm so happy to get here though. I've been looking forward to this for months!" As she said it, she realized the truth in the words. Despite her misgivings, starting over was exciting, and a welcome respite from the gossip and tears back home. No, not home, not anymore.

Vivian handed her a ticket. "First ferry ride is free for you; you'll want to buy a punch card when it's time to make a trip to the mainland. It'll save you some money, especially if you plan to make frequent crossings. Now hang on, I'll call one of my boys over here to get those suitcases."

# Chapter Three

The air was fresher, that's the first thing she noticed once she disembarked from the ferry and got away from the docks. She inhaled deeply, trying to take it all in, and smelled nothing but pine. A shift in the breeze brought the delightful scent of fresh roasted coffee, perhaps wafting from the bakery on the corner. She would definitely investigate that place later.

The road into Whispering Pines Village was paved, which she hadn't expected. When she read that there were no cars on the island, she just assumed the streets would be dirt or gravel. It was busier than she expected too, with bicyclists and a solitary electric cart vying for the right of way amongst all the pedestrians.

"It's probably always like this when the ferry arrives," she said out loud to herself and then looked around to make sure nobody noticed. That was a habit she needed to break.

She had booked an apartment, sight unseen, but it should be easy to find. *Look for the drugstore, it's upstairs*, the email from the landlord said. *Stairs go up the side of the building*. Yes, there it was. *Laska's Drugs, Est. 1971*. All of the buildings on this stretch of road were two stories, with the second story set back creating a wide balcony. That's what sold her on the apartment, the idea of sitting on her balcony sipping her morning coffee and looking out over the small town. She took a step backward for a better view, but something yelped under her foot, and she almost lost her balance.

"Christ, lady, watch where you're going!"

"I'm so sorry!" She had nearly stepped on a small corgi. Its owner knelt down, to smooth its fur and glare at her. He looked out of place here, with his shaggy sun-kissed blond hair and his Hawaiian shirt and cargo shorts. Vacationer from California maybe?

"Be more careful," he snapped. "Lucky for you Tristan moved out of your way."

"It's okay, he's probably just having a bad day. It has nothing to do with you," she told herself, then realized she had spoken out loud.

"Excuse me?"

"Sorry, I'm not mentally ill. I promise. I've just driven two days to get here and had nobody to talk to so I guess I've developed the habit of talking to myself. Don't worry, I'm not some crazy person wandering the streets." She laughed to show that she was joking, and expected him to smile back. After all, small towns were friendly, and she hadn't actually hurt his dog. She reached out to pet the corgi, but the man scooped him up in his arms before she could.

"Well I'm glad to know you aren't mentally ill. Wouldn't want anyone like that walking around, would we?" He stormed off, and she watched him go, chagrined. She hoped her first encounter wasn't a portent of what was to come. At least he was a tourist and not a local, so she didn't embarrass herself in front of anyone she'd have to see again.

She sighed and rolled her suitcases toward the stairs. Home. This was her home now. She swallowed the sudden lump in her throat and began dragging her luggage up the wooden steps.

🌲 🌲 🌲 🌲 🌲

The apartment was cheerful, though it was decorated in a nautical theme, which would not have been her first choice. She supposed she could always take down the fishing net suspended between two large faux shells on the living room wall. The rest of it would do until she gathered enough motivation to change it.

She did a walk through, examining the furniture. Sturdy, likely old, but well-made. The bedroom held a queen bed and one dresser, nothing else. She'd have to buy a nightstand, then. She sat on the bare mattress and sighed. Boxes lined the wall, with her name and new address on them. She'd have to go through and unpack, find her sheets and towels and pillow. Had she ordered a new pillow? She could no longer remember. The frenzied afternoon of online shopping seemed so long ago, a time when she was optimistic about her future, unlike now. Now that she was here, she felt empty and so very tired.

"I can do this." Somehow she managed to startle herself with her own voice, which led to giggles, giving her enough energy to go back out through the living room to check out the kitchen. She needed a drink of water and some ibuprofen to drive away the headache that started pounding at her temples.

In the kitchen, also nautically themed, she found something that instantly made her feel better, a note on the counter:

*Ms. Waites,*

*Welcome to Whispering Pines! We all look forward to meeting you! I hope your trip wasn't too tiring.*

*I took the liberty of stocking your pantry and fridge with a few necessities. Monger's Fish Market sent over some lake whitefish for you. It's in the freezer already filleted, and there are cooking suggestions imprinted on the wrapper.*

*Several businesses contributed to a welcome package. I put it on the kitchen table. There's also a telephone guide of winter residents that will come in handy. If you need anything at all, you can call anyone on that list; we're always happy to help out.*

*When you get yourself settled in, come down the street to The Digs—that's my bar. I'll be the one pouring drinks.*

*Tim Diggins, property manager*

She smiled to herself. That's the small-town life she expected, friendly people, welcoming people, not like that dog-walker outside. She could do this, she could start over and fit in here. She checked the basket on the table, and smiled at all the goodies inside: chocolates from Darling's Chocolatiers (she sampled those first); a bag of coffee from Piney Islands Roasters; and an envelope containing gift certificates and coupons for various restaurants.

Further explorations revealed that, true to his word, her landlord stocked her fridge with basics—milk and butter, some vegetables and cheese, as well as a small cake in a box labeled Margaux's Corner Bakery. The freezer did indeed contain the promised frozen fish with instructions, along with a bonus treat—a small carton of ice cream from Creamation. Lovely.

And since she was an adult, and she was in charge of her own brand new life, she could do whatever she wanted. In this moment, what she wanted did not involve unpacking, no, all she wanted to do was take that ice cream, find a spoon, and head out to the balcony to savor the feeling of being welcome in her new home.

# Chapter Four

Cherry felt strange going to a bar alone. She'd never done it before, but then, she'd never been friendless before either. "This will be fun," she promised herself, and she opened the door.

The Digs matched her expectations of a dive bar, lots of dark wood in the interior, and tables full of chatting people. There were two dart machines and a jukebox, though she couldn't hear music over the sounds of the crowd. Tourist season, she reminded herself, but did so silently in her head so that nobody would think she was crazy.

She found an open bar stool where she could sit and look around. The place was packed, and she wondered how many were locals and how many were tourists, and how to tell the difference.

"Can I get you something, miss?" The bartender approached her. He was a big man, broad shouldered, with scruffy facial hair and a wide mouth that looked like it was meant for smiling and laughing loudly.

"Actually, I think I'm here to meet you. Are you Tim Diggins? I'm Cherry Waites. I'm renting the apartment above the drugstore."

"My new tenant! Are you all settled in?" She was right, his mouth was meant for smiling. "Before you answer, let me get you a drink, on the house, to celebrate your arrival on our island." He turned and selected a couple of bottles and began mixing without waiting for her to order. "Try this. It's a Piney Islands specialty. And by specialty, I mean I invented it last week."

She sipped carefully—she wasn't one for surprises. But it was good, she tasted cherries (how appropriate!) and lime. "Thanks. It's delicious. And thank you so much for your note and everything you left in my apartment."

"No problem at all. I'm happy to welcome you to the community. I tried to anticipate your needs, and obviously every other business owner did too. We're all glad you're here. Rumor has it you're a fantastic teacher, and we're lucky you took the job. I help out with PE and teach a unit on ice skating in the winter. Do you skate?"

Was he flirting with her or just being friendly? She had been out of the dating world for so long, she couldn't tell.

"I don't, yet, but I'd be happy to learn." Trying new things was an important part of starting her life over. Gary had never liked going out in the cold, so there were many winter sports she'd never even thought about attempting. But she didn't have Gary to hold her back anymore—not that she could blame everything on her ex-husband. She'd been too complacent for far too long.

Tim got called away to help another customer, so she sat and sipped her cocktail and wondered what to do next. Maybe she should ask the bartender to identify the locals, so she could start meeting people. She didn't want to admit it, but she was so very lonely. The sudden realization that she was hundreds of miles from anyone who ever cared about her magnified her sense of isolation.

That's when yet another extremely attractive man arrived and sat on the stool next to her. He belonged in a magazine, with his gorgeous dark curls and well-muscled physique. His presence made her nervous—what if he talked to her? Sure, she wanted to meet people, but she wasn't ready to be hit on, and any man who looked like that and came to a bar alone surely intended to leave with someone else. The man set a Tupperware container on the bar and glanced over at her, giving her a friendly nod.

Anyone who brought something like that into a bar must live here, she assumed, since why would a tourist have a plastic container of what appeared to be food scraps? She should probably introduce herself, right? That's what a confident new resident should do. She took another sip of her drink, for courage.

"Hi, I'm Cherry Waites, the new school teacher," she said, offering her hand.

"Really?" he looked her up and down for a second and then smiled, showing perfect teeth. "I'm Sam Vervaine. I'm the chef up at the inn and I also help run the school's culinary classes, so I guess we'll be working together this winter." He shook her hand, and she tried to keep from shaking with nerves. His attractiveness intimidated her. If she still had a cell phone, she would have tried to surreptitiously take a picture to send to Katie, her best friend back home.

"Nice to meet you," she told him, feeling a little awkward. She hadn't had conversations with anyone besides herself lately, and here she was talking to someone far out of her league, someone she'd have to work with on a regular basis.

"You too. Hey, let me buy you a drink. Or, rather, barter you a drink." He tapped his container of fruit peels.

"With that?" she asked skeptically.

"Just watch." He winked and then waved at Tim, but didn't seem to get the response he expected.

"Hey, you're not welcome here. You know that." Tim crossed his arms. "Get out of my bar."

"What? But I brought lemon peels to infuse. Shouldn't that buy me a drink? And one for the new teacher?"

"That'll buy her a drink, if she wants it. But you're *persona non grata*. This bar is firmly Team Cara."

"But I'm your business partner. And we were just at the gym together like eight hours ago! You never said I couldn't come here. Seriously, man."

"He isn't really my business partner. We're just experimenting with brewing beers and infusing liquors, like the one you're drinking now," Tim explained to Cherry as he stashed the Tupperware under the bar. "But that's got nothing to do with the actual bar, and the bar has declared itself on Team Cara, like I said. Sorry, Sammy, you have to leave. If Tyrell comes down and sees you here, I'm going to have domestic trouble."

"It's not fair. Everyone is taking her side. Vivian won't even let me on the ferry anymore. This is ridiculous." Sam threw his hands in the air. "One drink! Please, let me sit here for one drink."

Tim raised an eyebrow at him and a sly grin spread over his face. "Tell you what. Cherry's a teacher, so she probably has a lot of experience dealing with conflict and immaturity—yes, I said it, immaturity. So since she doesn't know you or Cara, I'll let her decide if you should be allowed in here."

Cherry felt a thrill go through her. This was exactly what she wanted—a chance to talk to people and feel included. This might help ease some of the loneliness, and it sounded like it might be fun.

"Sure, I'll help. Tell me what's going on."

"To give you the full effect, we'll need to role play it," Tim told her. "You're going to be Cara, and I'll play Sam. So I just need you to pretend to be my girlfriend and tell me . . .

ummmm . . ." He hesitated, and his cheeks above his beard turned slightly pink.

"Just say it, man." Sam laughed at his discomfort. "If you can't even say it, she's siding with me."

"Umm . . . okay, Cherry, as Cara, I need you to tell me . . . tell me your menses are late and ask what we should do." The last words came out in an embarrassed rush.

"Menses? Really?" Sam's voice carried, causing heads to turn towards them. As the only woman in the conversation, Cherry's face turned bright red. Was she about to discuss the female reproductive system with two gorgeous men? How embarrassing!

"I've been out of the closet since I was twelve. I don't know about what goes on down . . . there," Tim gestured vaguely in the direction of Cherry's waist. Okay, that was good information. He definitely hadn't been flirting earlier. That came as a relief.

"Alright, let's do this." If she was going to be drawn into this weird conversation, she was going to play it up as much as she could. She paused to channel her inner teacher. She'd taught the 'Understanding Our Bodies' portion of the health class for years, so, while menstruation was a rather personal and inappropriate topic, if she could explain it to a roomful of children, she could handle discussing it—in the abstract—with strangers.

"Ready?" Tim took both of her hands in his. He was the first man other than Gary to hold her hands, ever. "Alright, Cara, my sweetest darling sugar plum, did you have something to say to me?"

"I don't call her that," Sam objected.

Cherry giggled. "Sam, my . . . umm . . . my honey muffin, I have some news. The crimson tide has not surged, Aunt

Flo was a no-show, my red flag is not flying, my playground is not flooded, and the red moon hasn't risen . . ."

"Oh my god, please stop, I'm begging you." Tim pulled his hands away, eyes wide with horror, while Sam's laugh rang out heartily, attracting quite a bit of attention again.

"Sorry, I worked in a middle school. I've heard them all. Anyway, my, ahem, menses are late, what should we do?" Cherry felt triumphant. Bantering and making new friends, already, on her first night in town? Yes, this was going to be okay. She could find her place.

Tim blinked a few times and shuddered before he got back to the role playing. "Wow, that was horrifying. Well, Cara, I don't know what *you're* going to do now, but *I'm* swimming for the mainland."

There was a moment of silence while Cherry digested that. She turned to Sam.

"Oh, Sam."

"It was a joke. I was just joking!"

"Sorry," Cherry told him, "I don't know your girlfriend—or ex-girlfriend most likely?—but I'm on her side. That was the wrong response. You can't drink here."

"What?" Sam reacted in surprise to her judgment. "That's what any man would say in the same situation! It was supposed to be funny!"

"Any man would not say that," Tim corrected him. "Seriously, Sam, if it were possible to knock up my husband, I'd have done it on the first date."

"Yeah?" Sam leaned on the bar. "Come on, man, let me have a beer, while you tell me more about that first date."

"Shut up, Sammy. And sorry, but not that sorry. Get out of my bar. Cherry, I'll bring you another when you're finished with your first one. And I'm putting it on his tab." With that, Tim walked away to serve other customers.

"I paid with the peels! You asked for those!" Sam shouted at his retreating back and then sighed.

"Well, that sucks. I guess I'm leaving." Sam stood up to go, but Cherry stopped him.

"Can we talk a second? I'm new here, I don't know you or Cara, but maybe I can give you some advice?"

"Sure."

"How old is Cara?"

Sam frowned and considered the question. "She's thirty. I think. Yeah, thirty. Or thirty-one?"

"Do you want kids?"

He shrugged. "I don't know. Maybe. Maybe not. It isn't something that I've ever really planned."

"If you and Cara are still together, you need to break up with her."

"What? That's terrible advice! I'm never going to do that."

"It's not." Cherry closed her eyes for a second, and Gary's face appeared. "Look, Cara probably wants children. She's thirty-ish, apparently, which means she's running out of time. What happens five years from now, ten years from now, when you still don't know or decide you don't want any? She'll have wasted the last of her childbearing years on you. If you change your mind, you'll be able to find someone else, someone younger, and have as many kids as you want, but that's an option that won't be available to her. You're going to steal her chance to be a mother."

"But . . . but I love her!" Sam objected as though that was the only thing that mattered. Cherry had been in love once, too, and look how that turned out.

"You might love her, but if you don't want to have children with her, you'll have to let her go. That is, if she wants kids. I don't mean to make an assumption."

Sam hung his head, silent for a moment. When he looked up again, his expression was serious. "I never thought about that. You know, everyone else kept telling me to apologize—which I did, by the way—but she's still upset, and I think I get it now. I know she wants children, and if that's what will make her happy, that's what I'll give her. Maybe not immediately, not yet, I still need some time to adjust to the whole idea, but yeah, I'll do it. I'll give her all the kids she can handle."

"Maybe you should tell her that."

"You're right I should. And Tim's about to come throw me out, so I'm gonna go find her right now. Thank you, you might have saved my relationship." Sam gave her a friendly wave as he walked away.

At least I enabled someone else to have children, Cherry thought as she watched the door swing shut behind him. Too bad I've lost that option for myself. She finished her drink, but didn't wait for Tim to make her another. Instead, she went back to her empty apartment, laid on the bed, and thought about Gary—and let the hurt and resentment wash over her again.

# Chapter Five

Dear Gary,

My therapist told me to write you because it would help me sort out my feelings, even though you're obviously never going to get any of these letters.

Okay, I'm lying. It's from a self-help book that I read.

Well, I skimmed it. But there was this part about writing letters to the one who wronged you, and I mentioned it to Katie, and she said it was a good idea. And you know her undergrad degree is in psychology, so she's an expert. Maybe not an expert, but she's my best friend, and I'm not going to pay a therapist when she already gives me the advice I'm looking for.

Did you know I moved? Not just out of our house—the house I once loved that you soiled with your infidelity. Did you know I left Ohio entirely, fleeing the humiliation you caused? Do you ever ask any of our former mutual friends about me? About how I'm doing, or where I've gone?

Or are you too caught up in the drama of Megan's divorce?

I saw most of it on TV, lying on the couch at my parents' house this summer, watching the news. It was unbelievable how much airtime she was getting. Did all of Ohio really care? I guess so, but only because Tyler owns so many car dealerships, and there was that shady tabloid-esque stuff with the pre-nup agreement. I stopped paying attention, though, because every time I heard her name, it was a knife to my heart. My mom always came in when she heard me crying and turned off the news. And so I learned to stop paying attention.

And I moved away, far away, to a tiny island, where I will rest, and heal, and make a new life for myself.

I'm sitting out on my new balcony writing you this letter, a letter I'll never send. Why would I send it, so you can gloat? So you can laugh at me, and my naïveté? So you can smirk, and show my pain to your girlfriend? No, I'll never send it.

And you'll never know how broken I am. How lost, and how alone.

You'll never know how I second guess myself all the time.

Was it my fault? Was I not good enough for you? Was I not pretty enough? Were you unhappy the entire time?

How did I not see this coming?

I thought I knew you, Gary. I thought I knew you so well. I spent thirteen years knowing where you were every minute of every day. I knew your class schedule in college. And I knew when you were at your part-time job or at your (our!) friends' apartments. When you got your first teaching position, I was just down the hall. We had lunch together in the teacher's lounge every day. And we went home together, too. When I moved to the middle school, it was just across the parking lot, and I still knew your whereabouts all the time. I knew your schedule, I knew your free period, and I knew when you left to go to the high school for your assistant coaching job—the one that was supposed to bring in extra money so that we could take more vacations and maybe buy a nicer car. And I always knew where you were at night, sleeping on my left side, sometimes with your leg over mine, sometimes laying on your back and snoring.

I always knew where you were.

So I don't understand why I didn't know you were cheating on me. How could I have missed that? How could I have not known that you were getting blow jobs in the back of your classroom while your students went to gym class? How did I not know that you stopped by a hotel for a quickie between saying goodbye to your second graders and making your high school students run laps?

And how did I, the person who knew you best in the world, miss all of that, when everybody else knew?

My bitterness is coming through. Writing letters to you is not as cathartic as I had hoped.

How do I sign off on a letter like this? Sincerely? Yours truly? Regards? With love? No, none of those work.

Resentment and regrets,

Cherry

*No Longer Yours*

# *Chapter Six*

*Fourteen years earlier: Bowling Green State University, August 2000*

Cherry still can't believe it's finally here—the first week of college! It's already been super exciting, getting away from her parents and the tiny town she grew up in. Most people would consider Bowling Green a small town too, but it's a huge metropolis compared to the one she came from. There's more than one store, which is quite a novelty. Downtown has multiple restaurants and bars, though she can't get into those yet.

And now the next exciting thing is happening—she's going to orientation. She's always known she wanted to be a teacher, so selecting her major was easy. Cherry arrives in the lecture hall early-ish, but not as early as she would like. She doesn't want to seem too eager, like some kind of nerd. But she doesn't want to be too standoffish either. She needs to prove she isn't just the shy boring girl she was in high school. She is going to put herself out there and have the full college experience.

She doesn't want to sit in the front row because, again, she doesn't want to appear too nerdy and overeager. It's a big auditorium, so she thinks about five rows back will be okay. There are other people in the row, and she wonders if she should take one of the empty seats next to someone, or one of the isolated seats. Will she appear desperate for friends if she just plops down and starts a conversation? They're all Education majors here, so she's going to see everyone in class all the time anyway. But no, she doesn't want to look too needy.

She decides to take the second seat from the end of the row. That way, someone will be forced to sit next to her, because people always want aisle seats. Yes, that's a good plan. Someone will ask if the seat is taken, and she'll say no, and that's the opening to introduce herself as they sit.

It works. The room is starting to fill, and a boy approaches. "Hey, mind if I sit here?" he asks, and she smiles. Her roommate had told her there wouldn't be any boys here, having an outdated and sexist idea of the education system. But her roommate is mostly right. The room is full of female students, but not so many male ones.

"Hi, I'm Gary," the boy says as he awkwardly folds his limbs into the seat next to her. He's very tall, so much so that he has to stretch his left leg out in the aisle. She imagines he doesn't fit in airplanes either, but that's based on what she's seen on television. She's never actually been on a plane. She's never been anywhere.

"I'm Cherry," she tells him, and then feels a little silly about the rhyming.

"That's your actual name?" he asks, and she blushes.

"It's short for Cherish. My parents . . ." She rolls her eyes, because that's what college students are supposed to do when talking about their parents. The truth is, she loves them madly, and she loves her name. She was a late-in-life surprise to two people who had spent years trying to have a baby before giving up and accepting their childless fate, and they named her accordingly.

"Your parents must like you better than mine like me." He grins, revealing teeth that are crooked, but in an endearing kind of way. "Gary is short for Garish."

She wants to laugh classily, like a suave and confident adult. But what comes out is more of a high pitched giggle. She can't help it. Gary looks pleased. Could it be that he's flirting with her?

"So where are you from, Cherry?" he asks. Is this real? Is she making a new friend already? Or maybe he'll become her first ever boyfriend?

"Madrid," she tells him.

"You don't have an accent." He looks slightly suspicious. Maybe he thinks she's lying.

"I mean Madrid, Ohio," she says. They both laugh, and this time it isn't her silly girlish giggle. "What about you, where are you from?"

"Gary."

"Sorry. Where are you from, Gary?" Did he think she forgot his name?

"No, for real." Now he's the one who's embarrassed. "I'm from Gary, Indiana. Born and raised. See what I mean when I said your parents like you more than mine like me?"

The orientation starts, and Cherry listens to the speaker, but finds herself sneaking glances out of the corner of her eye at Gary. And she catches him doing the same thing. He couldn't possibly be interested in her, could he? After an hour, the students are given a break. Cherry wants to walk around and stretch her legs, but she's afraid to lose her seat. What if she forgets what row she was in and sits in the wrong place, and Gary thinks she's trying to get away from him? He stands, and she realizes it's a non-issue. He might be trying to get away from her.

"Hey, I need to go to the bathroom. Save my seat?" Gary asks, and she nods. Save his seat? He's coming back and still wants to sit with her!

He really does come back. And he really does sit next to her. She tries hard to keep from grinning.

"So, you live on campus?" he asks.

"I'm in Mac North." Wouldn't it be perfect if he was too?

"Hey, I'm in Offenhaur, I'm your neighbor," he says with that same grin as before. There's something so charming about his smile, about the way he looks in her eyes as he speaks.

"I heard those rooms are big." She immediately feels stupid. What kind of a comment is that? The rooms are big? She wishes she'd flirted more in high school so she'd have more experience with it.

"They're huge," he tells her. "In fact, I heard a couple of years ago some guy built an actual working drawbridge in his." That has to be a joke. She looks for the sly teasing grin, but it isn't there.

"That's weird. I don't believe you."

"It's true. My RA said so. If you ever want to see my room, I'll show you how big it is . . ." He trails off and blushes adorably. Cherry doesn't know what to say. And right then, the orientation starts again. She stares straight ahead and doesn't hear a word of it.

After the orientation, he walks with her back to her dorm, since they're going in the same direction anyway. "Well, I guess I'll see you around," he says, and her heart sinks. She knows what that means. She may run into him on campus, and he'll give her a friendly nod and keep walking. She probably ruined it somehow. She is so terrible at talking to boys!

"Yeah, I guess," she replies, because she doesn't know how else to answer.

"Ummm, well . . ." And now he's got his hands in his pockets and he looks awkward and uncomfortable. Why doesn't he just walk away and spare them both? "There's kind of a party tonight. Me and some guys from my floor are going. It's in an apartment over on East Merry. I guess my neighbor knows someone there. Maybe if you want to come, you know, maybe bring your roommate or something . . ."

"That sounds good," she says, shrugging and trying not to look or sound too excited. She can portray coolness. "Yeah, I'll talk to her."

"Okay, cool," Gary's face lights up, showing his relief. "So ummm, I guess you should give me your number or something?"

# Chapter Seven

*Whispering Pines, August 2014*

Matteo sat on the steps outside the school door, closed his eyes and enjoyed the breeze. The summer was nearing an end, so the days were slightly cooler— perfect weather for kayaking and biking—which kept his rental shop busy. He had left it in the capable hands of his summer employees, but he'd need to get back soon, once he finished dealing with the new teacher. That was the problem with being the Village Council member who lived and worked closest to the school—he was the one stuck showing the teacher around.

He wasn't someone who liked change, so altering his daily routine caused problems for him. He reminded himself that everything was fine, and there was nothing to worry about. But still, he found his hand reaching into his pocket for his worry stone, a smooth piece of onyx with a perfect thumb indentation. He rubbed it, focusing on the feel of the rock and the rhythm of his own breathing. When he opened his eyes again, someone was watching him. It was the same woman he had encountered the day before, the one who almost tripped over Tristan's leash and then made inappropriate jokes about mentally ill people. Fucking tourist, he thought to himself. If she asked for directions to something, he was going to send her the wrong way.

"Oh my goodness, are you the one I'm supposed to be meeting here?" she asked. He stared at her. Was this really the new teacher? No, she couldn't be. He'd been on the hiring committee and he was pretty sure he would have recognized this chipmunk-cheeked young woman, if she were the candidate they'd offered the job over his objections. He thought they needed someone older and more established, someone likely to stay long term. Apparently, his opinion didn't matter.

"Are you Cherish Waites?"

"I am. But please, call me Cherry." That was her nickname? God, she was already annoying him.

"I didn't recognize you from the interview. Oh, now I see it. You've changed your hair." He remembered it as long and wavy, pulled forward concealing the sides of her face, very unlike the chin-length frizz tucked behind the ears of the brunette standing in front of him.

She reached up and touched the ends of her hair awkwardly. "Everyone keeps saying that. I've just cut it, that's all. I don't remember you . . . oh, you changed your face. You were the one with the big bushy beard, weren't you?"

"That's my winter face. I'm Matteo Capen." He rose to his feet and crossed his arms. "Glad to know we didn't hire a mentally ill teacher." Her face fell.

"I'm so sorry about yesterday. I shouldn't have made a joke like that. I meditated on it this morning and . . ."

"You meditated on it?" He interrupted her in a more derisive tone than intended, and a blush spread over her round cheeks. He didn't mean to ask in an insulting manner, he'd just been surprised. He meditated daily as part of his self-care routine to stave off panic attacks. Sometimes it even worked.

"Yes, I . . . I've taken up meditation. And I realized I shouldn't have made light of mental illness. I was just embarrassed you caught me talking to myself. Though I admit

I didn't expect to run into you again. I assumed you were a tourist."

"Why would you think that?" He knew the answer. His summer look was carefully cultivated to appeal to the tourists renting equipment from him, but he wanted to make her say it.

"Just, you know . . ." She looked uncomfortable and gestured toward his flowery Hawaiian shirt. "You dress like you're on a beach vacation, that's all."

"I live on an island. My whole life is a beach vacation. Now come on, I'll show you the school." He opened the door and led her in. He didn't want to be here anyway, and he especially wasn't interested in being here with Cherry. He kept his hand on his worry stone to focus his thoughts. He could get through this. He could tolerate her long enough to show her the classrooms.

🌲 🌲 🌲 🌲 🌲

"Oh, this is wonderful," Cherry murmured as she wandered through the schoolhouse, lovingly trailing a hand over various surfaces. Matteo tried to see it through her eyes. He had attended the school, kindergarten through twelfth grade, so perhaps he was a bit jaded. To him, it was nothing more than a worn old building, constructed in the seventies and still looking like it. They needed better lighting; that would help. But cheerful sunlight did stream through the many windows, the walls were freshly painted, and the floors gleamed with wax.

"It's divided, somewhat. That's the elementary area, and that's middle school. High school is through that doorway. And you and Wanda share the office over there. She's your assistant, but she's out of town right now. Family wedding in Michigan, I think."

Matteo pointed out the classroom elements. The elementary students had shorter desks and art cubbies, and the middle schoolers had tables and desktop computers. The high school students were each issued a school laptop that they brought every day. While Cherry would teach some high school subjects, her primary role for those students would be coordinating them with the online system that brought certain classes to rural schools all over the state.

"I love it!" She didn't even sound sarcastic. Maybe she was actually interested in the job. She wouldn't last long though. She didn't look tough enough to handle the island winters.

"Sure you do. Listen, here are your keys. I gotta take off. Lock up when you're done. If you need me, I'll be at Cap'n Rentals." He hoped she wouldn't need him though. He had work to do, and no interest in further babysitting the new teacher. He'd be surprised if she made it through the year.

# Chapter Eight

Dear Gary,

I guess I'm getting settled in, though I haven't unpacked all my boxes yet. You know me, I tend to procrastinate. But I can't do that anymore, can I? I no longer have someone to help pick up my slack.

Instead of dealing with finding a place for my few things and shopping for what I lack, I spent today exploring my new school. I'm already in love with it. It's nice to feel positive about something again, to have a glimmer of hope that I'll be able to turn my life around.

It's a little intimidating to realize the school is mine, all mine. There's only one other full-time employee—an administrator whom I have yet to meet—though, apparently, every single person in town volunteers there in some capacity. It's not technically a one-room schoolhouse because there's an office and the high school is in a kind of divided alcove. We also have access to a gymnasium and a small theater at the community center. I was given keys to both of those, but haven't had the chance to check them out yet. There's a library at the center as well, though I've been warned that it's small and mostly children's books. (Good for my kindergartners, not for my high school seniors.)

Everything is surprisingly modern and clean on the inside, though the building is a bit old. The best part? The windows. The kids are going to be daydreaming and staring out at the lake, and I'll have to stop myself from doing the same. We overlook Lake Superior, and I bet it's gorgeous in the winter. It's beautiful now, though you can tell the water is cold just by looking at it. Boats pass by; I saw a couple of yachts, I think. Maybe not. They sure looked fancy to me though. I haven't ever been on a boat, besides the ferry to get here, and the catamaran when we celebrated our fifth anniversary in the Caribbean. Lovely, wasn't it? Have you gone on vacation with Megan yet?

I'm sorry. My last question was snide. I still hate you, just so you know, but I sometimes think of you with a sort of wistful sadness too. Would you have come with me if I had gotten this job during our marriage? I can picture you on this island. I can see you learning to play ice hockey in the winter and riding around on a bicycle the rest of the year. There isn't a rec league basketball program, but I bet you would start one. People would love you, they'd be drawn to you. Your goofy laugh and the way you look at people from under your lashes when you tell jokes would endear you to them. Maybe you'd get over your distaste of fish, and I would have to yell at you to descale your catch somewhere else when you tried to do it in my clean kitchen.

This would all be so much more fun if you were here. The old you, I mean. The one that loved me.

Regretfully no longer yours,

Cherry

# Chapter Nine

She called her mother to update her on her new home and school, but hanging up the phone alone in an empty apartment made her isolation unbearable. It was hard to start over as an adult, and here she was in a new town, knowing nobody. Well, that wasn't quite accurate. She had met several people, but she hadn't met anyone she could consider a friend yet.

Maybe the best thing now would be to get out of the house, go where she could be around others, hide her loneliness in a crowd. Yes, that was a good idea. She would go out to eat, she decided. She still had the fish in her freezer, but she wasn't ready to try cooking that yet. Fish took skill, probably. She had never cooked it before because Gary didn't like the smell. But Gary was long gone, and she could now eat whatever she liked without him making faces and holding his nose.

She went outside and looked around indecisively before choosing the Village Diner. She had always liked diners. She and Gary frequented one back home in Parsons where they graded papers late at night while drinking coffee and sharing a plate of french fries. But she shoved the bittersweet memory away. She couldn't keep wasting time remembering her old life.

The diner was crowded. She must have picked a busy time. "If you're alone, a seat is open at the counter," suggested the hostess.

That wasn't ideal. She'd have preferred a table, but she took it anyway and found herself next to the only person she didn't want to deal with. Well, the only person besides Gary and Megan, of course.

"Great, it's you again." Matteo barely looked over his shoulder at her and then turned back to his book. He seemed to be taking up more than his fair share of the space. She decided it didn't matter, she would be pleasant. She didn't have a reputation here yet, and she didn't want to start with a bad one.

"Well hello yourself," she greeted him cheerfully. "I didn't get a chance to thank you for showing me around the school yesterday." She forced a smile that she didn't quite feel. She liked to think of herself as a friendly person, but it was hard being pleasant to someone who didn't reflect any of it back.

"You're welcome," he muttered, still focused on reading. Cherry decided to ignore him right back, so she picked up the menu and began to study it. Typical diner food, though with a twist. She had never heard of some of the options, like lefse or Iron-Range porketta. Maybe she'd just order a burger? Something familiar. Or should she try something new? This was, after all, her attempt at a new life.

"You been to Minnesota before?" She looked up in surprise at Matteo's question. He had set the book aside.

"This is my first time. I was born and raised in Ohio," she told him.

"Well then there are a whole lot of things you need to try. You like fish?"

"I'm not sure," she admitted. "Maybe? Probably. It's not something I've been exposed to very much."

"Isn't Ohio a Great Lakes state too? Wait, never mind. Lake Erie caught on fire once, right? I wouldn't eat fresh fish from there either."

"That was just the Cuyahoga River," she informed him, feeling the need to defend her home state.

"The river that feeds into Lake Erie? Yeah, that's much better. Alright, now that you're at a cleaner, less flammable lake, start with the fish and chips. It's Walleye, it's delicious, and it's a good intro. Everybody likes fried food, right?"

"I don't know about everybody, but I do," she said. And apparently that ended the conversation as Matteo picked up his book again. For just a moment, she thought he had been being friendly. After she ordered her meal, she sighed and pulled out her own book.

Her shoulders itched, and she started to feel a strange sensation, like she was being watched. She looked up to see Matteo staring. His eyes were a hard to define hazel, somewhere between green and brown.

"What?" she asked, somewhat irritated.

"I was just looking at your book. *Great Lakes Shipwrecks of the 1800s*? Really?"

"Yes," she turned it to show the cover, somewhat defensively. Now he was mocking her literary choices? "I picked it up at that little shop that sells island merchandise. I thought it looked interesting."

"It is." He flipped his book over.

"Oh, wow, we're reading the same thing!" She thought that could be an opening, they could perhaps interact and have a conversation. Gosh, she must be desperate to want to talk to someone as surly and unpleasant as him. But it didn't matter. Matteo merely nodded and turned back to his reading, and they ate their meals next to each other in silence.

# Chapter Ten

*Six months earlier: Parsons, Ohio, February 2014*

Cherry walks in to the house, still in shock from her encounter with Tyler. Gary is seated at the table, papers spread out before him. The basketball team he coaches has a tournament coming up, and he likes to go over player statistics and strategize in advance.

"Hey hot mama," he says with his usual grin. Then he notices she isn't carrying groceries. "Didn't you stop at the store?"

"I guess I forgot." She is feeling weak and nauseous. In a few weeks, she would have wanted to feel this way, would have hoped it was morning sickness. It's something else now. Something worse.

"That's okay, I'm sure we have something here. Or should we start in the bedroom?" he waggles his eyebrows at her. She bites the insides of her cheeks because she's afraid she's going to scream. She opens the fridge to conceal her shaking.

"Interesting gossip I heard today," she tells him, looking from the corners of her eyes. "You know Megan Rivera, right? She teaches with you?"

"Yeah, she's down the hall. Why?" Cherry has known Gary for a long time. She recognizes the carefully light tone of his voice, the way his back infinitesimally straightens. He is pretending to study his papers, but he is holding very still.

"She's getting a divorce."

"Huh. Interesting. She hasn't mentioned anything." Gary's neck is turning pink. He is still trying to appear relaxed, but Cherry senses his nervous energy.

"Why would she tell you?" Cherry pulls a container from the refrigerator, pretends to read the label, and puts it back.

"She's part of the group I eat lunch with when we aren't on cafeteria duty, so we chat sometimes." The lie comes too easily from Gary's lips, and Cherry wants to burst into tears, but she holds them back. "How did you hear about it?"

The question hangs between them for a moment. Cherry closes the fridge and finally turns to look directly at her husband. "I talked to Tyler Rivera today," she says, watching Gary's face. He is clearly struggling to control his agitation.

"Really?"

"Yeah, it was the funniest thing. I ran into him in the parking lot. Oh, and he gave me something. Hang on, let me get it." She walks over to the counter where she had dropped the offensive envelope. She lifts the flap slowly. Gary's eyes haven't left her face. Her stomach is churning, and she swallows back bile. This is her last chance to pretend this never happened, her last chance to ignore those pictures and make a baby and continue her perfect life.

She reaches into the envelope.

"Gary, I think this is a particularly good shot. I've seen this expression on your face before, but never thought to take a picture. Hmmm, I rather like this one, the way Megan's legs are wrapped around your waist. The positioning makes it not quite so obscene, but anyone can still tell what's going on." She shuffles through the photos and holds back the scream rising in-side her.

"Cherry, babe, I can explain," Gary starts, but of course he can't. There is no explanation he can give.

"Sure, explain. Tell me this is all photoshopped. Or maybe you have a twin brother you've never introduced me to?"

"Cherry, I've been wanting to tell you." And that is it. That is the beginning of the end of their marriage. The first words out of his mouth aren't an apology, aren't a plea for forgiveness, aren't even an excuse for his behavior.

🌲 🌲 🌲 🌲 🌲

Returning to work the Monday after learning about Gary's betrayal is nerve-wracking. Her discovery had happened on a Friday night, and she'd immediately packed her suitcase and fled to the sanctuary of Katie's guestroom. All weekend, she lay around alternating between sobbing and raging, and waiting for a phone call. Surely Gary would call and explain what a terrible mistake this all was. Surely he would tell her it was an accident, a momentary lapse, that Megan came on to him, that he regretted it more than anything and would spend the rest of his life making it up to her. But her phone never rang.

Middle school faculty is not much different from the students in terms of how fast rumors spread, and Cherry can tell from the moment she enters the building that everybody has heard. People don't make eye contact with her, and she hears someone whisper, "poor thing," when she passes by.

She tries to hold her head high and not let them see that she's hurting. Things will work out, she knows it. She and Gary are strong, and even though she is angry and hurt now, she can forgive him for one minor indiscretion. They'll go to counseling and talk it out. She'll make him grovel, that's only fair. But their marriage will survive, scarred but intact.

When she goes into the office to make copies, the school secretary rises from her desk, comes around, and envelops Cherry in an overly-perfumed hug. "Oh, Cherry. I'm so sorry for you," Dulcie says, and Cherry struggles to get away. She doesn't want sympathy right now because she is barely holding herself together as it is.

"Thank you," she says, biting her lip. She can't let herself cry, not at school.

"It's just such a relief you finally found out," Dulcie continues. "It's been awful, nobody ever knew what to say."

"What?" Cherry can't possibly be interpreting the secretary's words correctly.

"It's like I told Reid and Bess, you deserve to know. But you remember Alec, he convinced us it was best to let Gary be the one to tell you, so I held my tongue."

Cherry is frozen. She sits with Reid and Bess at their team-planning meetings every week, and they've been keeping this horrible secret? And Alec? Last school year he moved to Kentucky. How does he know? Is her marriage fodder for long distance gossip? How did word spread so fast?

"This past year has been awful. I swear Cherry, I wish you had found out sooner. Everybody hated keeping it a secret, but it wasn't our place to say anything."

A year? This had been going on for a year? But she and Gary were so happy! And they were about to make a baby! Her head spins and she feels like she wants to vomit.

"I'm so glad everything is out in the open. We're all on your side, Cherry." Dulcie's smile is bright and sympathetic, and she keeps patting Cherry's arm. But Cherry can't feel it. Her entire body is numb.

"Dulcie, I need a substitute today. I think I'm coming down with something." She turns and walks out of the school. She's never done this before, she's never walked off the job. But she can't handle being there with all those eyes on her. They all knew. All of her colleagues knew her husband was having an affair and never said a word. People she'd known for years, people she respected, people she considered friends, they all helped Gary betray her.

She makes the long drive back to Katie's house in a daze. Even if Gary calls, crying and begging, she can't take him back. How could she ever consider forgiving such an epic betrayal? Why did he say he was ready to have a baby when he was already cheating on her? But then she realizes exactly why: that was his fail safe. He knew that if they had a child she'd never leave. He was going to trap her so he could continue doing whatever adulterous things he wanted with another woman.

When she makes it to Katie's, she takes a few moments to weep helplessly into a pillow before pulling out her laptop. She can't stay in Parsons, not with this humiliation hanging over her head. She needs to find a new job, far from here. She needs a fresh start.

# Chapter Eleven

Dear Gary,

I used to think divorce was for quitters. I used to think if you got a divorce, it showed that you weren't willing to work hard. I thought all relationships could be saved.

My parents have been married for forty-five years. That's a long time. They had their difficulties, like throughout their thirties when they struggled with infertility and my mother had all those miscarriages, and later, when two adoptions in a row fell through. Those were traumatizing events, but you know what happened? My parents grew closer together. They provided each other strength. They leaned on each other.

And that's the model I had for marriage going into ours.

When we stood in front of all of our friends and family and vowed to be together 'for better or for worse,' I thought we both meant it. I thought we agreed that when you married someone, it was for the good times and the bad. I thought if we truly worked as a team, we could survive anything.

If someone asked me a year ago what possible future threats there were to my marriage, I would have said there were none. There were things that could destroy other less solid couples, like illness, infertility, or job loss. In my vanity and naïveté, I thought we were so strong, so committed, that those sorts of things wouldn't hurt us; if we went through them, they'd bring struggles, not destruction. I didn't honestly believe there were any threats to my marriage, oh no, not me. I was above all of that. But a year ago, you were already sleeping with Megan.

Our divorce was easy, Gary. It was easy, and it shouldn't have been. The decision to get a divorce should weigh heavy on a person's soul. It should come from sleepless nights and tearful talks, and attempts to recover from the trauma. But no, not for us.

I'll never forget the expression on your face when I showed you the picture of you and Megan caught in the act. You didn't look guilty or sad, you looked relieved. Did it make you feel better, knowing your betrayal was all out in the open? Is that it? Or was it because now you could finally leave me? You kind of gasped out an explanation, but you didn't offer to break things off with her. You didn't offer to go to counseling. You didn't offer anything to save us.

You didn't say anything while you watched me pack my suitcase. Did you hear me hysterically calling Katie? Did you listen to my end of that phone call? Did you feel anything? Guilt, remorse, regret, anything?

And when we met a few days later to talk, to discuss where we stood, and I asked what you wanted, you said 'I don't know.' You didn't know what you wanted. Well I knew. If there had been anything salvageable on your end, you would have tried. You would have ended your affair with Megan and worked to rebuild trust between us. You would have apologized, you would have courted me, you would have convinced me to forgive you. And I'm almost ashamed to admit this now, but you would have succeeded, if you had tried.

So that was the end. Our marriage was reduced to paperwork between lawyers and a check you wrote me for my half of our assets. We walked into our marriage with next to nothing, two older model cars and some cheap furniture. We built up so much, we paid off our debts, we saved up a nest egg, we were preparing for a baby. A baby! How lucky am I that Tyler Rivera showed up with those pictures before and not after I went home to have conception sex with you? How lucky am I not to be pregnant and alone and scared? How lucky am I to have walked away with just a check?

And how lucky am I to be starting over again, in a new place, all alone? How lucky, indeed.

With anger and regret,

Cherry

## Chapter Twelve

Matteo liked to keep to his routines. They helped anchor him, kept his mind steady, kept him on an even keel. That's why he ate at the diner every Wednesday night, always on the same stool at the counter. It was his routine, his plan. And that's why discomfort rose up in him when he entered the restaurant and his stool was taken, and the occupant wasn't some random tourist, no, it was that irritating new teacher.

"You're in my seat." His voice came out more growly than necessary. She looked up, startled.

"There are other seats available," she said, in her annoyingly cheerful voice.

"Yes, but I always sit there." He reached his hand into his pocket and gripped his worry stone. Calm yourself, Matteo. "Why don't you move?"

"Because I'm already here and I'm settled in. You're welcome to join me," she replied, and had the nerve to return to her book. He honestly hadn't expected her to stand up to him, he assumed she would move, and he stood there, staring like an idiot for a second. *That's my seat,* he wanted to say again. Instead, he closed his eyes and took a few meditative breaths. He could do this. He was a grown man. He could sit somewhere else. So he did, right next to her, right next to his actual seat, so he could take it back as soon as she left. And then he noticed the menu still laying on the counter.

"You didn't order yet?" He felt a wave of panic start to rise. How long was she going to hijack his space? *No, stop.*

*You can do this. You are stronger than that*, he told himself. *Calm, calm, calm.*

"I haven't. Any recommendations? The fish and chips you suggested last week were delicious, but I'd like to try something different." This was maddening. She perched on his stool acting like nothing was wrong. No, no, she was acting correctly. His reaction was the problem. He took a deep breath and tried to let it all go.

"Get the lake whitefish, with a side of wild rice. That's what I'm having tonight. In the summer, it's fresh caught, in the winter it's frozen."

"Thanks," she smiled at him, and somehow he found himself smiling back, relaxing a little bit. He was just on edge because of the two panic attacks he suffered through yesterday, and his body still remained tensed for a third.

"Why are you in such a good mood?" he asked. He wasn't going to pull out his book, not while sitting in the wrong seat.

"First day of school," she said. He'd forgotten about that. Not having kids himself, he didn't pay much attention to that sort of thing. He only cared when the PE class would be kayaking, since he provided the gear and taught that unit, but it started in April. "It went really well." Her smile was genuine.

"Glad to hear it."

"You don't have children, do you?" she asked.

"Nope. Only dogs."

"Dogs, plural? You have more than just that adorable corgi I saw you with the other day?" Okay, now things were getting better. His anxiety receded further away. His dogs were his whole life, and he loved to talk about them.

"That one was Tristan, then there's my husky, Martha, and my keeshond, Beverly." He left off the part about Beverly being his trained psychiatric service dog. She didn't need to know everything.

"I love dogs so much. I've always wanted to get a Bernese mountain dog. Are you familiar with those? But I don't have time to train a puppy," she said, and his heart twisted a little. Of course she'd bring up Berners.

"I had one once. I named her Jessica, and she was the best damn dog ever." She had passed away a couple of years ago, and his throat still constricted when he thought about her. Poor Jessica, taken from him too soon. But somehow, talking about his dogs loosened him up, and the conversation flowed. It was actually pleasant to chat with her while they ate. He didn't even want to open up his book. Anyone who liked dogs was fine with him.

🌲 🌲 🌲 🌲 🌲

"Well," Cherry said, after paying her check. "I was thinking about going down to the bar for a celebratory first day of school drink. Do you want to come?"

For a second, he almost did.

"Can't," he told her, and her face fell. Guilt pricked at his conscience. She was new, she didn't know anybody, and maybe she was lonely. He understood loneliness, he experienced it every winter. He sighed and decided to make an attempt at being friendly. "I have to take my dogs to the dog park. But if you're bored and want to tag along, you can."

"Do you mean it?" Her face lit up, and she clapped her hands like a small child. He supposed that action made sense; she did willingly surround herself with the little rug rats. He never planned to have children. They were messy, loud, and prone to inheriting things he would never want to pass on.

"Well, you said you like dogs. It's no big deal." He shrugged. "Come on." He strode out the door without looking to see if she followed, though he heard her footsteps hurrying to keep up. He led her to his house outside of town, on the other side of the docks.

"You don't live above your shop?" she asked. "I thought everybody lived above their businesses."

"If I lived there, where would I store my rental skis in the off-season?" He then realized his reply came out a bit too snappish. Really, this woman put him on edge with her overly cheerful voice. It's not that he didn't like happy people, he just found them annoying. "Watch out."

He unlocked the door, opened it, and stepped out of the way. Tristan and Beverly shot out like rockets, and he knelt to pet them. For a minute, he forgot about Cherry while he buried his hands in Beverly's fur. Then he reached for Tristan and . . . stupid, stupid dog. Tristan had run right past him and was happily being petted by Cherry.

"Oh, look at you. Who's a good boy? Oh, it's you, you're such a good boy!" She laughed while rubbing Tristan's sides. The ridiculous beast actually rolled over and exposed his belly for her. Cherry's face glowed with joy. She looked almost pretty, for a second.

"Yeah, let me get the leashes." He stood and walked through the doorway to whistle for Martha. She came, but slowly. Poor girl was getting old. He clipped a leash to her collar and brought her outside, where he discovered Beverly the betrayer was also enjoying belly rubs.

"Here, take this." He tossed her Tristan's leash, while he snagged Bev.

"Is he a mix? I didn't think corgis had tails," Cherry asked, soon after Tristan whipped her in the eye with his. Served her right. She didn't need to be so close to his dog.

"He's a Cardigan Welsh, they have tails. Also, he likes wearing cardigans, so the breed name suits him," Matteo told her. From the expression on her face, she didn't believe him. "No, seriously, it's true. Tristan loves sweaters and jackets and other outlandish dog clothes. My friend Nessie makes them for him. He even likes hats."

"How adorable! I would love to see that!" God, her enthusiasm was irritating. All he wanted was a peaceful night with his dogs. But this was his fault, he had invited her.

"I'm sure you will sometime. Now let's go."

🌲 🌲 🌲 🌲 🌲

Matteo watched the dogs race around the park and struggled to make conversation. He'd been polite in inviting Cherry to come with him, but really, this was supposed to be his quiet time. He liked to sit and relax and watch the sunset while his babies played. However, it was annoyingly clear that Cherry wasn't the sit and be silent type. She kept chattering away about the first day of school as if he cared. He'd had plenty of first days of school, so he knew how they went. Kids showed up, they learned and argued and complained about homework, then went home. Not much to it.

"So, why'd you move here?" he finally interrupted her to ask. That should change the subject.

"For the job, of course," Cherry said in a chipper voice that somehow rang false.

"I know you took the job, but why? Why apply for a position on this tiny island when you'd never even been to this state before?"

"Oh, I guess I just thought it would be an adventure, and I was ready to make a change in my life." Her answer sounded rehearsed as though it was what she told herself when she looked in the mirror every night. He had his own pep talks, so he wasn't going to fall for it.

"Wasn't your name different on your résumé?" he prodded. He was going to push past this outer layer of fake happiness.

"Yes, well, I got a divorce since then." She pursed her lips and sat in silence for a moment, and Tristan came running over and put his paws on her lap. He was the most disloyal dog that ever existed.

"Because your husband didn't want to come with you?" Matteo tried to trigger an honest response. *Come on, lady, say something truthful, not these false platitudes about making changes in life.*

"Ummm . . ." Cherry hesitated, and her chipmunk cheeks turned slightly pink. She turned her face away momentarily, and when she looked back at him, he could swear she was blinking away tears. "I met my husband on the first day of college. He was the love of my life. We were together for over thirteen years. And in February, right when we started trying for a baby, I found out he was cheating on me. So that's why I'm here. I couldn't stay in our house, in our town, where everyone knew about him."

"Oh. Well, that sucks." It was Matteo's turn to be quiet, to process that information, and apparently, she mistook it as an invitation to spill more of her personal life on him.

"I still don't understand what happened. We were so happy. Or maybe that was just me and he was miserable, but he didn't act like it. I mean, we were planning on having a baby. I'm supposed to be pregnant right now. I'm supposed to be painting the nursery and reading books of baby names and complaining that my ankles are swollen. And instead, I'm here and I'm all alone. I don't know anybody, I don't talk to anybody, I'm so lonely. It's hard, you know? How do you start over from scratch as an adult?"

"You're asking the wrong person. I grew up here." Matteo whistled for Beverly, and she came running. Her fur was soft under his fingers, and she always made him feel better. But he wasn't the one who needed her now. "Here, Bev. Come up on the bench." The dog eagerly jumped up between them and curled herself into a ball, with her head on Cherry's lap. That brought a smile to Cherry's face.

"What a good girl you are," she whispered, rubbing Beverly's head. Beverly whined with pleasure.

"There, see, life here isn't so bad. You made friends with my dogs at least. So that's something. And I'm sure it takes a while to adjust, I don't know. But overall, this community is great. The people are friendly, really. It's just right now we're still in tourist season, so nobody has time for anything else. That's how we earn our money. Most of the business owners live off their summer earnings year-round, so from May to September, we do nothing but work. There's plenty of time to be social during the winter, and you'll start meeting people. I promise."

"For real?" The corners of her mouth twitched like she was trying to smile.

"I don't know. Probably." He didn't want to give her too much encouragement. He didn't want her to mistake him for somebody who wanted to be her friend.

# Chapter Thirteen

Dear Gary,

I've been on this island for two weeks. That's fourteen nights. Fourteen nights of sleeping alone, in my own place. Do you realize I've never lived alone? I went from my parents' house to a dorm room to that run down old apartment we rented with four roommates to just living with you. Even when you left me (or, rather, I left you), I stayed with Katie's family until the end of the school year and then back to my folks' again. I'd never fallen asleep in an empty apartment.

It feels strange, but I'm getting used to it. I deliberately sleep in the middle of the bed now. I take up all the space I want. I use that raggedy quilt, the one you've always hated, the one my aunt made when I was a child. And I have a big thick comforter that I picked out myself. The filling is down, which you're allergic to, and it's covered in loud pink flowers, a pattern I'm sure you'd hate. I bought it because I know it's something I never would have had if you were still in my life.

My coffeepot has a timer, so I don't rely on you to make it in the mornings anymore. Most days I don't bother, and instead buy a cup from the coffee shop on the corner. That would annoy you, because it isn't very frugal. And yes, frugality matters. I'm the only one funding my retirement now, I'm the only one saving for anything, I'm the one on the hook for all my bills. But I'm also not married to someone funneling away our money to pay for seedy motels. Did you get discounts since you only used the rooms for fifteen minutes?

I go to the coffee shop most mornings, so I can see someone and exchange a smile and a polite greeting, even if it's just with the barista. Such a minor interaction, but what else can I do? There isn't anyone sitting across from me at breakfast anymore. I no longer look across the table and into the face of the man I thought I loved, while he smiles at me and thinks about his mistress.

I don't like being alone, but it's better than being with you. At least there's only one person I hate at the table and not two.

Because, yes, I hate myself. I hate that I thought everything was fine. I hate that I missed the clues. I hate that I lost everything. And I hate myself for still missing you.

Bitterly not yours,

Cherry

# Chapter Fourteen

*Whispering Pines Island, September 2014*

Matteo loaded his dogs into the box bike and started pedaling. He usually worked on Saturdays. But after spending a busy morning in his shop, he handed control off to one of his part-timers and left. It was a glorious afternoon, likely one of the last warm days, and he wanted to savor it. His babies did too, he could tell by how eagerly they got into the box, although Martha required assistance. All three of them loved to ride, and he was taking them to his favorite hiking trail where they could explore the woods. It was on state park land, so he'd have to keep them leashed, but still, the adventure was a treat for everybody.

He traveled west from his house on the five-mile road that circumnavigated the island. He always enjoyed the ride, though he had to dodge packs of tourists on rental bikes. He couldn't even swear at them when they cut him off because they were all his customers.

Despite the occasional wet globs of dog saliva, the breeze on his face energized him. He hadn't had a panic attack since Tuesday, so hopefully he was on the way to another long run of mentally healthy weeks. Sometimes he could make it months—long enough that he thought he was cured.

The crowds thinned out once he passed the campsites on the west end of the island. They were still inhabited by visitors, but at this time of day everyone was probably either out hiking or had gone into the village for lunch. He pedaled harder, eliciting a yip of excitement from Beverly.

The wind came hard from the north, making the bike wobble. He could control it, no problem. He felt strong; he felt wonderful. He loved days like this—the open air, the warm sun, the temporary escape from the anxiety that so often plagued him.

Tristan began barking excitedly when Matteo stopped at the trailhead. A few weeks ago, they had seen a badger, so he wondered if Tris caught its scent again, or if he was just excited at the memory.

"Hang on, boy," Matteo told him, smiling. It was hard not to be happy on a day like this. He lifted Martha out of the box, and she staggered a bit before finding her footing. Okay, that dimmed his smile. Poor Martha. There was a decision he would have to make soon, a decision he would do everything in his power to avoid.

"Leashes, babies," he commanded the dogs, and Martha and Beverly sat obediently waiting for him to clip them in. Tristan, who normally behaved much better, took off running up the trail.

"Hey! Tristan! Damn it, come back here!" he called, but the corgi ignored him and disappeared into the woods. Shit, that was a problem. He'd gotten cited last year on this same trail when Deputy Mills came across a leash-less Beverly. That was $110 he'd never see again.

"Alright, my good girls. Let's find your brother," he told the others. Beverly started eagerly, but Martha was slow. That didn't matter. She had a keen nose, and even if she couldn't lead him to Tristan, he was sure Tristan would find his way back. After all, Matteo was the one with treats in his pocket.

A few minutes later, Tristan came running down the trail, but as soon as Matteo tried to grab him and fasten his leash, Tristan took off again. Stupid dog. "Tristan! Come now!" he shouted in as commanding a voice as possible. "I'm the leader of this pack, damn it."

"Matteo?" a woman's voice called. Oh, that's why Tristan ran off, he found a friend. And there she was, sitting on a fallen log. Cherry. Great. She'd probably want to tag along and talk his ear off.

"Hi, Cherry," he said, forcing himself to sound friendly. She was a decent enough person, notwithstanding her previous mockery of mental illnesses. "You enjoying the day?"

"Not especially. I sprained my ankle," she said. And then he noticed that her face was red from crying, not from her usual blushing. He sighed. This marked the end of his hike.

"Let me take a look." He knelt down and took her foot in his hands. Well, there was one reason. Flimsy, cheap tennis shoes with no ankle support. What the hell was she thinking, wearing something like that in the woods? He tried to be gentle, but she flinched and pulled away. "Yeah, it's pretty swollen. I'm going to bet you don't have a first-aid kit with you."

"I don't have anything with me," she said. He looked around. She really didn't. No backpack, no water bottle. She was the most unprepared person he'd ever encountered, and he dealt with tourists every day.

"Are you kidding?" he asked before he could stop himself. "What's wrong with you? You didn't even bring water? You could die, you know that? Did you bother telling anyone where you were going before you went wandering around in the forest?"

"You don't need to be so mean about it." She wiped her eyes with the back of her hand, and Tristan put his head in her lap. Stupid disloyal beast. "I was just going for a walk. I haven't explored much of the island yet. And when I saw the trail, I thought I'd only go a little ways in. I wasn't planning on a long hike, but there was a hole and I just . . ." She trailed off and turned her head away. Damn it, she was crying for real now.

"It's fine. Relax. Nothing bit you. You just found a woodchuck hole. Here, drink some of my water. And lucky for you, I do have a first-aid kit." Matteo always came prepared; it made good business sense. He led guided tours often, plus most tourists rented bikes from him, so being able to show up in emergencies with a bandage or a patch kit make him a hero in their eyes. Sometimes his preparedness earned him tips, or five-star reviews online, and occasionally, it got him some gratitude in the bedroom.

"Are you sure you know what you're doing?" Cherry asked as he opened up his backpack and pulled out a SAM splint and an ACE bandage.

"Yeah, I'm a first responder. You know this is a remote island, right? We don't have fancy things like hospitals and doctors, so we usually handle our own healthcare needs." Years ago, one of Matteo's first initiatives when he was elected to village council was to make arrangements to bring wilderness medicine certification courses to the island.

"That's not true. I saw a medical center," she protested, because she obviously hadn't bothered to do any research before moving here.

"A limited medical center that's only fully staffed during the summer. We have a nurse practitioner or sometimes a

*No Longer Yours*

physician's assistant that rotate through a couple of days a week in the winter, part of some rural medicine out-reach nonprofit something or other. If you get injured, you better hope it's on a day when someone is there. But we islanders are resilient and prepared for just about anything. Believe me, you'll appreciate it. Non-professional but qualified medical care is a hell of a lot cheaper than a helicopter ride to the hospital." He kept talking to distract her while he wrapped her ankle. She was clearly in a great deal of pain and she winced every time he moved it. He half wondered if it might be broken. "If you want revenge for your injury, I'll tell Timmy. He'll come up here, catch whatever woodchuck dug that burrow, and cook it up for you."

"Ewww. Nobody eats woodchuck." Cherry made a disgusted face, and he smiled. It worked. She wasn't thinking about the pain anymore.

"Sure they do. Woodchuck stew is delicious, and September is the best time of year for it. They're all fat and happy from eating the tender parts of plants. They aren't nearly as tasty in winter, surviving off bark and stored fat. I told you, this is a remote island and we all do what it takes to survive. Now, speaking of survival, what's your plan for getting yourself home?"

"My plan?" She stared at him with those great big teary eyes, and he decided maybe he shouldn't tease.

"I'm kidding. You are actually the luckiest injured hiker ever, because not only is your rescuer strong enough to carry you down the road, but there's a bike waiting at the trailhead."

"I can't ride a bike like this!" The waterworks were starting again. Maybe she was someone who didn't handle pain well. She sure picked the wrong place to live. Didn't matter though. By the end of the school year, she'd be on her way back to whatever safe little suburb she came from. Hell, she'd probably not make it much longer than the first snowfall.

"Don't worry, I got you covered. It's a bakfiets, a box bike. You can ride with my dogs. Now, you'll have to wear my backpack, and hop on my back." He repacked his first-aid supplies and handed her the bag. Once she tightened the straps and cinched the waist belt he turned around. "Alright lady, climb aboard." This was not the hike he had hoped for.

They made it back to the bike, followed by three frolicking dogs happy to be off-leash. Even Martha had more of a spring in her step. Matteo hesitated a moment when they got there—he didn't have a helmet for Cherry. Should he give her his? He didn't want to be responsible for cracking her skull if they got in an accident. But if he gave her his helmet, this could be the one time that he wrecked and then he . . . he realized he was starting an anxiety spiral. Yet another way she ruined his day.

"I have to ride in this?" Cherry asked, her voice cracking as he lowered her gently down. The pain was worsening, he could tell. Her face was paler than usual, and she kept biting her lower lip.

"Yeah, it's the only way. But Tristan will keep you company. Actually, they all will. So you'll have a nice comfy dog-filled ride." He helped adjust her so that she was on the bench seat and propped her leg up on the edge of the box before loading the dogs. He didn't want any of them to bump her injury and hurt her worse.

He managed the trip to her apartment without incident. He offered to take her down the street to the medical center, but she was worried about costs. That was fair enough. He was familiar with the health insurance that her job provided, and she had a high deductible. After moving, she likely didn't have enough money saved up to pay the expenses. So he gave her a piggyback ride up the stairs and settled her in on the couch.

"Matteo, I can't thank you enough," she told him, after he made her a sandwich and put it on the table next to her. "I was stuck in the woods for hours and I didn't know what to do. You saved me."

"Hours? Jeez, Cherry. You need to prepare yourself better when you go out in the wilderness." He regretted his words immediately. She was trying to express her gratitude, and he was being a jerk. But she had ruined his planned outing, and now that he knew she couldn't take care of herself at all, he felt some degree of responsibility toward her. "Get some rest. I'll send someone to check in on you later."

# Chapter Fifteen

Ever since her divorce, Cherry felt herself drifting, isolated and alone. She was no longer part of a team, she no longer had someone to count on, just herself. And that really hit home this morning, when she ended up sitting in the woods, pain shooting up her leg, and realized nobody knew where she was, and nobody would look for her until at least Monday morning.

When Tristan and Matteo found her, she had been so relieved. Matteo made her feel foolish and weak as he wrapped her ankle, but at least he acted like he knew what he was doing, and he took her home, too. She cried again when he left, from sheer relief. He had rescued her, and although he was grumpy while he did it, she was so grateful.

But now she didn't know what to do. She'd spent the rest of the afternoon lying on the couch, injured ankle elevated on a pillow with an ice pack. It hurt. It hurt a lot. And it turned an alarming shade of purple. She picked up the phone a few times, but she didn't have anyone to call. Her parents would be so worried about her, but they were too far away to do anything. And if she called Katie, they'd both break down in tears.

A knock on the door startled her, but she couldn't get up to answer it. She'd crawled to the bathroom earlier, but the pain was worse now and the idea of rolling off the couch to hobble to the door was unfathomable. "Come in," she shouted as loud as she could, hoping to see a friendly face. But since she didn't know anyone with a friendly face, she at least hoped it would be Matteo.

It was.

"Hey," he greeted her, entering her apartment and holding up a pizza box. "I brought you something."

She let him help her out to the balcony and prop her foot up. "It's too nice a day to be stuck inside," he told her. "Be warned. In a couple of months, it's going to be dark and cold, and you're going to be wondering why you moved here."

"I already am," she muttered.

"Oh, it's not that bad. Where's your usual optimism? You could have sprained your ankle on a city sidewalk, too. Here, pizza always makes everything better." He opened the box. "I asked Bryce, and he said you ordered this before, so I figured you'd like it. Personally, I prefer more vegetables on mine. This'll clog your arteries and send you to an early grave."

It was a pepperoni and sausage pizza, exactly what she ate last week when she ventured down to Antonio's for dinner. She hadn't liked it, actually. The meat was too greasy and heavy for her. She'd only ordered it because Gary hated meat on pizza, so for years she'd only had veggies and extra cheese, and she wanted to try something that didn't remind her of her failed marriage.

"Small town life," she smiled, not wanting to admit she didn't particularly enjoy those toppings. "Who's Bryce?"

"Pizza shop owner. Tourists want the authentic Italian experience, so he couldn't call it Bryce's, could he?" Matteo helped himself to a slice. "This is not my favorite. You know Bryce doesn't make his own sausage? You want good sausage, get it from Wayne at the diner. Or better yet, go up to the inn and tell Sam that you heard Wayne makes the best sausage. He'll load you down with free samples, as long as you don't mind listening to a lecture on cooking techniques."

Cherry tried to laugh, but she was in pain, and she didn't know most of the people Matteo was talking about anyway. "I do appreciate you bringing me this," she told him. "You didn't have to."

"I know. But I was getting my own dinner, when I thought about you, and I figured you weren't able to stand up to cook anything. I've needed help in the past, but I grew up here, I've got a network to rely on. I assume you don't yet. Also, Tristan would never forgive me if I didn't check on you. I don't know what you did to make that dumb dog like you so much."

"He's not dumb. He's the one who found me today."

"Yeah, true. Hey, hold on a second, I have an idea." Matteo stood up and leaned over the railing. "Ty! Tyrell! Wait, I need to talk to you!"

Cherry craned her neck to see who he was yelling at. It was an African-American man who had stopped an electric cart down the road to release some passengers. She didn't recognize him, so he wasn't a school parent.

"Be right back." Matteo ran off down the stairs.

Cherry took advantage of his absence to peel pepperonis off her pizza and hide them in her napkin. If she could hop fast enough, she would throw them away inside, but her ankle throbbed and even the thought of attempting to go anywhere was painful. She hated Gary in that moment, more than she had hated him before. He was the reason this all happened. And now she was stuck in her apartment, trapped with no family and no friends, and no idea how she would survive the next couple of weeks.

Matteo came back looking satisfied. "We're getting a special delivery in a few minutes. Have you taken any painkillers?"

"Ibuprofen. That's all," she said. Special delivery? Oh, she knew what that meant. He bought drugs. He wasn't going to try to make her get high, was he? "I don't . . . I don't do drugs, Matteo."

"Okay? So? I didn't think you did. I asked about medications to make sure you can still drink. You know your landlord Timmy, right? Well, I just talked to his husband and got us a six pack of some of their latest batch of beer. Beer makes everything better. It's a little hoppy, but not terrible. Their brewing skills are improving."

"I thought you said pizza made everything better." The promise of beer came as a relief. She didn't want to admit why she thought he tried to arrange a drug deal.

"That too. And because I'm awesome," Matteo continued, "I also got you crutches."

"What? How'd you do that?" Then she felt silly. She lived directly above a drugstore. They must sell them. She could have scooted down the stairs on her bottom and bought some.

"I should have thought of it earlier. If you need crutches, who do you ask?" Matteo gave her a self-satisfied grin.

"The drugstore," she said. Yep, that would have worked.

The grin faded from Matteo's face. "Oh, yeah, they probably have some too. I didn't think of that. No, if you want to borrow crutches, you ask your friendly neighborhood amputee. He's going to deliver them with the beer. See, it's all in who you know."

# Chapter Sixteen

Dear Gary,

Do you want to know the worst part of all this? The worst part of starting over, of leaving everything behind? It's that you weren't that bad.

You were great, actually. Everyone knew you were a good catch. Megan, especially, otherwise why would she take you from me? Why would she choose you over her rich husband?

I reflect back on all the happy memories of our life together and I am filled with bitter longing. Here I am, in my tiny apartment, with a sprained ankle. My injury has immobilized me. I can do nothing but sit on the couch and relax (relax? Ha!) and think. I suppose I could turn on the television, or read a book, but instead, I find myself staring at the ceiling, replaying scenes from our past.

We always threw the best parties. I loved hosting, even when it was for things I wasn't interested in, like watching televised basketball tournaments. I'd spend the day in the kitchen cooking, while you spent the day frantically cleaning so our friends wouldn't find out what secret slobs we were. I used to look around our parties and be consumed with deep happiness, surrounded by friends, enjoying good times.

*No Longer Yours*

That's all gone now, or at least, it is for me. You probably still host parties. Does Megan cook? She strikes me as someone who only knows how to hire a caterer, but you can't really afford that on two teachers' salaries, can you? Is she used to being poor yet? Did she move into our house with you? Did she bring her own furniture and redecorate?

Why can't I stop thinking about everything I lost? Here I am, in a beautiful place, with my dream job in an amazing school, and all I can think about is that overcrowded middle school in Parsons, and how much I miss it. I miss having colleagues to talk to during the day, a quick word in the teacher's lounge, a shared coffee before class.

I miss you, Gary. I miss the man I thought you were. You would have taken such good care of me if I'd sprained my ankle during our marriage. You'd have driven me to the hospital for X-rays, just in case. You'd have cooked meals for me, and carried me to bed, and rushed to give me things so I wouldn't have to get up. You'd have cared.

Why did you stop caring? What did I do to lose your love?

Struggling,

Cherry

## Chapter Seventeen

"It's been almost a month. How are things going?" The voice on the other end of the phone made Cherry want to cry. She held the receiver tightly to her ear.

"Everything is okay, but I miss you, Katie." She did, oh, she missed her so much. True, life had been busy for both of them the past couple of years, especially after Katie started having children, but she never stopped being Cherry's best friend and closest confidant. If it weren't for Katie, Cherry didn't know how she would have survived those first horrible months after her marriage disintegrated.

"Oh, I'm sure you've made tons of new friends. Whispering Pines is a small town, right? You've probably met everybody by now, and you're having a great time, and you're forgetting about all of us back here."

Cherry laughed at the rosy picture Katie painted. In truth, that was kind of what she had expected. She grew up in a small town where everyone was friendly, and there were always many community activities going on. Here, it was different. She'd discovered that because tourism was the only industry, all of the other residents seemed to work weekends. She tried going to The Digs on a Friday night, but it was full of tourists. While she didn't have a problem with tourists, vacationers weren't the ones she wanted to meet. She missed having a group of friends, people she could regularly talk to and socialize with.

"I'm lonely," Cherry admitted. "I've met a lot of people, and everybody seems to volunteer at the school in some capacity, but I haven't really made any friends yet. Well, there is one guy, but I don't know if he counts."

Was Matteo a friend? He acted so off-putting and slightly rude, but he brought her pizza when she sprained her ankle, and arranged not only for her to borrow crutches from Tyrell, but for Tyrell to check in on her later to make sure she could get around on them. But he wasn't friendly, *per se*. She half wondered if he only acted semi-nice to her out of a sense of professional obligation, since he was on the village council, and they were in charge of overseeing the school.

"Oooooh, you met a man? Is he cute? Tell me more!" Cherry closed her eyes and imagined Katie, curled up on her big red couch, toddler sleeping beside her. She missed her. She missed that life.

"Ha, no, not like that. He's just a surly grouch that I see at the diner every week. He has cute dogs though."

"Maybe you should sign up for a dating app? That'd be a good way of meeting people. It's time you put yourself out there, Cherry. Find yourself a new boyfriend."

"Am I ready for that?" Cherry wasn't sure. Part of her did want to meet someone special, but Gary's betrayal was still so raw and painful. How could she trust anyone again?

"At least promise me you'll think about it. I worry about you being alone and so far away." Katie's voice sounded wistful. They had been best friends for over a decade, and while sometimes jobs and obligations kept them from getting together as often as they liked, this was the first time they'd been geographically far apart. A sense of isolation descended upon Cherry again.

"I'll think about it."

# Chapter Eighteen

Dear Gary,

Well, I guess it's time. I'm going to start dating again. I spoke to Katie last night, and she says I need to set up a profile online. I don't know how to do these kinds of things. Remember when your friend Liam tried online dating, and we made such fun of him? He took all those shirtless pictures and he wanted me to choose the best one, since he wanted a feminine opinion.

He always came back with the most hilarious stories about terrible dates. Remember the one where the girl ran up a $60 bar tab and disappeared on him? Or the woman who brought her mother and sister along, and made Liam pay for them too? Or the psychotic one who thought going out on one date made him her exclusive boyfriend and she stole his phone and texted a message to every saved number in his contacts saying 'back off, he's mine now'?

We used to laugh at his stories and go to bed smug, secure in our marriage. I told you several times how grateful I was to never have to do any of that. How I didn't want to pick a guy like I was choosing from a catalog, and how fortunate I thought I was to meet my soulmate at such a young age. And you said you felt the same way. That's what you said, when you used to lie to me about the strength of our relationship.

*No Longer Yours*

But I'm going to do it. I'm going to create an account on MidWestSinglzNetwork. I'm going to put up a couple of pictures of myself for strangers to see and judge. I will select tasteful images that show what I really look like and I'll write a profile that sounds cheesy and dumb. Men will read it, and most will laugh and ignore me. Some will contact me, and maybe I'll like them, but maybe our conversations will be uncomfortable and strained. I'll go on some dates, and maybe they will be wonderful, or maybe I'll have horrible stories to tell later.

I've only been on one first date ever, and that was with you. It was lunch the day after we met, that was what we counted as our first date, even though we'd been out together with a big group of friends the night before. We ate in the Founder's Hall cafeteria because we had heard it was the nicest one. I remember being so excited about the assortment of desserts. Who eats dessert at lunchtime? Apparently college students.

Talking with you was so easy. We talked about orientation from the day before, we talked about the party we all went to, walking around with our upside down red Solo cups until we found the one we were looking for, and then leaving early when Katie got too drunk too fast. And we talked about our childhoods, and your parents, and teaching, and the future, and I walked out of the cafeteria half in love with you already. That was my only first date.

You were my only first kiss as well. We were in my dorm room, the first week of class. My awful roommate had gone to some sorority rush event, and you had come over to watch a movie. We were sitting on my bed—you were the first boy ever to sit on my bed—and you suddenly leaned over and our lips met, and afterwards, we both felt kind of surprised and dazed. That was your first kiss, too, or so you claimed.

Now I have to have a second first kiss with someone else. Will it be awkward? Will our teeth bump together? Will it be passionate? Will it make me feel alive again? Will I feel desired? Will I feel like I deserve to be loved? Will I ever feel anything like that ever again?

I don't know.

I am so alone.

I resent you, Gary.

# Chapter Nineteen

Cherry sat back and read what she had written.

*Hello! Thanks for checking out my profile! I'm a newly divorced single woman looking for friends and possibly more. I enjoy good books, fine wine, and intimate conversation. I'm originally from a small Ohio town, and now live on an island, where I teach in a one-room schoolhouse.*

She sounded boring. Would anyone actually click the winky face button, or whatever they were supposed to do? She wasn't quite familiar with this online dating thing. Her only prior experience was helping Katie fill out a profile on FirstDate, a profile that was never used because two days later Katie met the love of her life while standing in line at the DMV. *I met the love of my life the first day of orientation,* Cherry thought bitterly. *And look where that got me.*

She walked away to start getting ready for bed, when suddenly she heard the beep of an incoming message. Already? Internet dating was easier than she thought.

No, no it wasn't. She recognized the face on the profile contacting hers. Matteo. Well, this was embarrassing. Now he knew she signed up for a dating site.

His message lacked any pretense of friendliness. *Change your privacy settings!*

*Hello Matteo! What do you mean?*

*Anyone can message you. Go to the upper-right-hand corner under settings and change it to only let people you've matched with contact you.*

*Why? Isn't the point of this to meet people?*

*Do you want an inbox full of dick pics?*

*I know what that sounds like, but I don't know what that is.* She sat back and watched the screen.

*Penises. Do you want an inbox full of unsolicited pictures of penises?*

*You're very crude. People don't actually do those sorts of things.*

*Yes they do.*

*I don't believe you.*

*I'm taking a picture of my junk for you right now.*

*Don't you dare!*

The next message didn't contain words, just an image. Whatever he sent must have been a large file, it was taking such a long time to open. She clicked to make it fill her screen, but all she could see was an icon showing that it was still loading.

*Ha! You opened it! You want dick pics!*

*How can you tell?*

*When you do I get a notice saying picture viewed.*

*But I can't see anything. It's still loading.*

*Of course it is. I didn't actually send you a dick pic. I sent you a screenshot of the loading symbol. What kind of man do you take me for?*

*You said you were sending me . . . oh.*

*Well, now that I know you want it. Hang on, I need to adjust the light to get a better shot.*

*Don't you dare! The only thing you've done is demonstrate that you're a creepy jerk.*

*Hey, I was only teasing. Obviously, I'm not sending you anything. But I'm willing to bet when you wake up tomorrow morning, you'll find an inbox full of hard-ons. Not mine, of course, unless you ask nicely. Don't click to make any of them bigger, unless that's what you're in to.*

*Just because you're disgusting doesn't mean everybody else is. I'm ending this conversation now.*

She closed her laptop and sat back, fuming. Matteo was wrong. He was rude and he was wrong.

🌲 🌲 🌲 🌲 🌲

The next morning when she woke up, the first thing she did was check her dating account. There would be no private parts pictures whatsoever, and she would make Matteo eat his words. She logged in to MidWestSinglz to see fifteen new contacts. Wow, this really did work better than she expected. Maybe her profile wasn't as boring as she feared.

First message: Hey, you want some of this, with a picture of a . . . oh. Matteo was right. Twelve of the fifteen had an attached photo. That was okay, the other three didn't. She opened one of those, to find a link to something she definitely wasn't going to click on. The second one was another link. Darn it. And the third? Matteo again: *You awake yet? Tell me the magic number.*

*Twelve. You were right. I'm changing my settings.*

His response came almost instantaneously. *Ha! I knew it. See you tonight. You can tell me all about them.*

# Chapter Twenty

Cherry was almost too embarrassed to go to the diner that evening. She considered staying in and cooking to avoid getting teased by Matteo about her foray into the dating world. But no, she couldn't force herself to do that. She was too lonely to skip out on her one non-solitary meal.

He was already there when she arrived, and he turned and smiled at her from his seat. She took the stool next to him, leaning the crutches against the counter. Hopefully, she wouldn't need them much longer. Her ankle could almost support her weight.

"Why do we always sit at the counter? The tourists are gone, there are plenty of tables."

"*I* always sit at the counter because I dine alone, and it's polite to leave the tables for families. I have no idea why *you* sit here." He gave her a mocking look, and she was tempted to hobble to a table and leave him by himself.

"You said 'see you tonight,' so I assumed you meant here. And we've eaten together every Wednesday for over a month, so I thought . . ." she trailed off. What she had thought was that she had exactly one friend on the island and one regular social engagement. Her other interactions with actual adults were almost entirely with her assistant, Wanda, and with parents, so they consisted of nothing more than comments about students' progress and scheduling. She needed to be able to have a real conversation with someone.

"I was kidding. I told you before I like routines, and having dinner with you is a good one. I've actually been looking forward to tonight. Perhaps we can share some fine wine and intimate conversations?" He winked lewdly.

"Stop!" She put her hands over her cheeks to hide the blush. "Don't make fun of my profile! I'm humiliated enough to have to resort to Internet dating."

"Why would that be humiliating? That's how to meet people nowadays."

They were interrupted by Wayne delivering two plates of food. Cherry started to protest that she hadn't even looked at the menu yet.

"I ordered for both of us. Isn't it easier if the food arrives at the same time?" Matteo said. "Don't worry, you'll like it. And if you don't, I'll trade you."

She looked down at her plate, another fish dish, this one with potatoes. Maybe she shouldn't have mentioned wanting to try new things. But she wasn't going to complain—the fact that Matteo ordered for her meant he really did expect her to join him. It was the most welcome she'd felt in a long time.

"So continue," Matteo said as they began eating. "You were telling me about the utter humiliation of using modern technology to interact with strangers in a place where you know nobody."

"That's not what I meant," she tried to explain. "I guess I've always thought online dating was, well, for losers." This wasn't how romances were supposed to start. Dating services were for people who couldn't find anybody else, for the rejects who didn't know how to approach people in public or who didn't have any friends who could set them up with someone. She hated that she now fell into these categories.

"Wow. You do realize you're talking to someone who has a profile himself. Anyway, you're the one trolling for dick pics, not me."

"I'm not trolling for anything. I don't understand why so many guys sent me those."

"I can tell you exactly why. You announced you're recently divorced. They know you're newly on the market, and you're over thirty, so you probably have low standards, and they think if they show you their penis, you'll be impressed enough to want to touch it, or mad enough to reply to their message. Any response counts as a win for them. They have an interaction, they apologize, tell you they didn't mean to send that picture, but did you like it anyway?"

"That is not how reasonable men act."

"There are no reasonable men on MidWestSinglz. You haven't realized that yet? Look at where we live. There are so few single people within a two-hundred mile radius that as soon as someone new shows up on the app, everybody jumps on them."

"Why do you bother then? You were obviously using it yesterday, or you wouldn't have known I created an account."

"I received an alert telling me a hot new single was in my area, so I had to log in and check her out. And I'm not a reasonable man. And I'm not looking for a relationship."

"Then why are you on a dating service if you don't want to date someone?"

"Are you truly so hopelessly naïve, Cherry? I'm not looking to date, I'm looking to fuck."

Cherry's mouth gaped open in horror. Did people really talk that way? What the heck was wrong with him? "Don't use such foul language! You're awful!"

Matteo smirked at her. "You're joking, right? You're on a dating app, but you get to be a prude? Okay, I'll rephrase. I'm looking to make sweet and gentle love to a variety of willing women. It works great during tourist season, not so well in the winter time. My favorites are the unmarried older sisters at family reunions and the bridesmaids at their best friend's weddings. They want to feel pretty and desired, and I'm more than capable of desiring them, so everybody wins."

"Matteo, you are a terrible person! You're taking advantage of women when they're vulnerable!"

"Women have agency, you misogynist. I don't know what decade you came from, but in this one, women are allowed to choose to have sex with whomever they want. If they happen to choose me, so be it. I'm not complaining."

"You just said you manipulate them."

"No, I said women who are lonely and feeling bad about themselves want to feel better. Look, I never lie to anyone. I live on this island and I'm not leaving. If someone wants to come here and sleep with me, I'm not going to turn them away. But at least I'm honest and upfront about who I am, and what I'm looking for, and where I'm staying."

She definitely didn't want to talk to him anymore after hearing that. But then a new horrifying question came out before she could stop herself. "You don't . . . you don't send them pictures of your you-know-what, do you?"

He had just taken a bite of food and nearly choked on it when he laughed. "My you-know-what? Yes, actually, I do, but only when requested. Some ladies want to be sure they know what they're in for before they board the ferry. Personally, I'm wondering why you're so interested in my you-know-what. First you asked for a pic last night, now you bring it up again? I'm happy to show you right here so you can move on." Without breaking eye contact, he reached down and undid the top button of his jeans.

"Stop! Oh, you are a disgusting crude man! I don't know why I'm talking to you." She turned back to her food, planning to ignore him. Then another mortifying thought struck her. "Wait . . . you're not . . . I mean, you don't . . ."

"Don't what? Spit it out."

"You don't think I'm going to sleep with you, do you? Is that why you talk to me?"

Matteo stared at her for a second before letting out another loud burst of laughter. "Cherish Marie Waites, I assure you, I can do better. I have no interest in you whatsoever. You do have quite an ego though."

"Fine. I get it. Just so we're clear, I have no interest in you either." Now she really was going to ignore him for the rest of the meal. Except she couldn't, because he was wrong about something else, too. "And that's not my middle name!"

## Chapter Twenty-One

Dear Gary,

Today I saw two birds fighting. They were from different species.

I almost wore mismatched socks. Then I realized it, and considered wearing them anyway, and giving a piece of candy to whichever student noticed first. But then I decided that was silly and changed into a matching pair.

I got a papercut, which hurt.

One of my students got a haircut that makes her look just like your cousin's kid, minus the buckteeth, of course. I've never met anybody with teeth like your family.

These are all inconsequential things that nobody cares about. I used to tell you these mundane bits of my life. I'm not sure you really cared, but that didn't matter; you had your own bits of trivial nonsense you shared with me. That's what being in a relationship is. It's not just the big picture stuff, it's these tiny little pieces of our days that we share with each other that bring us closer. Except now we'll never be closer, we'll keep getting farther apart.

I have no one to share those small fractions of my life with anymore.

I wish I were a widow. It would be a different sort of pain—deeper, and more beautiful. Instead, here I sit, bitter and hateful. I didn't used to be that way. You used to tease me, remember, about my innate optimism? I could always find the good in every person, the silver lining in every cloud.

If you were dead, when people asked about my husband, I could wipe my eyes and look away sadly, and they would feel the urge to comfort me. They'd be mindful of my feelings. Friends and family would still be checking in with me to see if I was hanging in there and to make sure I was getting through the healing process. If you had died, my grief would be socially acceptable.

But you aren't dead. You're a lying cheater. And people pity me, but they also wonder what I did wrong, why wasn't I enough to keep you, did I push you away? Was I frigid? Did I nag too much? What was so terrible about me that my husband had to seek solace in another woman's arms? And they want me to move on. They tell me to join dating websites and they say 'put yourself out there' and 'there are plenty of fish in the sea.' You know what else is in the sea? Garbage. Big masses of floating garbage. I'm sure that's a metaphor for something. How can I find a fish in a sea of garbage? And why would I want to?

It'd be easier if you were dead. I'd have our house, both retirement accounts, and all the savings. And I would have been able to keep my job, and my friends, and my life, and I wouldn't have had to flee to this tiny island in the middle of nowhere.

*No Longer Yours*

Unfortunately your ex,

Cherry

# Chapter Twenty-Two

*Whispering Pines Island, October 2014*

Cherry's stomach twisted itself in knots as she waited for Jared down by the ferry dock. This was it. She was back on the dating scene. It wouldn't be terrible, right? She didn't expect magic, she wasn't going to fall in love or anything. No. But Jared seemed like a nice, safe choice. She was dipping her toe in the waters, and it was smart to start in the shallow end.

The man who approached her didn't quite match his profile picture, and it was obvious that he wore a hat in it to conceal his receding hairline. But that wasn't a big deal, right? Gary was losing his hair too. At her age, and in this remote location, she couldn't afford to be picky. And so what if he was very clearly not the advertised six feet tall? Just because Gary had been tall didn't mean she needed to date a tall man. Someone she could easily make eye contact with was fine.

"Are you Cherry?" Jared asked as he approached and handed her a bouquet of pink roses. "Wow, you look exactly like your picture. That never happens!"

"Thanks," Cherry said, accepting the roses and wondering what he expected her to do with them. Flowers were a sweet gesture when getting picked up at her apartment; they were less sweet if she had to carry them around all evening. "Did you enjoy the ferry ride?"

"It was neat!" Jared said enthusiastically. "You know, my family used to vacation here a long time ago. It's been so many years, I had forgotten all about this island. I'm glad you reminded me!" His excitement far exceeded hers. This was only supposed to be dinner, right?

This whole situation disconcerted her. She had zero experience with men and relationships other than Gary. Now she was starting over from scratch, looking at the possibility of many first dates beginning with this one, with a misleadingly short balding man who had kind of a weird smile.

"Shall we go eat?" she asked. "There's a diner with a varied menu, or a pizza place that's pretty good, or maybe Harbor Snax, where they host a big Friday night fish fry?" *Please pick the diner*, she silently willed him. Matteo had mentioned going to the fish fry, and she didn't need to run into him and hear his snarky comments about her date. He'd find out about it anyway, the way gossip in this town went, but she didn't want him to be the one spreading it.

Fortunately, Jared did want to go to the Village Diner and see if it had changed since his childhood vacations. It hadn't—as he exclaimed loudly—when they walked in the door. He eagerly pointed out where he and his sister once spilled lemonade, and the booth where his little brother had a meltdown and crawled under the table screaming throughout the meal.

"Come to think of it, maybe that's why we stopped going on vacations," he laughed, before beginning a rather pointless story about his earlier Piney Islands trips.

Cherry tried not to fidget as she sat at the table, head resting on her hand, and listened. Jared was extremely talkative, so much so that she could scarcely get a word in edgewise. Even when he asked her about herself, he would cut her off with yet another anecdote about his life, mostly about his youth. She learned that he used to be a picky eater, she found out every position he played in little league baseball, and he spent an inordinate amount of time describing his high school days and everyone he went to school with. She forced herself to pay polite attention, but occasionally felt her eyes glazing over. A hand on her back snapped her out of it.

"Well, hello Miss Waites. No fish fry for you tonight?" It was Matteo, with his broad grin and mockingly friendly expression.

"I'm on a date," she informed him, hoping to make him go away.

"Oh, you must be from MidWestSinglz." Matteo reached out to shake Jared's hand. "I've dabbled in that myself. I'm Matteo."

"Jared," he replied.

"Seriously? Oh my god, please tell me your nickname is Jerry, that's too perfect. First Gary, now Jerry. Good job, Cherry!" Matteo's face contorted in a smirk that made her want to throw something at him. He sounded like he was reading a Dr. Seuss book.

"Did you need something?" she asked.

"Hey, no need to be rude. I was just saying hello. Have fun you two. Jerry, take good care of our Cherry here." He winked and walked over to the counter.

"So who was that guy?" Jared asked. He put his hand over Cherry's on top of the table. "Ex-boyfriend?"

"No, he's just an annoying man who hangs out in the diner to harass people," she explained, which led to Jared telling an excruciating story only tangentially related to the subject. Cherry feigned more interest than she felt. Matteo was sitting in such a way that he could see them, and she did not want him to know how bored she was. He would make fun of her later.

After the interminable meal finally ended, Cherry brightly suggested, "Well, I guess we should get you back to the ferry, so you don't miss the next ride to the mainland."

"What? No way, I'm having a great time. Say, why don't we check out the bar down the street? That's a place I've never been."

She reluctantly agreed, picked up her bouquet from the table, and let Jared hold her hand on the way out. Matteo was watching, so she had to act like she was enjoying herself.

🌲 🌲 🌲 🌲 🌲

At The Digs, Jared expressed how impressed he was by everything. "This is so neat!" he kept saying, as if there were no other words in his vocabulary. "Look how old everything is. Neat! Oh, and the old newsletters on the walls, those are so neat!"

When Tim came over to take their order and raise an eyebrow at her, Cherry stopped herself from ordering a scotch, neat.

"I love this place." Jared was effusive in his praise as they looked for somewhere to sit. Cherry was just glad the tables in the darkest corners were taken. They ended up near the dart machine, a brighter area which seemed safer. "I could really see myself coming here often. It's so neat!"

"Yes, it sure is," Cherry agreed. She wished there was a clock visible from her position, and regretted not wearing a watch. Surely he needed to leave to catch the last ferry soon.

"I'm so glad I met you, Cherry," he told her, and tried to take her hand again. She pretended she didn't notice him reaching for it and used it to smooth back her hair. "I'm serious. You're amazing. I feel such a connection between us." He looked so earnest as he said it. Earnest and misguided. He didn't know a single thing about her, he hadn't let her talk all night.

"Thank you," she said politely. "But . . ."

"No, thank *you*. I can't believe how fortunate I am. I've been on MidWestSinglz for almost a year, and most females won't even respond to my messages. I can't count the number of times I've been rejected or ignored. But then you came along, and I'm really feeling this."

"Oh. Well, I . . ." she trailed off. Being nice had been ingrained in her from such an early age. She wanted to stand up, throw her drink in his face, and scream 'you haven't let me speak! What connection? You know nothing about me!' But she never had the courage to do that sort of thing.

Jared surprised her by getting up and moving to her side of the table, forcing her to slide down in the booth. "I've been wanting to get closer to you all night," he told her.

"Oh, hey guys, mind if I join you?" Matteo appeared from out of nowhere, dropping into Jared's recently vacated seat. Relief coursed through her veins, and she suddenly felt safer.

"We're still on a date," Jared informed him, putting an arm around Cherry's shoulders. Her eyes involuntarily widened, and she gave Matteo a look that she hoped he would interpret as 'help me!'

"Sorry, Jerry, didn't mean to interrupt," Matteo rose to his feet and started to walk away. He turned back abruptly. "Oh, there's no clock in here, so I should tell you the ferry is going to head out soon. I'll walk with you down to the docks. Let's go."

"I'm not taking the ferry," Jared said.

"What?" Cherry's stomach dropped. Had she been giving off the wrong vibes?

"Oh, you brought your own boat? Awesome. I've got a new nineteen-foot Yamaha FSH myself. What do you have?" Matteo sat back down as though he'd just been invited into a conversation.

"No, I'm staying overnight, aren't I, Cherry?" For perhaps the first time all evening, Jared actually appeared interested in what she had to say. She tried to be polite.

"We hadn't discussed that, and this is a first date," she said carefully.

"I know, but it's going so well, and we have such a great connection..."

"Jeez, you sound like you're on a dating show," Matteo interrupted. "Next you're going to say you're 'here for the right reasons,' aren't you?" He looked so smug that Cherry was tempted to invite Jared to spend the night on her couch just to wipe that look from Matteo's face, but there was no guarantee and a lot of doubt that Jared would be willing to remain on the couch.

"Cherry?" Jared looked at her expectantly. "Tell him."

"Jared, I...umm..." Why was this so difficult?

"I paid for your dinner," Jared reminded her as he put his hand on her thigh. He had obviously interpreted this date very differently than she had.

"You did? Well, Cherry, a diner meal has gotta be worth at least a handie. You could take care of it real quick under the table, and he can still catch the ferry. I'll wait." Matteo leaned back and crossed his arms, with a big stupid grin on his face.

"That's not . . ." Cherry started to argue, but as he had been doing all night, Jared cut her off.

"Who do you think you are, talking to my date like that?"

"I'm a mediator, I'm helping with the negotiations. You implied that buying her food was putting a down payment on her body, so I'm helping set a value. You're welcome by the way."

"Matteo, please stop," Cherry begged. This was the worst night she'd had since moving here. She wanted to run home and cry, but Jerry was blocking her in the booth.

"That's not what I meant. I just meant our date is going really well, and it doesn't end here, right Cherry? Can we just ditch this guy and go back to your place now?"

"Counter-offer," Matteo said. "Stay here. I'll buy you both a couple of drinks—top-shelf, of course—and then we all go back to my place, and you work off your debts." He winked lasciviously.

"This is ridiculous. We're leaving." Jared stood up and offered his hand to Cherry. She looked from him to Matteo.

"I'm not going anywhere with either of you," she finally got the courage to speak up. "You're both disgusting, talking about me like that. Jared, this was just a first date. You aren't coming to my apartment. And Matteo, you can never buy me anything, ever again."

"Finally. I was wondering what it would take to get you to stand up for yourself," Matteo rose to his feet and gave her that same self-satisfied smirk that always made her want to slap him. "Alright, buddy, let's go. Docks, now."

Matteo wasn't that much bigger, or even intimidating, but Jared still took a couple of steps backward.

"Fine. You're not that good looking anyway. I can do better," he snapped at Cherry and strode out the door.

"Good date?" Matteo asked, once again sitting down uninvited.

"Very funny. I hate you."

"No, you don't. Come on, relax. I'll buy you a drink, no strings attached, and you can explain why you're doing this to yourself. You just got divorced, you probably shouldn't rush into dating when you're so clearly not ready."

"Well, I have to move on sometime." She did, she hated being alone. Sometimes, she wasn't sure if it was Gary that she missed, or just the feeling of being part of a couple, of always having someone around. It was difficult to put it into words, but she tried. "Matteo, I've never been so alone in my life. I hate it. I hate being alone. I hate living alone. I need to find someone to fill up this hole in my life."

His mouth twitched, and she instantly realized the double entendre he was going to make. "Don't you dare!" she warned him before he could. She wasn't sure she could handle anymore tonight.

"Darn, you got me. Fine, I won't. But look, Cherry, you need to be more careful in your choices. Don't rush into anything."

"Why do you care so much?" she asked.

"I don't actually. In fact, I should be encouraging you. Tourism slows down this time of year, so I need something to entertain me. I can't wait to see the next guy you bring around."

"You aren't funny at all," she informed him. But she did allow him to buy her a drink. It was better than spending the rest of the evening alone.

# Chapter Twenty-Three

Dear Gary,

Remember how we used to talk about retirement? How, when we were old and gray, we'd buy a house by a lake with a big front porch, where we could sit and watch the water for hours? Our children and grandchildren would come to visit. Sometimes, in the summers, the grandkids would come to stay with us for a week or two, and we'd swim in the lake and make them pancakes for breakfast every day, fancy ones with chocolate chips and whipped cream, the kind of breakfast we would have never made for our children—because we would have been great parents and enforced healthy eating habits most of the time.

Remember Anita? That's the name I picked out for our daughter, but we mostly would have called her Annie. She would have had a little brother named George, after your beloved grandfather, and Annie would have called him Georgie and complained when he messed with her stuff, but they would have been the best of friends. Annie and I would have fought sometimes, when she was a teenager, but those fights would have been tempered with love. We would have gone to the beach for family vacations, and we would have celebrated birthdays, and baked cookies for Santa. We would have loved those kids so darn much.

But Annie doesn't exist, and she never will. Neither will George. You've taken them away. It wasn't just our relationship you destroyed. It was our potential children's lives. Anita Dryden will never be born, she will never lose a tooth, or draw a picture, or grow up and fall in love. George Dryden will never exist. He will never learn to play catch, or ride a bike, or beg for a dog, and we will never give in and get a puppy named Chewy and then another one named Luthor, so Chewy doesn't have to be alone during the day.

You took all of that away. You eliminated our children, our grandchildren, generations of descendants. They will never exist because of your selfishness.

I live near a lake now, just like we imagined. I can't see the lake from my apartment, but it's only a short walk, two minutes, max. I can walk down to the shore and stare out over the cold waters and imagine some kind of future. But Annie and George aren't in it, not anymore. I'll never meet them, I'll never nurse them and hold them and love them.

I hate you Gary. I hate you so much.

With bitterness,

Cherry

# Chapter Twenty-Four

The students always ran out the door so fast when Cherry dismissed them. They were in such a hurry these days, all of them. Jack, her only high school senior, had taken the time to explain—with the early sunset, they needed to get in their outdoor time immediately. The younger kids went straight to the playground, where a couple of parents waited with snacks, the others dispersed around the island to the woods and the trails.

Cherry watched them go with a smile on their face, admiring their youthful energy. Then she noticed the man leaning against the building, also watching them. "I remember those days. It's more fun when Lesser Lake freezes, and they can ice skate. Should be soon."

"What are you doing here?" she asked cheerfully.

"Why are you always in such a good mood?" Matteo responded. "I don't get it."

"Why aren't you always in one? Look around. We live in a beautiful place. We breathe fresh air every day. You're a successful business owner and you have the most amazing dogs I've ever met. You should be in a great mood too."

"Your optimism is annoying." He followed her back into the school and, uninvited, sat down on her desk. "Listen, I came by for a reason. You know I hate changing my routine, but I'm not eating at the diner tonight. Do you know my business partner, Cara? She and her boyfriend invited me over for dinner."

"Oh." Cherry felt strangely disappointed. Matteo was often surly and rude, but he was also her only friend, and eating with him was her main social interaction. "I haven't met her, but I think I met her boyfriend at the bar once."

"Big guy, lots of hair, kind of dumb? Yeah. He's a professional chef, so he makes a pretty good meal."

"How lucky for you. Well, have fun." She smiled as brightly as she could so that he wouldn't see how much it affected her. Her only plans, canceled.

"Here's the thing, though. I don't like changing my routine."

"You've said that." She didn't either, not when it meant she would be eating alone, again . . . as usual.

"So I was thinking, you're part of my Wednesday night routine, so why don't you come with me? The food there is always phenomenal. I think Tyrell and Tim are coming too, so there'll be a bunch of people. Might be fun for you, talking to grownups instead of kids for a change."

"Are you sure it's okay?" she asked, her heart soaring. An actual night with adults! A dinner party! This was her first invitation to anything since she'd gotten here.

"Yeah, I already told Cara I'd bring you. I'll come by your apartment at 5:30."

After he walked away, she sank down into her chair and covered her mouth so he couldn't hear her squeal of excitement. She couldn't contain her grin. Maybe she'd make a real friend tonight!

# Chapter Twenty-Five

Matteo arrived precisely on time and parked a tandem bike at the foot of Cherry's stairs. He assumed she knew how to ride, though he hadn't actually asked. He'd guessed at her helmet size, too. Her head was medium, right? It looked medium-ish. If he was wrong, he'd race back to his shop and grab another one.

He knocked on the door and was about to turn the knob, but stopped himself. Usually, he strolled right in to his friend's houses, but Cherry wasn't a friend, not really. More of an acquaintance. She was just somebody who liked to play with his dogs and he felt sorry for her being all alone. He knew about loneliness.

"Come in, I'm almost ready," she greeted him, stepping aside to let him pass. He looked around.

"I love what you've done with the place," he said.

"I didn't do anything. It came fully furnished."

He walked over and sat down on the couch. "I know, I was being sarcastic. I used to manage this property. Everything looks exactly the same. Same terribly uncomfortable couch, too. You ought to get a new one. Tim can store whatever you don't want."

"Oh, well, I . . . I don't want to redecorate. I'm not ready to have to buy new things," she said, and her cheeks turned pink. Was she embarrassed? Who cared if she couldn't afford to decorate? He wasn't one to judge.

"When you do, don't take down that ugly old fishing net. I think it's structural."

"Are you serious? Oh dear, that's the one thing I was planning on removing." Was she really that gullible?

"No, but if you twist one of those big shells just right, it opens the secret passage."

"You aren't as funny as you think you are." She picked up two bottles of wine from the counter. "What should I bring? Red or white?"

"Don't bring anything."

"Are you being sarcastic again? I can't tell."

"Trust me. We show up with any kind of food or beverage contribution, we get treated to a lecture about wine pairings and how Sam already chose the perfect combination. You only take something to Cara and Sam's if they specifically request it. I promise, it saves a lot of headaches that way."

"Are you sure?" Cherry chewed on her lower lip and looked so uncomfortable with the idea that Matteo almost second guessed himself. Was it rude to not bring anything? He had an unopened bottle of tequila at home, and Cara always appreciated that. No, it was fine. He'd been there many times and seen many people make the same mistake Cherry was about to make. Sam was obsessively particular about his food.

"I promise. Don't worry, I'll tell them you wanted to bring something and I stopped you. Seriously, once Tim took hotdish, and I swear Sam was so confused and horrified. It throws off his meal planning and his tiny brain can't handle it."

"That's different. I can understand not bringing a cooked dish, but bringing a bottle of wine is traditional," she objected.

"I forgot, you aren't from around here. It's not *a hotdish*, just *hotdish*. It's basically tater-tot casserole. People bring it to potlucks all the time. Everybody and their grandmother has a recipe."

Cherry giggled. "I still can't tell if you're kidding. But honestly, tater tot casserole sounds pretty good to me."

"Great. I'll tell Wayne to make it part of the special next Wednesday. Now come on, we have to go. I brought a bike."

"The bakfiets again?"

He shook his head. "Even better. A tandem bike."

Her eyes widened. "A tandem bike? Now I know you're joking. Right?"

"That wouldn't be a very funny joke, Cherry."

"I assumed we were walking. I haven't ridden a bike since I was a child. I don't even know if I remember how anymore."

"Cherish Louise Waites, you always say you want to try new things, so you are getting on my bike and riding. No arguments." He folded his arms and tried to look stern, though he felt a little silly.

"That's not my middle name!" Her chipmunk cheeks reddened, and she looked like she wanted to yell at him. Good, that snapped her out of whatever self-pitying fear that was making her hesitate.

"You're going to have to mount up, lady. I don't want to sound too cliché, but it really is just like riding a bike."

# Chapter Twenty-Six

Cherry committed to trying new things when she moved to the island. That's why she hiked every weekend, and went on near daily long walks, and actually started thinking about taking up jogging. But getting on a tandem bicycle? That was a whole different level of newness. Matteo held the bike for her, and she mounted the rear half—the stoker, as he called it. As soon as she placed her bottom on the seat, it wobbled beneath her, and she put her feet back on the ground.

"I'm going to fall off and sprain my ankle again!" She wrapped her fingers around the handlebars in a death grip and tried to force herself to get back on.

"Oh, relax Cherry Blossom," he responded. "It's easy as long as you trust me. You do trust me, right?"

She actually paused before she answered. Instinct was to say yes, of course, but did she? He was abrasive and rude, but he had rescued her when she injured herself. And he was a good, if surly, conversationalist. And, most importantly, he'd never given her reason not to trust him.

"Sure, I trust you. But don't call me Cherry Blossom."

"Your hesitation has been noted. Now get your ass on the seat, and your feet on the pedals. When I say 'on' you start pedaling. That's when I'm going to mount and pedal too. But you have to start. It'll feel weird for you, but I promise, I won't let you fall."

They managed to start the bike without her falling to her death or breaking any bones and then they were off, riding through the village. Matteo waved at a couple of people as they passed, but Cherry kept her hands firmly on the grips. She wasn't going to let go until they were safely stopped.

The ride went well. She listened to Matteo's shouted instructions, telling herself to relax and follow along. He obviously knew what he was doing, and if they crashed, he'd be hurt too, so surely he wouldn't do anything to cause that. As they pedaled, she slowly became comfortable enough to start enjoying herself. As soon as she settled in to the rhythm and they started going faster, he slowed them down again.

"Here we are," Matteo said, steering them on a narrow path behind the main building of the Inn at Whispering Pines. They stopped in front of a small house, and he straddled the bike so she could dismount first.

"Oh my goodness, that was fun!" She felt exhilarated. She did it! She rode a tandem bike!

"You're the best first-timer I've ever taken out. I brought a light, so on the way back, we can take the longer route, go all the way around the island. Unless, of course, you're too scared." He raised an eyebrow to accompany his annoyingly cocky grin.

She smiled back. "I'm up for the challenge."

🌲 🌲 🌲 🌲 🌲

The success of the ride helped quell some of her anxiety about the dinner party. She couldn't help but feel nervous. This would be her first evening associating with island adults in this context—as opposed to friendly superficial chats at the bar or coffee shop—and she wanted to fit in so she'd be invited back for more.

Matteo leaned his bike against the porch railing and led her to the door, where he didn't bother knocking. He just opened it, and they walked in—apparently, he acted as rude to other people as he did to her. A pretty auburn-haired woman Cherry had never seen before was kneeling at the fireplace, jamming logs in.

"Good, you both made it." She stood up and brushed her hands on her jeans before walking over. "Hi, I'm Cara. You must be Cherry. I've heard all about you."

"It's nice to finally meet you," Cherry told her politely. Normally, this would be the moment she'd hand over a hostess gift, but Matteo had talked her out of that. She hoped Cara wouldn't take her lack of bringing anything as a slight.

"You too. I've been wondering about the person who role-played me and gave Tim nightmares."

"I . . ." Cherry had forgotten about that first night in the bar. Her face started to turn red, betraying her emotions as always. Gary used to tease her about that.

"Relax, it was hilarious. In the version I heard, Tim was so freaked out he had to go hide in the back for a few minutes to compose himself. Hey, Matty, if you finish making the fire, I'll go get us all a drink."

"Sure." Matteo ambled over to the fireplace, and Cara disappeared into the kitchen, leaving Cherry uncomfortably alone by the door. When it got too awkward standing there, she went over to watch Matteo.

"I wish I knew how to build fires," she commented. "I've got a fireplace in my apartment, but I don't know if it even works."

Matteo grunted in response, but didn't even look at her. Was she really welcome here? Why ask her to come if he wasn't going to talk to her at all? It reminded her that she was still an outsider.

"I hope you like red." Cara returned balancing three wineglasses and handing one to Cherry. "It's a Barolo that my cousin sent me from Italy. We're having duck tonight, so this is all Sam will let us drink until dessert. Something about flavor profiles and palettes. Cherry, I should warn you, my boyfriend is extremely particular about food."

"I already warned her." Matteo stood up and closed the screen in front of the fire before taking his glass. "She wanted to bring something, but I let her know your man is crazier than me when it comes to some things." Cherry was grateful he brought it up, so that she didn't look like the rude one.

"Oh my god, remember the time Tim brought over hotdish? Sam was so horrified. He whispered 'do I have to serve this?' to me. And when I told him he did, I thought he might cry."

"I wasn't going to cry, I was rethinking the entire meal plan and wondering if I had time to make sausage," Sam yelled from the kitchen.

"See? He's sensitive," Matteo whispered loudly.

"I heard that!" Sam came into the living room wearing a bandanna tied around his head and an actual chef's coat, the first time Cherry had seen one on a real person. She always thought of them as a television chef gimmick. "Cherry! Glad you could make it! We need to talk about school. I had a new idea for the elementary students . . ."

"No. No shop talk tonight," Cara interrupted. "You can discuss it during business hours. This is supposed to be a fun evening."

"Whatever you say, boss." He leaned down and kissed Cara's cheek, and watching the interaction sent a sharp pain into Cherry's chest. They were so beautiful and so happy. She could tell just by looking at them that they were the kind of people who'd never had anything bad happen to them in life. Cherry used to have the same healthy loving glow, before Tyler Rivera showed up and destroyed that illusion.

"No kissing either. You two make me sick," Matteo said. His surliness seemed to be as universal as his rudeness. He dropped down on to the couch. "Be polite to our girl Cherry here. She just got divorced, you know."

"Oh, I'm so sorry," Cara said, and Cherry didn't know if she was apologizing for the kiss or expressing sympathy for the divorce itself.

Cherry was the guest here; she would never place a burden on her hosts and ask them to pretend to be unhappy just to spare her the pain of seeing other's joy. But talking about her divorce with a near stranger made her uncomfortable, so she smiled and lied. "It's fine. I'm fine, I'm moving on."

"Yeah, she's using MidWestSinglz. She's met some real winners too." Matteo just liked to needle her, and anyway, that was an inaccurate statement. She'd only had the one date so far.

"Been there, done that. Let me give you a tip for weeding out the creeps," Cara advised Cherry. "What you do is read their messages, but don't reply for at least forty-five minutes."

"Good one. I should have told her that," Matteo agreed.

"Why? If I see it, I write back right away. I'm an honest person, I don't play games," Cherry said. Thus far she had responded to everybody who inboxed her, even if she didn't have any interest in them. It was the polite thing to do. She did block them when they tried to send pictures of their private parts though. She had blocked a surprisingly large number of people.

"God, you are so naïve," Matteo said quite rudely, in her opinion. "Here's what happens. Guy sees you read but didn't reply. The actual decent human beings—of which there are very few—will wait. The ones you need to avoid will follow up their first message with a demand for a reply, followed by a string of insults."

"People don't really do that." Cherry was quite confident Matteo was making things up again. He acted like he knew so much about dating, but he already admitted he wasn't using the app for anything other than nefarious purposes. He was probably exactly the kind of creep he was describing.

"Sadly, they do," Cara said.

"Wait, how do you know what guys do on those apps?" Sam, who had returned to the kitchen, called out.

"Don't worry, sweetheart. My cousins told me about it," she said back, then added in a whisper, "I used to meet guys that way, but it's been years."

"I can still hear you. Why does everyone think that sound doesn't carry around corners?" Sam came back in carrying a plate of hors d'oeuvres. "Everything is almost ready. Where are the Diggins boys?"

Matteo burst out laughing. "The Diggins boys? Is that seriously what you call them?"

"How do you say it? The Digginses? Digginsii? That doesn't sound right." Sam's voice was defensive, but then Cara giggled, and he started laughing as well. It was the same laugh Cherry remembered from the bar, loud and hearty and contagious, and soon it spread to all four of them, even though Sam's comment hadn't been that funny to begin with. A sense of joy and belonging suffused Cherry. This was what she had been craving for so long.

# Chapter Twenty-Seven

Matteo helped himself to some of the appetizers Sam provided. "You know Cara, these weird bread things are good, but every time I come over, I get a craving for those double-fudge brownies your mom always made."

"Those aren't weird bread things, those are crostini with red onion jam. You don't have to eat them," Sam said, grabbing the plate and moving it out of Matteo's reach. God, he was sensitive.

"Yeah, whatever. Weird but kind of tasty. Doesn't stop me from missing Cara's mom's cooking." He shoved another one in his mouth. They were delicious, but sometimes Sam needed to be brought back down a peg.

"You grew up here too?" Cherry asked Cara, deftly changing the subject. She sat down on the couch and politely took only one crostini. Her face glowed with happiness. It was just as he suspected: she had been isolated for too long. She was the kind of person who enjoyed being part of a crowd.

"No, I'm from Texas. But my mother and I lived here for a couple of years. There weren't many kids my age, so you can see who I got stuck with."

"Yeah, I was the poor local boy who was forced to show the new girl around. I tolerated her pretty well though. Still do. For the same reasons, too."

"Careful, Matty. My boyfriend can kick your ass," Cara warned. She was probably right, although Sam always struck him as a lover, not a fighter. He worked out daily for vanity's sake, not to keep in fighting trim.

"What? I wasn't going to be insulting. I come here for the food. Man, Cherry, I have such good memories of coming over here and just devouring her mom's brownies. They were so good, they made putting up with Cara's nonsense worth it." His own mother never baked anything. She worked long hours on the mainland, especially after his father couldn't work anymore.

"To be fair, those brownies were made with black beans and zucchini." Cara gave him an evil grin. She had to be lying, right? He could remember her mother cutting him the biggest one, every time. She hadn't really spiked it with veggies, had she?

"No! You're tainting my childhood memories! Damn it, I hate you!"

"It's true. My dad found one of her old recipe binders. She took copious notes. She was increasing the amount of zucchini, waiting for you to notice. Mom thought you were undernourished." A lump formed in Matteo's throat. He used to envy Cara so much for having a mother like hers, and he had been devastated when she was killed in a car accident. Poor Cara had been through so many untimely deaths, first her mother, then, just a couple of years ago, her fiancé. Truth be told, Matteo wasn't sad about that last one, there was always something he mistrusted about that guy. But Cara was his best friend, and he mourned with her.

"I was undernourished. Still am. Those Digginsii better show up soon. They're going to miss out on these odd, unusual, but not definitely not weird bread things." He grabbed another one. He was certainly getting better food here than he would have if he'd kept to his diner routine tonight.

Cara just laughed at him. "I'm going for a refill. You guys want some more wine?"

"Slow down, save some for dinner," Matteo told her. She used to have a bit of a drinking problem, and he'd spent far too many nights holding her hair back while she spewed tequila in the toilet. That had changed in the past year, since she and Sam became an item. She was happier now, her moods were lighter, and she no longer drowned her problems. He hoped it lasted.

"It's ok, we have an entire case." She smiled saucily and walked off to the kitchen, so he suspected she wasn't really going for alcohol. She probably wanted a quick make-out session.

"So you've been friends for a while?" Cherry asked him, with her bright-eyed smile. She seemed less brittle than usual. He knew bringing her along was a good idea.

"Yeah. Since we were kids, obviously. She came back and visited every year, so we saw each other a lot. And we were roommates for a couple of summers while I worked at the inn."

"Oh, I didn't know you worked here, too. No wonder you bought those cabanas."

"Built. I built the cabanas, mostly with my own two hands." Matteo and Cara had bought the land for their cabanas over a year ago, but the first ones weren't complete until this past spring. They, with a lot of hired help, had spent every possible moment constructing the tiny cabins and getting them ready for the summer tourist season.

"No you didn't!" Sam shouted from the kitchen, where he was putting the finishing touches on the meal.

"Well, I supervised most of it. That counts!" he shouted back and then continued in a normal tone. "I worked here while I was saving money to open my rental shop. I even lived in this house for a few winters. Paddy—you know him from the Village Council—let me stay for free in exchange for maintenance work. I painted every room in the inn." The work had been good for his mental health, the calming Zen-like actions, the feeling of accomplishment.

"They need a touch-up if you want to move back in. We'll give you the same deal, plus you can eat Sam's cooking." Cara returned to the living room, and he noted with amusement that her hair was mussed, and she didn't have a wine glass in her hand.

"Forget it. I'm not living with you gross lovebirds. Solitary life is awesome, right Cherry?" He tipped his glass at her, and caught a brief glimpse of sadness in her eyes. Damn, he shouldn't have brought that up. For himself, living alone was the best option, but he could understand how she might be lonely. She was hardly self-sufficient. He reminded himself that there were topics he needed to avoid if he wanted her to relax and enjoy herself. That was the goal, wasn't it? Get her to have fun and make new friends so she didn't seem so lonely all the time?

# Chapter Twenty-Eight

Dear Gary,

I went to a dinner party last night. When I was invited I was so excited. It was the first real social gathering I had been invited to, and I've been lonely. It's hard to make friends, especially after my ex-husband taught me I can't trust anyone.

The food was exquisite, a three-course meal by a professional chef. Two of the other guests were a married couple, still newlyweds, and they called each other Love and Baby, and they held hands, and fed each other bites of food, and made my heart ache for what we used to have. Were we ever that happy? I don't even remember. But the group of us sat around the table, talking and laughing, and I had a glimmer of hope that I could find some sense of contentment again.

But it all went to heck, and I was left roiling in bitterness.

And do you know what set everything off? What made me so miserable? The hosts announced their engagement. That's right, they put the whole event together because they wanted to share their joy with their friends. When Cara (the bride) started showing off her ring, I couldn't help it; I felt so angry and bitter and betrayed, not by her, but by you.

Engagement is such a hopeful time. It's when you think about your future and put on your rose-colored glasses and imagine long weekends in bed, and buying your first house, and what will you name the kids? You think about this long shared life, and how someday, you'll retire together and maybe go on those old-people cruises and play shuffleboard and golf, and tell stories about the good old days.

I'll never forget your proposal. It was Christmas break, our senior year, and you came home with me. You were nervous on the drive, and I thought your agitation was due to it being your first time not spending the holidays with your own family. And yes, I remember your mom screaming at you on the phone about it. On Christmas Eve, you and my dad 'went to the store' and were gone for two hours and came back smelling like a bar and Dad gave me a big hug, and I thought 'ah-ha! He asked permission!'

The present you had wrapped under the tree for me was very clearly a jewelry box—a necklace. You handed it to me on Christmas morning, and I tried to hide my disappointment. I opened the box and lifted out a cheap gold necklace with a heart pendant. "Thank you, it's beautiful," I lied. And you told me that wasn't all. And you removed the insert and there, underneath, was a hidden diamond ring.

"Marry me, Cherry," you said. And then you looked embarrassed by rhyming at what was supposed to be a serious moment. And how could I say anything other than yes? I knew you were the love of my life, I knew we were destined to be together forever.

That's what I thought about last night when Cara showed me her ring, a custom-made one her fiancé ordered from some designer he knows in Italy. Everyone was hugging and grinning and talking over each other, and I had to sit back and put a fake smile on my face and try not to cry. All I could think about was how someone can have something so beautiful and perfect and full of hope, but it can all be taken away in an instant.

I wish them all the happiness that you took from me. Surely some marriages work out, right? There are some men who don't cheat, who stay faithful and loving, who don't take their wives' hearts and shatter them and then stomp on the pieces, right? I wish I'd met one.

With bitter regrets,

Cherry

# Chapter Twenty-Nine

Cherry was trying to relax after a long day of work when she heard heavy footsteps coming up her stairs, followed by something being dropped in front of her door. There was no knock, and the footsteps retreated. Curious, she went and checked outside, to find a small pile of logs. And then she spotted Matteo, coming back up the stairs with another armful.

"What are you doing?" she asked in surprise. If she had known she'd have a visitor, she wouldn't have changed into sweatpants and an old T-shirt. She reached up and touched her hair. It was messy, of course. Why didn't he ever call before stopping by? Had he no manners?

"It's a cold evening, and you said you didn't know how to build a fire."

"So you're going to build one for me?"

"Why would I do that? No, I'm going to teach you how. You need to learn how to be a bit more self-sufficient."

"Sometimes you act like I'm a child, Matteo. I am self-sufficient." He was right though. She wasn't, not really. Her adulthood had been stunted by marrying so young and never actually living on her own. There were so many things she didn't know how to do. Much as she wanted to, she couldn't blame Gary for her lack of home maintenance skills. She could have taken the time to learn. But she never expected to need to—Gary was supposed to always be there for her. That's what he had vowed, when he stood up in front of all their family and friends and lied.

"Yeah, sure you are. Help bring this wood in." He walked right past her, without waiting for an invitation. Sighing, she picked up some of the logs and followed him into her apartment. "I'm not disturbing anything am I?" he asked, looking around. "I probably should have called first."

"No, you're fine. I was going to have a glass of wine and read a novel." She left off the part of her plan involving doing so in a hot bath. She didn't need to listen to whatever salacious remarks he would be sure to make.

"Sounds great, pour me a glass while I make sure the damper is open." He kicked off his shoes and hung up his coat without bothering to wait for her to actually respond. He was really making himself at home. She was going to object, but realized her objection was on general principle. He might be ill-mannered, but she enjoyed spending time with him more than she liked to admit. It was definitely better than spending yet another evening alone.

As it turned out, Matteo was a patient and thorough teacher. Not only did he teach her how to build the fire, he talked to her about the principles behind the techniques. He showed her how to prime the flue by warming it first, and she thought about the time Gary had tried to make a fire in the house they rented after college. After accidentally filling the living room with smoke, Gary determined that it was broken, and they never used it again. It never occurred to her to question his knowledge on the matter.

When the fire was burning brightly, and Matteo completed his safety lecture, he turned to go, and Cherry felt a pang of disappointment. "You can stay and hang out," she invited, trying to sound casual.

"Shall we drink some more wine and have long intimate conversations?" he asked, raising an eyebrow.

"No, I save those for my dates," she snapped, and considered revoking the invitation. Sometimes he was just plain unpleasant.

"I was only teasing." He sank down onto her couch. "Jeez, lady, you really need to trash this old thing. I hear there's a decent furniture store in Two Harbors, or there's a thrift shop with a good selection in Grand Marais, if you don't mind used stuff. Or head down to Duluth. The ferry brothers run a delivery service, if you pay them enough one of them will go down there with a truck."

"Do you want to come with me? You could use an update yourself."

"Nah." He waved his hand dismissively. "I don't need anything and I'm not much of a shopper."

"I've seen your couch. It's held together with duct tape. And since you're the one who complains about my furniture, you should be happy to help replace it."

"The duct tape is an aesthetic choice. My couch is perfectly functional, so no need to buy another. But when you finally decide to replace this monstrosity, I'll help you drag the new one up your stairs."

They sat in companionable silence for a while. It was pleasant, watching the fire, drinking and relaxing. Cherry almost felt content.

"Did you enjoy yourself the other night? Hanging out at Cara's?" Matteo asked abruptly.

"I did. Oh, it was so lovely. I feel like I still haven't found my niche here, so I enjoyed feeling like I was part of a group again. It reminded me of back home. I felt a little sad . . . no, not sad, exactly, maybe wistful?"

"You miss your friends in Ohio?"

"No, not that. I mean, yes. Yes I do, very much. My real friends, that is, not all the ones who knew for a year that Gary was cheating on me. I hate all those awful fopdoodles."

"Language, Miss Waites!" Matteo laughed. "I do believe that's the first time I've heard you use a naughty word. Or at least, I assume that's what you were trying to do."

"Well, this is my second glass of wine. I'm sorry, that was terrible of me to say. They're all good people. They just didn't want to hurt me and didn't think it was their place to say anything. No, I was talking about how Sam looked at Cara. Did you notice that?"

"You mean how he leered at her like he wanted to bend her over the counter and bang her brains out?"

"Matteo!" She was shocked and horrified. Nobody back home spoke like that! What the heck was wrong with him? "You're horrible! I thought Cara was your friend! Why would you say such things?"

"Don't worry, she likes it," he said, but that didn't make it better.

"She likes you making snide comments about her intimate relations?"

"I don't know about that. I just meant she likes being bent over the counter. What's your problem? Don't tell me you and your old friends never talked about sex."

"Not so graphically, we didn't." She had never really had sexual conversations with anyone, not even Gary. Sometimes she and Katie would allude to it, saying things like 'Well my husband sure kept me up last night' or 'I've been getting some exercise lately if-you-know-what-I-mean,' but never anything so descriptive. She had never met anybody as crude as Matteo.

"Your loss. Talking is how people exchange ideas, learn new ways of doing things."

"You should be ashamed of yourself, Matteo. The way you're talking about your friend is terrible. And that wasn't what I meant, anyway. Didn't you see how Sam looked at her, the expression on his face . . . oh, it was pure love, like he could see nothing else but her. In the over thirteen years I spent with Gary, he never once looked at me like that. Never. Not even on our wedding day." Their wedding, which should have been a portent of things to come, when Gary was hungover from the bachelor party and Cherry was stressed out from dealing with his trashy family.

"I guess I'm not very observant. Maybe he did look like that, I don't know. But I'll tell you something, if you don't have a man who looks at you like you're the only woman in the room, you're with the wrong person. You deserve better than Gary, and you know it. I'm sure you're going to find someone to look at you that way," Matteo promised, and leaned over to clink his glass against hers. He held it up in a toast. "To finding someone for our prudish Miss Waites."

"I'm not drinking to that," she told him. "And I'm not a prude. Just because I think private parts should remain private doesn't make me a prude."

"I think you're trying to date in the wrong era. You're a throwback to, I don't know, sometime last century. You want a gentleman who considers it scandalous to do anything beyond holding your hand before you're properly wed. Times have changed, Cherry Blossom. This is the modern age. Women are allowed to enjoy and talk about sex."

"I didn't say women shouldn't enjoy . . . it. I'm not being anti-feminist here. I just think some things should be personal. People don't have to brag about their conquests, for example. And they don't have to describe their favorite positions. What happens in the bedroom should stay in the bedroom."

"What if you use other rooms? What then?"

"Matteo, stop being disgusting."

"Cherry, you need to relax a little. How are you going to survive in the dating world, especially using an app that allows people to send dick pics so easily? You aren't."

"Why should I have to relax? Why should I have to change? I need to meet someone who's on the same wavelength, someone who is respectful and patient, and understands that I think physical intimacy is for relationships, not one-night stands."

"Are you holding out for marriage?" She could tell by his tone he was mocking her.

"Enough! Stop teasing me. Seriously, I'm about to kick you out of my apartment. You're being very judgmental. Why can't you accept that some people have different needs? And I need an emotional connection first. Why are you making it sound like a big deal?" Her voice cracked, and she was afraid she might cry in front of him.

"Okay, hey, I'm sorry," Matteo said. "Maybe I shouldn't tease you about this. I don't get it though, what difference does it make? You're an adult, right? And clearly you have some sexual experience. Why use a dating app if you aren't interested in hooking up?"

"Look, I've only been ... intimate ... with one man, ever, and that was my husband. He was my first everything, and it was all very special to me. I never expected to end up single again, and I never thought I'd have to go through the whole process again. Healthy relationships are hard to find, you know?"

Matteo sipped his wine and stared at the fire for a moment before answering. "I know. To be honest, I've only had one relationship ever, and that only lasted two weeks."

He frowned, and the angles of his face changed, making him look like someone much older and tireder. "Tell me about it," she encouraged, and was surprised when he did. She half expected him to make another crude joke.

"She was a summer employee. I had known her for a long time, even before she started working on the island, and I had a crush on her for years, actually. She was everything I wasn't, so pretty and open and free."

"Why didn't it work out?" Probably got tired of his rudeness, she imagined.

"Turns out she was allergic to dogs. She didn't ask me to choose between her and them or anything, she knew better. But we wouldn't have worked out in the long-term anyway, she's too much of a wanderer, and she'd never settle down in one place. But for the next couple of summers, when she came out to work, she'd occasionally surprise me at my shop, and we'd have this crazy intense sex in the backroom. She made me promise not to tell anyone, so I never did. But I used to tease her about our two-week relationship a lot, trying to make her say something. Never worked, she was too smart for that." He smiled at the memory.

"What happened to her?" Cherry asked. She thought back to the few summer employees she had met before the season ended. There was a very attractive woman who worked in the ice cream shop. Could he mean her? He would like someone like that, with her flirty smile and perfect figure. Ugh, he was annoying.

"She's with someone else now. Last year, when all the businesses started talking about extending to a year-round tourist season, I got so excited. I thought she'd come back and stay, and even if she couldn't come around my dogs, we could maybe try again. But that summer, she came back and talked about nothing but her new man, and how in love they were, and that ended everything. Broke my heart, which was weird, because I thought I was over her. I guess I wasn't." He fixated on the flames as he spoke. Cherry wanted to reach out and touch his arm, but she didn't want to break the spell. This was the first time she'd seen Matteo lower his walls. He finally shook his head as if to shake the memories from his mind and turned to her.

"Enough about me and my nonsense. Explain why you've only been in one relationship."

"It wasn't on purpose. I didn't date in high school, not because my parents wouldn't let me or anything, I was just kind of awkward. Boys thought of me as the bubbly friend, the one the cute guy's wingman had to distract, not the one you date. When I started college, I was determined to change that, I planned to have lots of boyfriends and go out all the time, but it turned out that's not how I am. And anyway, I met Gary on the first day of orientation, and we hit it off so well. We started dating soon after that, and by junior year we were living together. When we graduated, we got married and found jobs teaching in the same school. I was so naïvely happy. I felt like I had been spared all the awkwardness of trying out different relationships. I'm not going to lie. I was so smug about it. My best friend Katie went on all these awful dates and came home with terrible stories, and I'd sit there and think how I was above all that, how lucky I was to meet the love of my life at such a young age. If he hadn't cheated on me, we'd still be together. He destroyed our marriage."

"Well, to be fair, that was your decision."

"What was?"

"Destroying your marriage. Cheating doesn't have to end everything. You could have gotten marriage counseling to get to the root of why he strayed, or you could have forgiven him and moved on, or even decided to have an open marriage. But you chose to end it."

Cherry had never been so angry at anyone in her life, except, well, of course Gary and that hussy Megan.

"How dare you?" she hissed. "How dare you blame me? I didn't make him cheat. That was his choice. His, not mine." Was she being foolish, defending herself when deep down inside she suspected Matteo was right?

"Yes, but you could have kept him around. Relationships can survive cheating. It happens."

"Get out." Cherry reached her limit. "Get out of my apartment right now."

"You're only angry because you know I'm right. Divorce was your choice, Cherry Blossom. And finally letting yourself move on will be your choice too." He put on his coat and then paused with his hand on the doorknob. "See you Wednesday."

She wanted to throw something at him. "Just go," she told him, hoping he'd leave before she broke down crying. Matteo had touched on her deepest fears. What if it had been her fault? What if she should have been the one to compromise, to save her marriage? And was it so terrible that she hadn't wanted to?

# Chapter Thirty

He probably shouldn't have said any of that, he reflected later. Who was he to give advice on relationships anyway? It's not like he knew anything about them. And now Cherry was probably mad at him, and he would need to apologize. But would she accept his apology? Or would she stay mad? Maybe Wednesday he would show up for dinner at the diner, and she wouldn't be there. And then what if that evening she decided to start a fire in her fireplace, and she hadn't really been listening to his instructions, and the fire spread through the apartment? Would she be able to get out in time? Probably not, there was only one door. Maybe he shouldn't have taught her how to build a fire, this was going to be all his fault. And if the fire didn't get put out right away, it would destroy the drugstore and . . .

Beverly whined and climbed into his bed, on top of his chest. She always sensed when his mind started the downward spiral. Sometimes the comforting pressure of her weight was enough to stop an anxiety attack. It's what she had been trained to do. Unfortunately, it didn't always work.

"I know baby, I'm trying," he whispered, rubbing her head. He started his deep-breathing exercises to break the cycle. He needed to overcome these thoughts before things got worse, before his heart started racing and he couldn't breathe and the panic clouded his mind and . . . Beverly whined again.

Holding back panic attacks was difficult, but at least this time he was dealing with the easier of his two forms of anxiety. This was the small one, the one he thought of as his mouse, an internal mouse that scrabbled around in his guts and occasionally gnawed at his heart. He could feel it running, claws digging in, stirring things up, making his heart beat faster and more painfully. The mouse always whispered that something was wrong, that he needed to be concerned, that if he didn't focus on it, if he didn't follow the trail of his thoughts in their spirals, then his body would collapse, he'd have a heart attack, and he would die horribly and painfully.

As bad as that was, the other type was worse. The doctors liked to use the clinical term, agoraphobia, but he thought of it as a formless, fathomless, black dread that threatened to overwhelm him. The feeling was almost tangible, a heavy dark presence he could almost see out of the corner of his eye. It wasn't always there, but when it was, it was terrifying. Its presence made him feel like death stalked him. Sometimes it camped right outside his door, paralyzing him, preventing him from leaving the house, threatening to destroy him.

He kept the dread at bay, most of the time, in part because he learned what he needed to avoid. That didn't keep it away entirely though. He always felt its presence like a malevolent shadow. Sometimes it pressed closer, looming over him and forcing him to retreat into smaller and smaller circles until he couldn't leave his bed.

The fear was a thousand times worse on the mainland though. His agoraphobia blocked him from ever setting foot over there. The last time he had defied it was two years ago, when Cara's first fiancé died, and the funeral was held in Chicago, a mere nine hour drive away. Everyone told him he didn't need to go. He'd never forget the pain in Cara's voice, crying on the phone and assuring him, "You don't have to come, I understand." He thought their friendship and her great need would strengthen him enough that he could stand up to his own mind, to keep his disorder from controlling his life.

"You're my best friend. I'll be there," he had promised, and he did go. Given the state he arrived in, he probably hadn't been any comfort to her. The dark dread descended upon him while crossing on the ferry, and he popped some emergency pills. They didn't help, they made him dizzy and weak, and left him shaking and terrified. Fortunately his distant cousin Margaux was part of the group, and she let him hold tightly to her hand the entire time. She helped load him into the back seat of the inn's van, where he laid down, covered his eyes, and tried not to scream throughout the interminable drive.

Somehow, he survived the trip. Afterward, he thought perhaps, if he faced down the dread once, he could do it again. He gathered his courage and his dogs and made an attempt, taking his boat over and pulling up to the docks. But as he started to tie it up, his heart started racing, his chest tightened, and chills ran through his entire body. He would die if he stepped out of the boat, he just knew it. His death was lurking, waiting for him. And he wasn't ready to die, so he turned around and sped off, back to the island, back to his safe space. It was nearly a week before he gathered enough mental capacity leave his house again.

He hated the dread, he hated the weakness it created in his mind, and he hated himself for giving in so often. Just like he hated himself now as the mouse scrabbled around in his chest and meditative breathing couldn't make it go away.

Matteo swung his legs over the side of the bed. "Come on, Beverly, let's go." The anxiety attack was really bearing down on him now, the panic coursed through his veins and a heart attack threatened. If he couldn't control it with breathing, his next best option was to go for a run. That's what he would do. He'd take Beverly and Tristan and jog the adrenaline down. And he could pass by Cherry's apartment, verify that it wasn't on fire. That might help, too.

# Chapter Thirty-One

The first message from Oliver sounded promising: *Hello! I see you're a teacher, so am I. Middle school for me, how about yourself?*

That was a much more engaging opening than the typical 'hey' or 'what's up?' She clicked on the profile. Oliver was rather ordinary looking, which suited her just fine. He had a full head of hair, he enjoyed cycling, and one of his pictures included a dog. Dogs were always a positive sign—it showed that he was friendly, likable, and had excellent taste in pets.

*I used to teach middle school, too. Now I teach k-12 in a one-room schoolhouse.* She left it at that, no follow up questions. This was how to tell if the potential suitor could carry his end of the conversation.

It turned out he could. He wrote back, and before she knew it, they had been chatting for a half hour, and she needed to go to bed. Not once did he ask for naked pictures of her or threaten to send any of him. Had she done it? Had she finally found a reasonable man online? Oh, she was going to rub Matteo's nose in this one.

The next morning, she woke up to a long message:

*Cherry, it was wonderful 'meeting' you last night. No pressure, and I don't want to be too forward, but I'm going to be near Ferry's Landing this weekend. Any chance you're free to meet up for coffee and continue our conversation? I can take the ferry across the lake Saturday morning, if you like?*

Cherry smiled as she read it. She did it, she found a polite and decent man.

🌲 🌲 🌲 🌲 🌲

Oliver matched his profile picture, another plus. He smiled when he saw her, and they conversed easily as they walked from the docks to the coffee shop. He even offered to pay for her cappuccino, though of course she didn't let him. She might let him buy her dinner sometime though.

"I'm very curious as to how you went from teaching middle school in Ohio to running an entire school in Minnesota." Oliver rested his arms casually on the table and leaned forward. He actually seemed interested in what she had to say. How refreshing!

"Well, after eight years of teaching, I wanted to take on a bigger challenge. When I found this job posting, I sent in an application, and I guess they liked me." She left off the desperation she felt as she dropped the envelope in the mailbox, the tears, the hope, and the need to flee as far away from her failed marriage and the petty gossip as possible.

"I guess they did," he smiled, though something seemed off, like it didn't quite meet his eyes. No, she was reading him wrong.

"Lucky for me, right?"

"I bet there was quite an application process, though. How did that go?" For a second, she wondered if he asked because he wanted to learn more about her, or if he was trying to get career advice in a search for a similar job. No, he wouldn't come all the way out to the island just for that, would he? And anyway, jobs like hers were rare.

"It was very different. For one thing, there was no hiring fair."

"Ah, yes, the dreaded hiring fair," Oliver smiled. "I think we've all been through those."

"Right. Well, instead, this one started out with the usual, submitting a résumé and cover letter. After that, I was told they whittled down the number of candidates and mailed out a packet of essay questions about teaching philosophies and methods. Some of them were intense. It took me hours. One of the village council members told me that only about thirty applicants even bothered answering all of them. They ended up doing conference-call interviews with ten people, then a second round with five, and two days later I received the job offer. Although it was a lot of work, everything came together more quickly than I expected."

Oliver listened attentively, nodding his head and making encouraging noises at exactly the right times. "That's a long drawn-out process. What do you think made them choose you?"

Had he overemphasized 'you' as though he was criticizing? No, that was her imagination. "You mean besides my résumé? I'm good with students, I'm forever an optimist, and I think they saw I'm the kind of person who would work hard and do anything for my classroom. I'm also from a small town originally, and I think that was a point in my favor—I can handle living in tiny communities."

"Interesting," Oliver said. "Did you ever meet any of the hiring committee members in person?"

"No, I never visited the island until it was time to move. It was a twelve-hour drive, and probably just as much travel time if I flew. Why do you ask? Are you trying to find a job at a small school?"

"I was. Now I'm trying to figure out why they chose you over me. This was my dream job, I have six years more experience than you, I've taught at every level, I was already licensed in this state, I did everything right, and for some reason they picked you instead."

"Oh. I didn't realize you'd applied for the same job," she said slowly as she reevaluated the situation. So this wasn't a date? He'd suddenly become hostile.

"I did. And I made it all the way to the final round. The job should have been mine. I'm better qualified than you. Well, not in all ways." He cast his eyes rather obviously down to her chest. "You do have some better assets than I do." His face changed. He was no longer the friendly, open guy she had been talking to. He transformed into somebody completely different.

A voice interrupted them. "If by assets you mean a better personality, then yes, you're correct, she does have much finer assets than you." Cherry looked up to see Matteo standing next to their table. Why was he always around? And why was she so relieved to see him?

"This is a private discussion," Oliver told him coldly.

"Not really. You're being pretty loud. And as a member of the committee that made the decision, I think I can speak on the matter. Don't you recognize me from the video interview?"

Oliver looked from Matteo to Cherry. "Ah. I get it. Of course. No wonder you hired her. Damn it, I knew it was rigged."

"Language!" Cherry said, horrified. Oliver was definitely not the person she thought he was.

"Yeah, no swearing in here, asshole. And, for your information, her selection wasn't unanimous. I voted for someone else, a high school teacher from downstate with a longer career than both of you combined. Everyone else preferred Miss Waites. So you, guy whose name I can't remember, weren't even the second choice. But please, do continue insulting our new teacher and making your insinuations." Matteo folded his arms across his chest and stared down at Oliver. Cherry, as always, was torn between the desire to punch Matteo or to hug him.

"Is this the only reason you connected with me on MidWestSinglz? So you could harass me about why I was hired?" That hurt. That hurt a lot.

"Your profile said you taught on Whispering Pines Island, so I figured I may as well contact you and find out if you were the one they chose over me. And yeah, I still don't understand why."

"You never had any interest in me at all then?"

"Why would I? I have a girlfriend, and she's way prettier and younger than you."

"Wow, that was blunt. Can I throw this guy out now?" Matteo asked Cherry. She couldn't talk because she was trying not to cry, so she bit her lip and nodded.

"I don't think you have the right to kick me out, but I'm leaving anyway." Oliver stood up. Cherry braced for a fight, but Matteo didn't move. He stood there with his arms crossed, forcing Oliver to walk around him to leave.

When her not-actually-a-date was gone, Matteo sat down. "You sure do know how to pick winners."

"Aren't you supposed to be at work? Stop harassing me."

"I close for an hour at lunch to grab a bite to eat and let my dogs out. You should be glad I stopped by."

"Why? So you could laugh at me?"

"I'm not laughing. Not yet. But later, when you see the humor in this, I'll laugh with you. Also, from now on, can I please screen your dates? Your taste in men is atrocious."

# Chapter Thirty-Two

Dear Gary,

What did you do with the Halloween decorations this year? Did you get them out of the attic? Did Megan help you string the trees with those purple lights? Did she hold the ladder for you as you hung the ghosts? Did the two of you go to the pumpkin patch and each pick out the two largest you could find, one for a funny face, one for a scary one? Did you roast the seeds and drink pumpkin beer while you carved them?

Or did you let those traditions die, too?

I only carved one jack-o-lantern this year. I went to the mainland and bought it at a grocery store, not at a pumpkin patch. It was a smallish one, something I could carry myself (you kept both the wagons we always used—are they still in the garage?). I didn't buy pumpkin ale, either. I'll admit, I never liked the taste; I only drank it because you liked it, and it was our funny-yet-gross tradition. I carved a happy smiling face, to mask how I really felt, and I put a candle inside and set it on the base of my stairs. Some of my students passed by, and one girl very shyly said it was the best pumpkin she'd ever seen. It was sweet of her to say, but I knew she was lying. I went up by Gallery Row and saw what some of the local artists made, and they're spectacular. The yarn shop had a huge crocheted jack-o-lantern, the blacksmith had an iron headless horseman with a pumpkin in its arms, and the glass collective filled their window with delicate gourds of all colors.

There was a Halloween party at the community center. I went; it was lovely. I didn't bother with a costume though. Remember how you and I used to dress up? We always made the best costumes, and we always went as a couple. We had such fun at the elementary school fall festival—we couldn't call it Halloween, because that awful parent's group protested 'the devil's holiday,' remember that? If I recall correctly, Megan was one of the strongest advocates for keeping Halloween in the name. Did you bond over that? Over your mutual love for the holiday? Did the two of you make an adorable couple this year? Maybe she went as your mistress?

I hope you missed me. I hope you looked around at all of the decorations and remembered the fun we used to have, the traditions we created. I hope you felt regret. I hope it hurt. I hope you suffered.

Is my anger coming through to you? It should. This was always our holiday, Gary. Ours. We loved it.

Do you ever think about our annual tour of Northwest Ohio haunted houses, when we enjoyed the thrill of being scared? Well, I don't enjoy being scared anymore. It seems like I'm scared all the time, but not of witches and zombies and things that go bump in the night. No, my fears are much more mundane, and much more realistic.

Will I be alone forever? What will happen to me, when I'm old and have nobody to take care of me? What will I do if I get sick or injured and can't work anymore? Will I lose everything, again? Will I ever find my place in the world?

If I die, will anybody care? Or am I already a ghost? I must be. I am dead to everyone back home in Parsons. There's nothing left of me there. Maybe people still talk about me, but they don't talk about my teaching skills or the parties we threw, or the fabulous pie I brought to the bake sale. No, they talk about me in gossipy whispers as the woman who couldn't hold on to her man, the woman whose husband left her oh-so-publicly, the woman whose coworkers knew exactly what was going on and conspired to keep it a secret. My ghost is a joke there, isn't it?

I hope I haunt you, too.

Cherry

# Chapter Thirty-Three

*Whispering Pines Island, November 2014*

The day after Halloween, Cherry had another date. His name was Alex, and he seemed nice enough when he messaged her. She tried Cara's suggestion and waited to respond to his messages, and he didn't insult her at all, so he passed the creep test. Truthfully, he was a little dull, but maybe he was just uncomfortable talking via the computer. It didn't matter, she had to put herself out there, like everyone told her. She certainly wouldn't meet someone sitting around the island.

Alex offered to come out to Whispering Pines, so she proposed getting a happy hour drink at The Digs. That sounded safe enough, and after the interminable date with Jared, it was definitely better than meeting for dinner. Drinks required less of a commitment. She could order one beer and then, if they didn't hit it off, she'd close her tab and go home. Easy. He agreed to meet her at the bar, so she didn't have to stand around the docks in the freezing cold.

When she walked into The Digs, the sheer mass of people took her aback. The place hadn't been so packed since the summer tourist season ended. Was there some event she didn't know about?

"Hi Cherry!" Cara waved at her, and Cherry made her way through the crowd, glad to find a friendly face. Cara stood at a table with Nessie Ryan, a petite school mom with a daughter in first grade.

"Hi! Oh my goodness, why is it so busy tonight? What's going on?"

"Oh god, you don't know?" Cara rolled her eyes, and Nessie laughed.

"It's the most asinine thing," Nessie explained. "This is the famed 'Night of the Last Shave.' It's an annual tradition."

"What does that mean?" Was this some strange Minnesota holiday she had never heard of?

"See the queue over there? A professional barber came out from the mainland with a straight razor. He's giving shaves to all the men. And they can't shave again until the beginning of April. It's some kind of manliness contest." Cara shook her head. "I'm not a fan."

"It keeps their faces warmer in the snow," Nessie said. "And I think beards are kind of hot."

"Neatly maintained beards are hot," Cara corrected. "I like the first few weeks of the contest, but after that it gets out of hand. Nessie, you've seen my uncle and that enormous red and gray bush he grows under his chin. And Tim's face practically disappears under all his hair. Oh, and they take such pride in it too, like it takes skill to not shave your face."

"I bet Sam looks good with a beard," Cherry ventured, trying to participate in the conversation. Would it be too forward to make a comment like that about another woman's fiancé?

"I bet he does," Cara said. "But he protests the whole thing. He has a long speech about beard nets in kitchens that you don't want to hear. He still got a shave though, and now he's working behind the bar, hoping that people will order a 'surprise me' cocktail so he can try out some of his fancy new bartending skills."

"That's . . . that's . . ." Cherry tried to think of a response, but failed. "Do all the other men on the island really do it?"

"Yep. Except Tyrell."

"No, Tyrell participates," Nessie said. "He doesn't shave until April either. It just doesn't count because he can't grow facial hair anyway. So he spends the winter complaining that Tim's beard is too scratchy. I told him that's what he deserves for marrying a Midwestern outdoorsman."

"Feel my face. It's so smooooooooth." Matteo appeared out of nowhere to interrupt them. He stumbled, and grabbed Cara's arm for balance. Cara touched his face.

"Yes, very smooth, drunky. Cherry, I forgot to add that after their shaves they start doing shots."

"Your turn, Cherry Blossom." He grabbed both of Cherry's hands and held them to his cheeks. "That's what a straight razor will get you. Like a baby's bottom."

Cherry giggled and tried to pull her hands away. "Stop, I don't want to touch you."

"Are you sure? Last chance for all this smoothness. After tomorrow, you won't recognize me," Matteo told her, finally releasing his grip. He reached past her to grab Cara's drink and quickly downed it. "I'm going to be ruggedly handsome, with a glorious beard, and I'm going to win this year."

"Hey, you owe me a drink now." Cara smacked his arm.

"How about a round? Cherry, Ness, you both in? I'll be back." Matteo staggered off. The three women watched him go, laughing.

"I've never seen him so cheerful. He's usually so . . ." Cherry cut herself off before she could describe Matteo as surly and mockingly crude. It wasn't polite to talk about him that way, especially to his friends. Plus, he was kind of growing on her.

"Who, Matty? Don't let his outer act fool you. He's a friendly guy. So what brought you out tonight, if you didn't know about this travesty of an event?"

"Oh no! I'm meeting a date here and I completely forgot!" Cherry scanned the room, but she didn't see anyone who matched Alex's picture. "Did the ferry already arrive?"

"Duncan is here, so it must have," Nessie said, pointing out one of the ferry brothers waiting in line for the barber. "He and Everett were trading off runs so they could both come to this."

Cherry still couldn't see him. Maybe he'd missed the boat and would arrive on the next one? That could be, and since Whispering Pines lacked cell service, there was no way he'd be able to call and let her know. How fortunate she'd found a crowd of people—friends?—to talk to while she waited.

"Drinks for all!" Matteo returned with four shot glasses. "Tequila!"

Cherry hesitated before taking one. She didn't want to get too intoxicated before her date arrived, and she wasn't very fond of tequila. But she also desperately wanted to fit in. She drank the shot, and managed to keep from immediately spitting it back out.

"Tim's yelling for you," Nessie said suddenly.

"Me?" Cherry looked over at the bar where Tim was waving a phone at her. Ah, that was it. She hadn't been stood up after all, Alex had missed the ferry. "Maybe it's my date!"

"You have a date? I gotta hear this." Matteo followed Cherry, uninvited, as always.

She took the phone. "Hello?"

"I'm at the docks."

"Is this Alex?" His unexpectedly harsh tone surprised her.

"Did you forget my name already? Figures. I'm here, waiting for you."

"I'm sorry, I thought we were meeting at the bar."

"We were, but when I got there you were flirting with some other guy and feeling up his face. I don't have to stand around and watch that. I decided to give you another chance, but you need to come down here and apologize first."

"Apologize for what? I'm here, waiting for you, like we planned." This didn't make any sense. Why wouldn't he talk to her while he was here? Why would he leave? It should have been obvious she wasn't touching Matteo's face because she wanted to, he was holding her wrists.

"Give me that." Matteo snatched the phone right out of Cherry's hand. "Who is this? . . . Oh, yeah? . . . Funny, she said she had a date with a man, not a sniveling little boy . . . Great idea, I'll meet you outside." He tossed the receiver to Tim.

"Matteo!"

"He says he's on his way back here to kick my ass. Who should we send out in my place? I'm thinking Duncan. He's brutal."

"You can't start fights with my dates! That's so rude!"

"Rude? You're worried about *me* being rude, when that guy stood you up and pouted because he saw you daring to speak to someone of the opposite sex? Yeah, you need a control freak like that in your life. The only reason he wants you to apologize is so he has an excuse to come back in here and wait for the ferry where it's warm."

Cherry hated to admit it, but Matteo was probably right. Alex's reaction was a bit of a red flag. "Darn it, I thought he was a nice guy."

"Oh ho! Such language! Come on, I keep telling you there's no such thing as a nice guy. Let me buy you another drink. Want one of Sam's surprises?" Matteo signaled Sam, and the next thing Cherry knew, she had a flaming shot in her hands with no idea how to consume it.

"New things, right? Drink up." Matteo clinked his glass against hers. "But don't forget to blow out the flames first."

🌲 🌲 🌲 🌲 🌲

Hours later, she went home alone, slightly intoxicated and completely exhilarated. This was the best night she'd had since moving to the island, even if her date did abandon her. She learned how to play darts, and had teamed up with Nessie to actually win an impromptu tournament. Matteo had bought several rounds of drinks and then led the entire crowd in a cacophony of drinking songs. Cherry hadn't known any of the words, but she did her best to follow along and sing-shout the choruses like everybody else.

I did it, she told herself sinking onto her couch. For the first time, she felt like a part of something, like she might belong here. Her elation carried over until she opened up her laptop and read the message from Alex.

*Thanks, slut. Thanks for making me take the ferry to your island just to show off your boyfriend. Jokes on you. I'm a great guy, and he probably beats you like you deserve. I would have treated you like a queen. You missed out.*

# Chapter Thirty-Four

Dear Gary,

Did you know one of my 'friends' told me you cheated on me because I had 'let myself go'? Like your infidelity was my fault? I haven't changed that much from when we met. I've gone up what, two sizes? I could probably still fit into my wedding dress, if Katie and I hadn't burned it in a bonfire in her backyard late one night when we were drinking and talking about how much we hate you.

I haven't changed.

You have. Oh my goodness, I remember how excited you were when we got our first jobs and had actual dental insurance. You'd never had any before, and you were always so embarrassed about your teeth. You used to cover your mouth with your hand when you smiled. They never bothered me; you know that. Sure, they were crooked and you had an overbite, but so what? But when we got insurance, the first thing you did was get a consultation for braces.

I still remember the horrifyingly huge cost estimate they gave us, and we were looking at paying thousands out-of-pocket. We had just started our first jobs. There were student loans and bills to pay, but we scrimped and saved. I didn't buy new clothes for a year. We lived off of rice and beans, and celebrated our anniversary with sandwiches and a fancy $5 bottle of wine. My parents sent us $200 for

Christmas, and we used it toward your braces. Every extra penny went to getting your teeth fixed. In the end, you had a beautiful smile. I didn't care about your smile as much as I cared about the confidence it gave you. I was proud of you, and seeing you happy made me happy.

Was it your newfound confidence that led you to flirt with Megan? I suppose it doesn't matter.

Anyway, I've taken a look at myself. I've always been comfortable in my body. Really. Sure, I'm a little soft and I have a few extra pounds. I don't run or jog, because my chest is too big, but that was always something you liked, wasn't it? I can see that I'm not beautiful. Megan is beautiful, with her long straight hair and sculpted cheekbones. She is a teacher, sure, but her husband owned all those car dealerships, so she had money, at least when you first got involved. And I know she was one of those women who could afford private trainers and went to the gym and did Pilates and ran in charity 5k's. She was skinnier than me, and in better shape. Is that why you chose her?

I'm exercising more now. I have a friend who owns three wonderful dogs, so I help him take them on walks sometimes. The other day he didn't feel well, so I walked them before and after school, and again in the evening. I was sore the next day, but the good kind of sore, where your muscles know something has happened. Even without the dogs, I'm walking at least a half hour each day. On weekends, I find it therapeutic to put my headphones on and walk the entire road around the island. It's about five miles, a longer distance than I've ever walked before. I like it. Sometimes, I sit down on a bench at the halfway mark, on the north side, and I stare out over the lake and I almost feel happy.

The snows are going to start soon, and I'm going to learn how to snowshoe and cross-country ski. I'll develop nice thigh muscles and an amazing rear, one you will never see or touch. I'm going to keep exercising and breathing deeply of the fresh clean air and I'm going to continue meditating every day. And someday, maybe my heart won't be so broken. And maybe I'll feel good about myself again.

Cherry

# Chapter Thirty-Five

Matteo spread papers out on the table in front of him. The numbers weren't great. New businesses usually took years to break even, but watching money slip away was nerve-wracking. Their losses were slow and steady, not crisis level yet, but he and Cara needed to work out a concrete plan to slow the bleed.

"We can always raise the prices," he mused. Rates for everything dropped in the winter season, but if they lowered them too much, they couldn't afford to operate. They'd already canceled their contract with the maid service; he and Cara were capable of doing that themselves. What else could they cut?

"Our priority needs to be filling beds," Cara corrected. Just because she ran an inn, she assumed she knew more than him about the hospitality business. "We need better marketing."

"Also true. We did well this summer. The problem is the only access when it snows is going to be via skiing. I think in the winter we should have guests check in at my shop, and include cross-country skis in the price. I can even tow their luggage out for them." Last year at this time, the cabins were nothing but concrete foundations, so this would be their first actual winter.

"That might help, depending on snow levels. But if you're doing those runs right when the ferry arrives, what about the other tourists who make your shop their first stop? We'll need to manage the logistics. And also . . . oh, hey don't look now, but your girlfriend just walked in."

"Who, Nessie?" She was a friend with benefits, not a girlfriend, and they hadn't hooked up in a while. Maybe he should change that.

"Ha ha. You know I'm talking about the new schoolteacher. I've been hearing all kinds of rumors about you."

"We eat dinner together occasionally because I feel sorry for her. She's new and doesn't know anybody. Why don't you ask her to join your rather sexist ladies-only coffee group that you purposely exclude me from even though I'm your best friend?"

"You're excluded because you aren't a lady and you annoy everyone there. I did invite her, but she works. She's kind of on an opposite schedule than everybody else." Cara made a valid point. He hadn't thought about how difficult it must be for Cherry, working during the week when the other islanders were free and then being off on weekends when the rest of the population was dealing with tourists. "And actually, Matty, the rumors that reached me are that she's been going on dates and you've been sabotaging them. Is there a reason?"

"Whoa, hey, I'm not ruining anything. She has terrible taste in men, that's all. She keeps bringing around these jerks that aren't good enough for her, and they are rude and they have certain expectations, and she's . . . well she's not the type of woman who should be using a dating site. She's too reserved and sweet and strangely naïve for someone who was married for as long as she was. She deserves better."

"Better like you?"

"Stop it, Cara. I don't date. I don't do relationships."

"You could."

"You're not funny."

"I'm not joking, Matty. Anyway, stop talking about it. She's on a date—that you need to promise not to ruin—and they just took the table behind you."

# Chapter Thirty-Six

Perhaps going to Antonio's was a bad idea, Cherry realized as soon as Darren opened the door for her. Of all the places to be on a Friday night, there was Matteo, sitting and chatting with Cara. From the looks of their table, they hadn't eaten yet, so no chance Matteo was on his way out. She almost suggested going somewhere else, but before she could, Darren took her by the hand and led her to a seat—the table right behind Matteo. Fortunately, he didn't appear to notice them.

"Are you sure you want pizza?" Darren asked as they examined the menus. Cherry tilted her head and looked at him, confused.

"This is a pizza restaurant, that's what they serve. It's pretty good, too." Hadn't they talked about that, when they made their plans? Pizza, and possibly drinks afterward if it went well? And it should go well, right? Her date was an attractive man, with a deep voice and dark eyes. They had gotten along chatting online, and he liked the same movies she did, so they should have plenty to talk about.

"I know, but I thought that at your age, your metabolism might be slowing down, so a salad might be better." Darren smiled endearingly. "I mean, *I* think you're beautiful just the way you are."

"Thank you," Cherry responded automatically, but his comment confused her. Did he call her old or beautiful? Both? Was it meant to be some sort of backhanded compliment?

When the waiter came to take their order, Darren requested an individual pizza for himself, a house salad with dressing on the side for Cherry, a beer for himself, and a white wine spritzer for her.

"Actually, I'd also like a pizza," Cherry corrected, "with pepperoni and olives. And instead of a wine spritzer, I'll have a glass of the house red, thanks." Did she imagine things, or did a look of annoyance cross Darren's face?

"I suppose it's fine to eat like that, for now," Darren said. She started to ask what he meant, but he changed the subject. "So how long have you been on MidWestSinglz?"

"Only a couple of months, since I moved here. Yourself?"

"About two years. It's been enjoyable, I've met a lot of women, had some fun times. I'm a bit picky, though, so it's tough."

"Oh, really?" That was possibly the most flattering thing he had said all evening.

"Yeah, my friends always criticize my choices, too. But what can I say, I'm not interested in conventionally attractive women, I like them much ... softer. Not fat, of course, I have standards, but I don't want one of those skinny bitches who works out all the time. I like a woman who is comfortable with her curves, like you."

Cherry glanced down at herself. She had thought she looked nice, her sweater hugged her body in a non-slutty but date-appropriate manner. Maybe it was too thick? Did she look fat in it? No, that couldn't be what Darren meant.

"You do have the right body type for bearing children, has anyone ever told you that? How many kids do you want?"

"Two, maybe three." The way the conversation shifted threw her off, and she couldn't tell where Darren's questions were going.

"Well, that's something you'll need to start soon, before you get too old. You should probably limit yourself to two, to make sure you have enough time, without worrying about rotten eggs or whatever. Lucky for you, I only want two, preferably both boys."

"Why not one of each?" Cherry always fantasized about having two children, though the faces she used to imagine had dissolved, cast aside by her husband's infidelity.

"Who wants to raise a daughter? I know what boys are like, I know how they think. This is a man's world."

"I see." This level of misogyny hadn't been apparent in their earlier conversations. Had she known he thought this way, she wouldn't have agreed to a date. She hoped the food would arrive soon so she could get this over with.

"I bet you'd be a good mother though. You're a teacher, so you have a lot of experience with kids, and that's the kind of job you can quit easily so you can stay at home with them."

"If I have kids, I'm planning to continue working." Why wouldn't she? Sure, she'd use her maternity leave, but of course she'd come back from it. She loved her job and every single one of the children in her classroom.

He laughed. "I'd never let my wife work. What kind of man would I be? Men are supposed to be the breadwinners, you know that. When things get serious between us, I'll expect you to leave your job. I want to take care of you." He reached across the table and took her hand. Did he think he was being charming?

"Now there's a man with the right idea," Matteo interrupted them. "I'm so tired of these females coming out of the kitchen. It's like, where's my sandwich, lady? Come on."

"Excuse me?" Cherry glanced over at Matteo, and he had the nerve to wink at her. Great, two jerks to deal with.

"Sorry, didn't mean to listen in. But obviously, I wasn't talking to you. I would never address a female without her man's permission." With that, he turned back to Cara, ignoring them again.

"Well, that guy was rude, but he did have a valid point," Darren said. Cherry was about to ask him to elaborate, but the food arrived. "Why don't you ask for a box now, so you can set half of your pizza aside for later? That's what my ex always did, and she had a rocking body."

"Thanks, but I'm fine." Cherry took a bite, even though it was way too hot. She burned the roof of her mouth, but she didn't care. She was going to devour this entire thing, even if she felt full partway through, just to spite him.

"Darren, I don't understand your opposition to women working."

"It's because they're too delicate," Matteo's voice carried. They both ignored him.

"The division of labor is basic human nature," Darren explained. He spoke as though he were indulging a small child. "You see, men are stronger and smarter. We're the ones who need to go out and earn money. That's the hard work. Women are soft and weak and overly emotional. That's why they're better at raising children and running the household. Marriage is a symbiotic relationship."

"I actually think marriage is a partnership," she said. She tried not to sound angry, so he wouldn't dismiss her as an irrational woman. "Men and women should work together.

I was married for ten years, and we both held jobs outside the home, and we shared household chores."

"And how did that work out for you?" Darren's overly confident tone irritated her. "Maybe you wouldn't be divorced, if you'd kept a better house."

Cherry froze for a moment and stared down at the table to gather her thoughts. His words cut her to the core—she did sometimes blame herself for Gary's betrayal, but she had been learning that it wasn't her fault. She wasn't in charge of his decisions. Finally, she figured out exactly what to say in response, she was going to inform him how wrong he was and end this date immediately, she was going to . . .

"What the hell?" Darren suddenly shouted and jumped to his feet, covered in liquid.

"And maybe you wouldn't have beer in your lap if you were politer to your date." Matteo stood next to him, holding an empty pitcher and grinning.

Darren wiped ineffectively at his pants with a pile of napkins before getting in Matteo's face. "You sonofabitch!"

"You're not the first to call me that. Maybe you should leave. Don't worry, I'll cover your meal. I hope your balls don't freeze off. It's awfully cold to be walking around in wet pants."

Darren clenched his fists like he was going to throw a punch, but was interrupted by the sound of chairs scraping on the floor. All over the restaurant men started to rise, looking in their direction. Cherry recognized some of them as dads from the school, all locals, all ready to defend Matteo. And her! They were defending her! She was being treated like one of their own!

"We're done. Don't call me again," Darren spat at Cherry as though she were the one being rejected and not the other way around. He stomped out of the restaurant, pausing to extend both middle fingers. Cherry didn't know whether they were directed at her or Matteo.

When the door slammed shut, Matteo turned to Cherry. "Well, that was another exciting date. You can join us if you like, though we're going to have to order another pitcher of beer. We inexplicably ran out."

"Why did you do that?"

The grin faded from Matteo's face. "It was an accident. My hand slipped. Sometimes rampant misogyny and uncalled for insults trigger clumsiness in me, I can't help it."

"I was going to handle it, you know. I was just preparing my speech." She knew she shouldn't take out her frustration on him, but he had stolen her chance to stand up for herself.

"Oh, I'm sure it was scathing." Matteo's sarcasm made her want to dump a pitcher of beer on him.

"Enough." Cara interrupted them both. "Cherry, bring your food over here and sit down. Matteo, I see Bryce coming with a mop. When you're done cleaning up your mess, you can order another pitcher and join us."

Cherry laughed, a real honest laugh. Despite the terrible date, this was going to be a fun evening. First, she had a room full of people from her new community getting ready to defend her, now she got to have pizza and beer with friends? Yes, please.

*No Longer Yours*

# Chapter Thirty-Seven

Dear Gary,

I saw a strange sight today. In our old life, I would have come home from work and described it to you, maybe while we cooked dinner together. You would tell me what you thought, and, in a situation like this one, we'd both come up with some kind of entertaining story to explain it. But you're not here.

So I'll never actually tell you about the strange old man. I'll never tell you that while I was sitting in the coffee shop sipping a latte (yes, I drink lattes now, I've become fancy), an old man walked to the edge of the town square. The coffee shop is right on the corner, and from the front windows, you can see everything. The square is covered in grass, a little brown now, glistening with frost every morning, and soon to be blanketed in snow. The old man stood at the edge, and everyone who was outside turned their backs on him.

Yes, that's right, in this tiny supposedly progressive town, they all turned around and shunned him like he was some kind of leper. Even some of my students who were tossing a ball around stopped and walked to the edge of the grass and wouldn't look at him.

You know me, I'm nosy. So I asked Margaux, the lovely and very pregnant lady who runs the shop, what was going on, because everyone inside had turned away from the windows as well, and do you know what she said? She told me it was nothing, don't pay any attention.

Is this a literal shunning? Doesn't that seem puritanical? There wasn't a scarlet 'A' across his chest. There was nothing to differentiate him from anybody else. He certainly dressed like he belonged, in a faded old coat and knit cap, just like everyone wears. He didn't look ill or threatening or in any way that would merit being ignored.

If you and I could talk, you'd come up with a creative story. Perhaps the old man has a super power that makes him invisible, but instead of the traditional light-passes-through type of invisibility, the power takes the form of making people not willing to see him? Or he's a Gorgon, and his looks will turn them to stone? You would suggest those things, and we would laugh. And I might investigate further or I might never encounter him again, and we would forget all about it.

But you aren't here. We don't have these little jokes between us anymore. We don't talk, and it hurts. It hurts to have you gone from my life, but I don't want you back in it either.

I miss us. I miss the us we used to be.

Wistfully no longer yours,

Cherry

## Chapter Thirty-Eight

It was mid-November before the mysterious old man made his second appearance. Cherry was on her way to the schoolhouse early, hurrying with her head down in the chill wind, when an odd stillness descended. Movement in the square stopped, and that's when she saw him. Grey hair peeked out from under a black knit hat, sparse grey-blond beard, old brown coat, and he was hunched over and walking as though his steps pained him. The old man, again, and the few others who were out had their backs turned. Even in the cheerfully warm coffee shop windows, all she could see was a row of backs.

This was not going to happen, not again, she decided. In a rush of boldness, she hurried over to him to break this awful wall between the stranger and the townspeople. She stopped in front of him and gave him her biggest, friendliest smile.

"Good morning, I saw you out walking and realized we haven't met yet. I just wanted to introduce myself, my name is Cherry Waites. I'm the new schoolteacher." She offered a hand to shake, but the old man disregarded it. She smiled as brightly as she could, trying to demonstrate that she was friendly and non-threatening. He took several deep breaths and struggled to speak. Finally, the words came out.

"Get. Out. Of. My. Way."

She had not expected that response. "Oh, I'm sorry, I'll walk with you. I wanted to meet you, since I hadn't before. What's your name?" He didn't move, just stared at her with strangely familiar eyes. She tried again.

"I noticed you walking by yourself, and I wanted to . . ." A hand over her mouth silenced her and another arm wrapped tightly around her torso, lifting her off her feet and carrying her away.

She struggled and fought, but her assailant was much stronger than her. She was terrified! Someone was kidnapping her in broad daylight, and since everybody was carefully avoiding looking at the old man, there were no witnesses! This was all Gary's fault! If he hadn't cheated on her, she wouldn't be here right now, battling for her life!

"Jeez lady, stop fighting. What's wrong with you?" Oh. She recognized that voice. Matteo.

"Wrong with me? What the heck is wrong with you?" she managed to gasp as he set her down on the sidewalk.

"Hey, that's the foulest language I've ever heard from you, naughty Miss Waites."

"Why did you do that? I thought I was being kidnapped!"

He started laughing. "Are you joking? You think this is such a dangerous place that someone would kidnap you? Right out of the main square during the day? That's hilarious! No, he told you to move out of his way, and you wouldn't. Leave him alone."

"Why? Everybody is shunning him, like he's a leper or something. That's not right, Matteo. He's a human being, he shouldn't be treated that way."

"What?" Matteo's voice was incredulous. "You think we're shunning him? What is this, a Hawthorne novel? No, we're giving him privacy, that's all."

"Privacy for what? He walked across the square, why does he need privacy for that?"

"He walked across the square?" Matteo turned and looked and his eyes widened. The old man stood on the far side, looking around, seemingly bewildered. "Holy shit, he did it! He crossed the square!"

"So what? What's the big deal?"

But Matteo ignored her. He had already taken off running and shouting, "Dad! Dad, you did it! You made it!" Cherry watched him race over and hug the old man, tears in his eyes. What the heck was going on?

# Chapter Thirty-Nine

"So I guess I owe you an explanation," Matteo told Cherry. He had come by the schoolhouse and waited on the porch for class to end. All three of his dogs had been sitting patiently at his feet, though when they saw Cherry, Tristan immediately jumped up and strained against the leash trying to reach her.

"I guess you do," she said. He studied her face. She looked annoyed, which was unfair. She didn't know everything. She bent down to rub Tristan's head, and the ridiculous traitor dog happily rolled over and offered his belly.

"Why don't you ever rub my belly like that?" Matteo couldn't help himself. He wasn't actually flirting. He just liked the way her cheeks would turn pink and she would glare at him. Her glares were adorable—her face was made for happiness, so anger made her look like a pouting toddler.

"Matteo!"

"Sorry. Come to the dog park with me, please?" He expected her to say no, but instead, she went back into the school and grabbed her coat. She locked the door and started walking in the direction of the park without saying a word. "Hey, wait, are you mad at me? Here, take a leash," he gave her Martha to slow her down. Poor Martha was getting weaker. Mouse claws scrabbled at his heart, and he tried to ignore them. He couldn't focus on Martha right now.

🌲 🌲 🌲 🌲 🌲

When they arrived at the park, Matteo slipped off their leashes and set them free, and he and Cherry sat down on his usual bench. They watched the dogs frolic for a few minutes.

"That was my dad," he finally said, when it appeared she wouldn't initiate the conversation.

"I got that."

"He runs the lighthouse. He lives in a little cottage at the base."

"How nice."

"It's a tiny cottage. He usually can't get more than fifty feet away from it."

"Because he needs to stay to guard the lighthouse?"

"We're not at war with Canada. Why would he need to guard anything?" Matteo almost laughed at her, but held back. He didn't like having this conversation, but it was time. "No, he can't go very far from it because he has severe agoraphobia and panic attacks. They've gotten worse over the years. When I was a kid, he could go anywhere on the island, but his world has been shrinking. When you saw him this morning, that's because he's been working on getting out more. Every day he makes an attempt. His goal has been to cross the square. Sometimes he can't even make it out of his yard."

"But why was everyone ignoring him? Shouldn't they be more supportive?"

"They weren't ignoring him. They were being polite. He can't stand to have people watch him struggle. Everybody out there is his friend. People stop by and visit him all the time. He can handle guests. It's a sign of respect when they turn their backs and let him try. He doesn't want witnesses to his failures, and so they honor that."

"Oh." Cherry fell silent, and Matteo struggled with what to say. He knew he should tell her about himself, but the words caught in his throat. What if she stopped being his friend? No, she wouldn't do that, would she? Maybe. No? His thoughts started racing around in his head and his heart rate increased. *Not now. Come on, stupid brain, don't do this now!*

Beverly bounded across the grass and practically jumped into his lap. "Oh, there's my girl, there's my good girl." He focused on the soft feel of her fur and his own breathing.

"It must have been difficult."

He opened his eyes to see Cherry watching him, frowning sympathetically. "What must have been difficult?"

"Growing up with a father like that. Now I understand why you got so mad at me the first time we met, when I joked about not letting people with mental illnesses wander around town. You were thinking of your dad. I'm so sorry, Matteo."

"I wasn't only thinking about my dad." Now was the time, this was the moment, he had to say it. Surely she had heard though? Wouldn't someone else have mentioned it? "You know mental illness can be inherited."

"Good thing you avoided it," she started to smile, but froze when she noticed his expression. "I'm so sorry, that was insensitive. Do you have a sibling?"

"No, Cherry, I don't. I'm talking about myself."

"But you're so . . . so . . ." She seemed to be unable to form complete sentences. He didn't like the way her eyes crawled over his face, as though she was trying to see if the insanity was visible there.

"I'm so . . . what? So handsome? Is that what you're trying to say?"

"No, that's not what . . . I mean, I'm not saying you aren't but . . ." She stuttered over her words.

"Relax, I was kidding. Cherry, I'm agoraphobic, and I have panic attacks, too. Fortunately not daily, but often enough that they're destroying my life. I've only set foot on the mainland once in the past decade, and it required so much medication and assistance that I can't face going again. Even the thought of it can bring on an attack."

"Oh, Matteo, I had no idea." God, she had an expressive face. He didn't like the pity he saw reflected in it.

"I hide it well," Matteo told her. "No, not really. Everybody here knows. This island is like a big family. We take care of each other. When I'm having my worst days, people bring food to my house and stop in to check on me. When my dogs need to go to the vet, Nessie takes them, because I can't do it myself. If I didn't live in such a supportive community, I don't know how I'd survive. But I fight every single day to keep what I've got, to be able to travel all around the island, so my world doesn't shrink like my dad's did."

"That's . . . that's awful you have to suffer too. I'm so sorry. Have you ever tried talking to a therapist about it?"

"My goodness gracious! Cherish Evangeline Waites, you may have saved my sanity! A therapist? I never thought of that! Why, you're a genuine hero!"

"Stop, stop, don't make fun of me." Her cheeks turned red. She blushed so easily and adorably. "I was only trying to help. And that's not my middle name!"

"Yeah, sure. And yes, I've done it all. I've had therapy. I've tried anti-anxiety meds, and those really fucked me up . . ."

"Language!" she interrupted. Sometimes he felt like interjecting swears every other word just to annoy her.

"Swearing helps my anxiety."

"No it doesn't."

"Ok, but the way you shout 'language' every time I swear does."

"Stop! Why can't we have a serious conversation?"

"We were, until you interrupted me to criticize my linguistic choices. Can I continue?" At her nod, he did so.

"I've had the meds. I've tried various behavioral modifications. I meditate regularly. I've experimented with changing my diet. I've tried cognitive therapy. And I've given up. I can reduce the panic attacks, and I can mostly handle the agoraphobia, but I can't make them go away. My choice is to live with them as best I can."

"Matteo," she reached out a hand as though she wanted to comfort him. He didn't need that from her. That's what Beverly was for. Besides, his annoyance with Cherry for harassing his dad this morning outweighed any desire for a comforting touch.

"Alright, that's it. This conversation is over. I don't want to talk about it anymore. Come on, let's go," Matteo whistled for the other dogs and started clipping their leashes back on.

"Are you talking to me or them?"

"Everybody. We're dropping my babies off at home and then you're buying me a drink at The Digs."

"But it's a school night!" she protested as though they'd never gone out to a bar on a weeknight before.

"Yeah, well you should have thought of that before you brought up my mental illness and made me need a drink. Here, take Tristan." He handed her the leash and started walking away, sure that she would follow.

# Chapter Forty

Cherry's assistant Wanda came back from the community center with a cart full of books, arriving just as Cherry was about to dismiss school for the day.

"The interlibrary loans are here," Wanda announced, and started handing them out to students as they walked out the door. When all the kids had left, Cherry went to the cart to retrieve her own books.

"Interesting selection," Wanda commented. Cherry liked working with her, but she didn't necessarily need to hear her observations.

"Sure is," Cherry replied.

"I hope Matteo doesn't see you reading those."

"Why would Matteo care what I read?"

"Oh, come on, everybody has seen the two of you flirting. But I don't think he'd appreciate you doing all this reading on his condition. What are you trying to do, find a magic cure?"

Yes, actually she was. But now she was too embarrassed to admit that. "I just want to understand it better," she replied a bit defensively. She had requested several heavy books with titles like *Understanding Panic Disorders* and *Free Yourself from Your Own Mind*. She hoped they'd help her learn more about Matteo's illnesses without forcing him to talk about it. He wasn't very forthcoming, and she didn't want to embarrass him with her questions.

"If you actually wanted to understand better, you'd ask him. He can explain his own mind better than any strangers. Or talk to his dad."

"I have talked to him about it. I just like reading, that's all," Cherry said, taking her books and walking away. Before she left the school though, she took off her scarf and arranged it carefully over the book covers so nobody could read the titles. She didn't need any more rumors to spread.

🌲 🌲 🌲 🌲 🌲

The next evening she made her way to the diner for dinner and was surprised to see that not only was Matteo there before her, but he sat at the counter with a meal already in front of him. How odd. Lately they had begun eating at a table—it was easier to converse that way.

"Back at the counter?" she asked cheerfully, taking the seat next to him.

"This is where I sit when I eat alone," he told her.

"Oh." She paused for a moment. She thought they had a solid routine going. Did she have the wrong night? This was Wednesday, right? She'd never needed to confirm it with him before. "You weren't expecting me?"

"I figured you were too busy reading the DSM or something." He didn't look at her when he spoke.

"The DSM?" she repeated. "What's that?"

"Very funny."

"No, I genuinely don't know what you're talking about."

Now, finally, he turned toward her, and she was struck by the utter coldness in his eyes. "The book shrinks use for diagnosing mental illness. Sorry, I guess I assumed you got that when you checked out all the other books about me."

"I didn't ... that's not ..." Darn it! She should have known word would spread. "Matteo, I wasn't trying to invade your privacy or anything."

"If you had questions, you could have asked me. You didn't need to sneak around behind my back. But I'm happy to give you a chance to explain." He folded his arms, and she felt their friendship fading away.

"Matteo, I didn't want to pester you with questions. I thought that would be invasive. And you know me, I'm a teacher and a reader, so it seemed like a good idea to learn what I could. Honestly, I was trying to help you."

"Help me with what? Did you think you'd find a way to fix me? Because there isn't one."

"Well, maybe with coping mechanisms or something. It's so unfair you have to deal with this condition. You're so smart and you're being denied the opportunity to do things like go to college or travel..."

"Hold up. Did you just say you think I'm uneducated?"

"That's not what I meant. I know you're extremely intelligent, and you would do great in school..."

His laugh cut her off. "You are making an awful lot of assumptions. There's this thing, you may have heard of it, it's called the Internet. Universities offer online degree programs these days. That's how I did my Bachelor's. Oh, and my Master's in Public Policy. And my Master's in History. I did that one just for the hell of it."

"I didn't know."

"Because you didn't ask. You know I'm on the Village Council, right? Did you think that was just a sympathy election, everyone felt sorry for me so they wanted to give me a task keep me from worrying about my shortcomings? It certainly couldn't be because I was qualified and got a fucking degree in it. I run two successful businesses, I manage my life just fine."

"Matteo . . ." She tried to interrupt him, but he wouldn't let her explain.

"No. You don't get to look at me with pity. You don't get to come here and act all superior and . . . and fixy, just because I'm not perfectly fine in the head. I'm not some project for you to take on to distract yourself from your own shitty life." With that, he got up and walked away leaving an uneaten plate of food behind.

# Chapter Forty-One

Dear Gary,

I've lost my only close friend, and it has shown me how isolated I am here. I have nobody to talk to outside of work, nobody to laugh with, nobody to cry with. All of my other relationships are so superficial, just greetings, chats about the weather, or how their children are doing in school. I only had one real connection, one person with whom I could relax and argue and open up. And now he's gone, just like you.

You know those feel-good movies where the thirty-something woman comes out of a long relationship, and she travels and explores and finds herself? She discovers she doesn't need a man, she is strong and independent and beautiful (though how they pretend gorgeous Hollywood actresses aren't beautiful before this realization is absurd). Well, that's not me, and it never will be.

I wish I could revel in solitude. I hate living alone, Gary. I hate it. At first I thought it would be great, I could decorate to my tastes (though this is a fully furnished rental, so I haven't). I can watch whatever I want on television. I can leave dirty dishes in the sink overnight. I can let my laundry pile up. My front entryway can become my shoe closet. I know,

I'm starting to sound like a terrible slob now. But I thought hey, my apartment, my rules.

But it's actually lonely and sad. If I leave the dishes overnight because I'm too tired to deal with them, then I have to wash them myself the next day, and it's harder, everything is caked on and I have to bust my knuckles scrubbing. If I leave my shoes in the entry, I'm the one who trips over them. There's nobody here to pick up the slack. Nobody shares chores, nobody takes turns with me.

And worst of all, there's no one to talk to. When I come home from work and put my feet up after a long day, I am greeted only by silence. When I wake up on the weekend and realize I've slept until 10, no warm body lies in the bed next to me, nobody sits in the kitchen playing with his phone and waiting for me.

I have my freedom, but I don't want it. I don't want to be alone. I'm not meant for this.

Feeling lost,

Cherry

# Chapter Forty-Two

Cherry had no idea what her reception might be or what to expect, but she needed to go through with this. She took a deep breath and knocked on the door. It opened almost immediately, and she found herself once again looking into a familiar set of hazel eyes.

"Mr. Capen?" she asked tentatively. "Could I talk to you for a few minutes about your son?"

"You're the teacher from the other day, aren't you? It's been years since someone from the schoolhouse had to come here. Did he release a flock of ducks in the classroom again? That boy of mine . . . so undisciplined."

Cherry hesitated, biting her lip. Was he senile? Did he think Matteo was still a little boy? She didn't expect him to have dementia, too. He stared at her a moment before he burst out laughing.

"Oh, the look on your face. Let me guess. Matty told you I'm crazy, and now you're wondering just how crazy. Come on in. I don't bite, I promise." He gestured for her to enter the house, and she didn't want to be rude, so she did.

"I brought you some coffee." She offered him the package she'd picked up at the bakery. Margaux had assured her that it was his favorite.

"Decaf? Lovely. Take a seat, and I'll make us a cup."

She sat down at the kitchen table and looked around. Was this the house Matteo grew up in? She could picture him eating his breakfast here as a child. Given the avocado-green color of the appliances, she was sure the decor hadn't changed in years. It reminded her of visiting her grandparent's house, a time capsule from another decade.

"So what brings you here?" Mr. Capen asked as he placed a mug, a bowl of sugar, and a pitcher of cream in front of her. She watched his hands—they were so much like his son's, strong, with blunt fingertips and squared-off nails. All of him was so familiar. She knew exactly what Matteo would look like in thirty years. "Is it something he's done, or something you're trying to convince him to do?"

"It's sort of awkward to explain," she began. "You see, Matteo and I have become friends, but I made a mistake, and now he's angry with me. I'd like to get advice from you on how to make it right with him." She went on to tell him about the library books, and how Matteo stormed out of the diner. He listened, eyes fixed on her face. She expected recriminations, when she finished, but he only shook his head and laughed.

"Don't you worry about my boy. He can't hold a grudge. It isn't in him. He's not one for apologies either. He'll come around eventually. You just need to wait."

"But I don't want to do that, I want to take the initiative and work things out," she protested. She was the one who needed to apologize and she had always valued open and honest communication. Well, she had until Tyler Rivera showed up and honestly communicated the truth about her marriage.

"You have to respect his process. Trust me, I know my son. His anxiety means he can't stay mad for too long. It eats away at him. But his pride won't let him apologize himself, so he'll pretend it never happened."

"That seems like manipulating him. I think I hurt his feelings, I need to make him understand how sorry I am."

"You did hurt his feelings. You implied that he was uneducated, and that's a sensitive subject for him. He probably never mentioned this, but he did attempt to go to college. He moved into a dorm room and everything."

"He did? I thought he never left the island."

"His disorder didn't manifest until he turned eighteen. He was so smug before that too, so sure he was better than me. Growing up, he always hated me. He thought of me as pathetic and embarrassing."

"I'm sure that's an exaggeration," Cherry said. She knew Matteo loved his father, she saw it all over his face when he talked about him. It was very similar to the expression on Mr. Capen's face now.

"No, it's true. He told me often. He resented me because his mother worked full time on the mainland and attended night school. She'd leave every day on the first ferry, and return, exhausted, on the last one. He grew up practically motherless, and always said that if I wasn't so lazy and weak, his mother wouldn't have to work so hard. Honestly, he was right. My condition forced an unwanted burden on them both."

This conversation made Cherry uncomfortable and slightly guilty. The whole reason Matteo got upset with her in the first place was because she hadn't come to him to learn about his condition. She was probably making it worse, asking his father for help instead of resolving it directly with him. Surely he wouldn't appreciate that, especially with his father gossiping and sharing details that Matteo himself hadn't. She only intended to seek insight on the best way to apologize, like maybe what kind of pie did he like best, or was there a favorite type of cookie she could bake. That's what she thought they would discuss.

"When he started college, he had such grand plans," Mr. Capen continued. "He told me he was never coming back. His mother said the same thing when she loaded up her car to take him, and she at least told the truth. Matteo only made it about six weeks. He called me crying from the hospital emergency room—he had his first panic attack, and thought for sure he was dying. I think it's the first time he realized my mental illness was a real thing. Vivian—you know her, right?—drove down and picked him up, and moved him back home. He was absolutely devastated."

Cherry wanted to cry as she thought about Matteo and his somewhat arrogant attitude. That was all a cover, he ached inside. And she made his pain so much worse, especially with her comment about his education. No wonder he walked out on her!

"He's doing so much better now, right?" Cherry asked. He seemed to be. Matteo was always out and active in the village. If he hadn't told her, she never would have guessed that there was anything wrong with him. Well, anything clinically wrong. He had a lot of other issues, like his inability to have a conversation without swear words and his generally rude attitude.

"He forces himself to do better. Truthfully, Cherry, he's afraid. He's terrified of any setbacks that might crash down upon him. He never wants to be like me, and I don't blame him." Mr. Capen hung his head, and Cherry reached out to pat his arm.

"I know he loves you. He talks about you with pride. I think he sees how much you've overcome, and he understands your struggle now."

"He can love me and resent me at the same time." He rose to his feet. "Come with me. I want to show you something."

He led her through his living room—which was packed with books, another similarity to his son—to a small door. "Are you ready for this?"

He opened the door to reveal a rickety metal staircase curving up an interior column. The lighthouse! Was she going to get to go inside a real lighthouse? That was definitely a new experience!

"Are you sure it's safe?" she asked with trepidation.

"If I can do it, you can too. You aren't scared of heights are you?" Just like his son, he passed her and started walking up without bothering to check if she followed. Now she knew how Matteo had developed that obnoxious habit.

She forced herself to put one foot on the stairs, then another. Mr. Capen weighed more than her, and he was going up, no problem. If the stairs held his weight, surely they must be able to support hers. She held on to the railing and watched her feet as she carefully followed him upwards.

"I can't believe you do this every day!" she called out as they climbed. Had she tried this a couple of months ago, she would have been winded, but her daily walks on the island were getting her in better shape.

"I don't. Lighthouses have been automated since the '80s. I just keep it clean, and occasionally bring up the tourists or school field trips."

"Oh." She hadn't thought of that. For some reason, when Matteo told her his father ran the lighthouse, she assumed that he polished the mirrors and checked the beacon and trimmed the wicks. Perhaps she had read too much historical fiction.

The stairs led to an area below the massive light. The rotating support base for the lightbulb came through the center of the room. "Wow, this is really interesting," Cherry said as she examined the base. "Thanks."

There had to be a reason he brought her up here. Was there a hidden meaning? The light must represent something, perhaps Matteo? She needed to find a way to turn him on ... no, that certainly wasn't right. Maybe the light symbolized mental illness, and she had to examine it to understand how it worked? She continued studying the light fixture as she tried to parse the metaphor.

"I didn't bring you up here to show you the bulb," Mr. Capen said in the same exasperated tone Matteo used sometimes. They were far too similar. It was uncanny. "Step outside." He opened a door and a blast of cold air hit her in the face.

*Step outside? Are you insane?* she wanted to ask, but stopped herself before she could say something so offensive. Instead, she went with, "I'm fine inside, thanks."

"Trust me, it's safe. The walkway is solidly attached, and there's a railing. I promise, I won't let anything bad happen."

Cherry thought back to the night Matteo convinced her to ride a tandem bike. *Trust me*, he had said, and she ended up having a fantastic time and gaining confidence. Her faith in Matteo made her feel like she could trust his father as well, so she gathered her courage and stepped out on to the walkway.

When she finally managed to pull her eyes away from concentrating on the platform under her feet and insuring that it was still firmly connected to the wall and there were no suspicious cracks or holes, she looked out at the view, and saw all of Lake Superior's blue-grey glory spread before her. She gasped in delight. "Oh my goodness! This is amazing!"

"Isn't it?" He seemed proud of himself, yet another common trait. Was Matteo actually his son or his clone? "You can see the ferry in the distance, and some fisherman way out there, on their way home. I love when I can come up here. Take a deep breath, let the air rejuvenate you."

"I love it!" Cherry said. "Thank you so much for showing me this!"

"I invited you up here for a reason." Mr. Capen suddenly looked serious. "There's something my son always forgets. He thinks he's trapped on this island and he acts like it's a prison. Even if it was, he's the luckiest prisoner that ever existed. Look around, we live in a beautiful place, and we have everything we need for happiness: good friends, fresh air, and the acceptance and understanding of our community."

His words struck a chord with her. She had been feeling almost the same way, not trapped, not exactly, but like she had nowhere else to go. Instead of pitying herself, perhaps she needed this reminder. She lived in a peaceful, beautiful place, and even if she wasn't fully integrated into the community yet, that would come with time.

"Thank you," she said again, wiping an unexpected tear from her eye. "This means more to me than you could possibly understand."

# Chapter Forty-Three

Matteo was unloading his box bike when his father opened the door. "Hey, dad, brought you some more firewood. I'll trade it to you for a hot toddy." His muscles still radiated heat from the exertions of chopping wood up near the cabanas, but the air was crisp with the promise of snow. Nothing tasted better than a hot drink on a cold day.

"Lucky for you my grocery order just arrived too. Otherwise, I'd be offering you a hot water and beef jerky." Monty smiled as he said it, so Matteo hoped that meant he was joking. For years he had been telling his father he needed to keep at least a month's supply of food handy at all times. What if a massive storm hit and nobody could get to him? He'd starve. Monty's only concession to his son's concerns was to purchase a fifty-pound bag of rice that he kept in the linen closet. The same bag had been there, unopened, for years. It was probably full of weevils by now. At least that would provide protein in an emergency.

In the kitchen, Monty put the tea kettle on the stove and got out his bottle of bourbon. "Your girlfriend came by the other day."

"I've told you a million times, Cara's not my girlfriend. And she's engaged, remember?" This conversation had taken place hundreds of times over the years, between Matteo and just about everybody on the island. It sometimes seemed that nobody understood platonic friendships these days.

"I wasn't talking about Cara. I meant Cherry, the one that actually likes you."

"Everybody likes me," Matteo retorted. "But Cherry doesn't like me like that." Actually, she probably didn't like him at all anymore, even as a friend. Not after the way he'd yelled at her and abandoned her in the diner. He felt a little guilty about it, but wasn't quite sure how to fix it.

"Oh, I don't know. Maybe she does."

"Dad, you're getting blind and stupid in your old age."

"Am I? Or are you choosing not to see what is right in front of you?" The two men stared at one another for a moment, matching expressions of annoyance on their faces before Matteo looked away. He liked his father, really. Monty was the only one who truly understood all of his issues. Of course, it was his father's genetics that he blamed for having those issues in the first place.

"Look, Dad, Cherry and I are just friends. She's not sticking around. She's actually been dating a lot. She's looking for a man who can give her children. I predict she's here for one more year, max, before she moves back to the mainland and starts popping out babies."

"She could stay and do that here. I wouldn't mind being a grandfather."

Matteo didn't answer right away. Was his father serious? Matteo couldn't have children, ever. Why would he want to consign a child to a life trapped like this? Having panic attacks was bad enough; guaranteeing someone else a lifetime of them would be worse.

"Why would I spread my illness to a child?" he finally asked, and a look of pain crossed his father's face.

"Do you regret being born?"

Maybe he did, sometimes, in his darkest moments.

"No," he lied.

"Do you wish you didn't exist?"

"Irrelevant question. I didn't have a choice in it. Yes, I'm glad I'm alive. Yes, most of the time I'm happy. But I'm also mentally ill. I can see my future and I see my world shrinking. I'm not going to ever marry someone, because I don't want my wife to resent being trapped. And I'm not going to bring a child into this world and force them to suffer the way I have."

Monty shook his head sorrowfully. "Matteo, son, I don't think you know what you're talking about. Go home. Go home and call your mother."

"Call mom? And tell her what, that you're getting senile on top of everything else? I'm not sure she'll care." His words were cruel, and he regretted them as soon as he said them, but not enough to apologize.

# Chapter Forty-Four

It had been one week since Matteo stormed out of the diner. She hadn't seen him at all around town, but she hadn't had much opportunity to look. The sun set so early these days, she barely had time for a walk after school before it got dark, and, silly as it sounded, she didn't feel comfortable walking alone at night. Sometimes she wrapped herself up in a blanket and sat on her balcony and stared down into the mostly empty streets. She'd give anything to have her friend back.

Should she go back to the diner tonight? Maybe Matteo would be there. He didn't like to change his routine, so she could probably find him sitting at the counter and maybe strike up a conversation. It would be better than taking his father's advice and waiting him out. Yes, that's what she would do. Resolved, she put on her jacket and started down the stairs. And was startled to see a shadowy figure waiting at the bottom.

"Matteo? Is that you?"

He turned and looked up at her. "Who else would it be? We're almost late for dinner. If you don't hurry, we're going to lose our table."

"What are you talking about? I thought you were mad at me."

He shrugged. "I was. Now I'm not. So are you coming or what? If you hurry up, I'll even pay. It's cold out here."

"Fine. But if you're paying, I'm ordering dessert." Was Mr. Capen right and everything was better now? Is time really all it took? Matteo's smile indicated that it was.

They started off down the street together, when he suddenly stopped. "Wait, did you feel that?"

"What?" She hadn't felt anything. But then, there it was, the lightest of touches on her face. Snow! It was snowing!

"First snowfall of the year. Hey, I have an idea. Go back up and get your winter coat."

"This is my winter coat," she said, looking down at herself. She wore a nice leather jacket that she'd bought just last year. She thought she looked sophisticated, though perhaps it was a bit too fancy for a small town.

"What the hell is wrong with you? You are going to die this winter. It doesn't even cover your ass." He sounded exasperated. "Okay, fine. Here's what we're going to do. Go to the diner and order meals for both of us, I don't care what. Surprise me. Dessert, too. Ask Wayne to pack everything up to go, and wait for me." He took off running in the direction of his house.

"I thought you said you'd pay," she shouted after him, but he didn't stop. He was the most infuriating man.

🌲 🌲 🌲 🌲 🌲

Cherry waited patiently at the counter, and Matteo arrived just as Wayne handed her the boxes of food. Matteo's arms were full—he was carrying a large coat and an insulated food carrier.

"Here," he tossed her the coat. "Put this on, while I pack our food. Hey, Wayne, did you put the meals on my tab?"

Cherry examined it. It was definitely a woman's coat, a very thick one that came almost to her knees. Did he keep this around in case any of his paramours got cold? He saw her confusion.

"It's my mom's. You can borrow it until you buy yourself something functional."

"I didn't know you had a mom," she responded thoughtlessly and then realized how dumb that sounded. "I mean, I know you had one. I thought your dad told me she didn't live here."

"She doesn't, she lives in Florida. She rarely visits in the wintertime, but when she does, she needs a coat, so she leaves it at my place. Because unlike you, she prepares for the weather. Hurry up and put it on so we can go."

She followed him out the door and down the street. He walked much faster than her, and she had to hurry to catch up. "Where are we going? To your house?"

"Why would we go there? No, we're going to my boat launch."

She stopped in her tracks. "Boat? But it's dark and snowing!"

"You are such a baby. We're going on my boat. New things, remember?" He kept walking, and after a moment, she followed.

# Chapter Forty-Five

"Life jackets are under the bench seat. Grab one and put it on," Matteo told Cherry. He buckled his own and then looked over and burst out laughing.

"Don't make fun of me!" she said indignantly, still struggling with the life vest. "I'm not used to these things."

"Of course you aren't, or you'd know that one is Martha's. The human ones are on the other side." It was too dark to tell, but he was positive her face turned scarlet.

When she was safely ready, he started the boat and took them out into the icy waters. Whispering Pines was the largest—and only inhabited—island of the Piney Islands archipelago. Their destination, the smallest and most distant, was called Lonely Pines. He dropped anchor in the shallow water near its shores.

"We're going on another island?" she asked, and he heard the delight in her voice. Damn, maybe that's what they should have done.

"No, sorry, not this time. I thought we'd sit out here to eat. The back of the boat has a swim platform, with comfy seats. We can stare out into the Canadian waters and let the snow fall on our faces."

"Oh my goodness, that sounds so lovely!" He wanted her to be happy, but her enthusiasm was a little over the top. Couldn't she be just *mildly* excited?

They ate in silence, hunched over their Styrofoam containers to keep snow off the food. The snowfall was quiet and soft, and so gentle over the lake. He loved moments like these, no sound but the water lapping against the sides of his boat, and the occasional hoot of a snowy owl from the nearby forest. There had already been a few owl sightings this year as they came south from the Arctic. He kept his eyes peeled in case it made an appearance. That would make the night even more special, since he was quite certain Cherry had never seen one before.

"Thank you so much for bringing me out here," Cherry finally said. "Matteo, I can't apologize enough for what I did, checking out those books instead of talking directly to you. I thought I was helping, but now I understand how wrong I was."

"It's fine," he replied. He'd probably overreacted anyway, though he certainly wasn't going to admit it.

"But you know, you owe me an apology, too."

"For what?" What the hell? He was the victim here.

"You should have told me sooner. We spend a lot of time together, we talk all the time, and yet you chose to keep a major part of your life secret from me. I tell you everything."

"That's because you're chatty, whereas I'm stoic and reserved."

"You are not!"

"I thought I was. No, listen, I wasn't keeping it a secret. I was just waiting for the topic to come up organically, and it never did."

"Matteo! You've asked me to walk your dogs when you weren't feeling well, and I did it, no questions asked. I thought you had a cold or something. But you didn't, did you? You were having a . . . I don't know what to call it. An episode? An attack? That would have been an ideal time to tell me."

He supposed she did have a point. Also, maybe he took advantage of her a little bit, because she had brought over crackers and ginger ale when she thought he was ill. He liked having someone treat him like an ordinary person and not a mental patient. He took a deep breath and decided he might as well be honest.

"Whatever, I'm sorry. I didn't tell you because you were the only one who didn't treat me differently. Everyone else looks at me with pity. You look at me with annoyance. I like that you don't cut me any slack. I worried that if I told you the truth, you'd see me as weak and broken. Maybe I enjoyed pretending that I wasn't."

"Matteo," she began, and he didn't like the sympathy in her tone, so he interrupted.

"No, we're done. We've talked it out, we've made our apologies. Move on, Cherry Blossom." They sat in silence for a moment, but then he had to break it to ask the question that had been nagging at him. "What did you talk to my dad about?"

"Ummm . . . not much, actually. I went to visit him and I told him what happened, and he said . . . well, never mind what he said. But he showed me around the lighthouse and took me up on the walkway. You can see so far from up there!"

"Yeah, he likes the view. I'm glad he made it up the stairs. He can't always climb them. So, you won't tell me either. That's fantastic. I love having people gossiping behind my back. You should make it a weekly event." He couldn't contain his sarcasm, but then felt slightly guilty about it.

"I wanted to help."

"I know." Apparently, they weren't finished with their discussion after all. "Alright, nosy Miss Waites, assuming you're done chatting him up and reading about my condition, is there anything you want to ask me?"

"What do you go through when you're having an attack?" Her question was earnest, and she looked at him like she could really see him, like she truly wanted to understand what went on in his head. The intensity of her gaze made him uncomfortable.

"Do you ever watch horror movies? There's a part just before the killer strikes, when you're looking at the victim and you know there's something dangerous, you know she's about to get killed, the soundtrack music is all tense and even though you're watching from the safety of the couch, you feel the fear in your body. Imagine being that victim, in that frightening place, knowing you're in danger, something malevolent wants to hurt you and it's right there, ready to attack."

"So it's like being scared?" He obviously hadn't explained things very well, if that's all she got from it. He tried again.

"It's like your whole body is on alert warning you something is wrong, and your brain is screaming. Think about when your body fills with cortisol and adrenaline after your fight or flight reflex gets triggered, and imagine feeling that for a long time, long after you should be back to normal."

"But you know what it is right? You can identify the feeling and you know nothing is actually wrong, so why can't you fight it off? That's what I don't understand. I've worked with so many students over the years who are scared of things, but once they acknowledge their fears and face them, they can overcome them. Once I had a sixth grader with a paralyzing fear of public speaking, to the point she skipped class to avoid being called on. But I helped her figure out exactly what she was afraid of and then she took baby steps to face those fears. She's in high school now, and last I heard, she got cast in a play. It works."

He laughed, a short harsh burst, and she turned away. "Look, Cherry, that's a sweet story. But that's not how panic disorders work. Intellectually, I know the problem. From an outside perspective, I can tell myself 'hey, dumbass, you aren't having a heart attack, you aren't dying, get over yourself.' But that doesn't work when I'm in the middle of one because my lizard brain is in control. Maybe it's overdeveloped and powerful, I don't know. But it overrules everything else and screams at me, and it always wins. You can't reason with it. Do you understand what I'm talking about?" It wasn't something he had to explain often. Everybody in town knew about his particular situation.

"I do. I'm a teacher, I know about the limbic system. And so I sort of get what you're saying, but I find it difficult to connect you with someone who doesn't have complete control over himself."

"Excuse me? You make me sound like I'm incontinent. Fuck, Cherry. It's a mental illness. You can't tell if someone has one just by looking at them."

"Stop using such foul language! You don't have to swear to prove your point!" She sounded annoyed, which was gratifying, because he was getting annoyed himself.

"Look, you don't have to hang out with me. You don't have to be my friend if my being crazy makes you uncomfortable."

"Are we friends?" Her smile lit up her face more than the moonlight did, and for a moment she looked beautiful.

"Yeah, whatever. I guess." He tried to hide his own smile. "If we weren't, I'd make you swim home."

*No Longer Yours*

# Chapter Forty-Six

Dear Gary,

Last night was magical. I went for a boat ride out past the farthest island in the chain, almost to Canada. The weather was freezing, but it was so peaceful, especially with the gently falling snow, like icy little kisses upon my face. I ate my dinner while sitting on the back of the boat, enjoying the pleasant rocking sensation caused by the wind and the water. And for a moment, staring out over the lake, I felt at peace.

Do you know anything about snowy owls? They're these huge white birds that live in the Arctic, but they come further south in the winter. I saw one swooping over the water and then landing in a tree on Lonely Pines. And I stared at it, and I thought 'I am like that bird.'

Am I vain to compare myself to something so beautiful?

But I am like that owl, far from home, needing to move and to adapt. They live in the flat cold tundra, and yet here was one on a pine-covered island, just as out of place as me.

I'm an Ohio girl, born and raised. I cheer for the Buckeyes, I put chili on spaghetti, I say pop rather than soda. And now I'm here, where people trap and eat groundhogs, where all events are scheduled based on the ferry's arrival, where most of the houses stand vacant for much of the year, and where everybody knows everybody but me.

It's hard, it's rough, and yet, seeing that snowy owl grounded me a bit. That bird probably doesn't want to come south, it wants to stay where it breeds, stay in its own lands, its own home, but instead, it's here. And it's going to survive.

So will I. I will survive. I am hardening. I am learning a new way of life.

And I have a friend who will help me.

So there, Gary. I have a friend, someone I met without you, someone who likes to talk to me and hang out with me. He sees me, and even though I am sad and broken and lost, he doesn't care, because in a way, he is too. Maybe everyone is. Maybe I'm not the only one alone and suffering. Maybe I'm not the only one who hates myself.

Things are turning around.

Cherry

# Chapter Forty-Seven

*Whispering Pines Island, December 2014*

"I haven't seen you on MidWestSinglz lately," Matteo told her as they sat down in the diner. He had to admit, he liked sitting at a table better than the counter, though he didn't appreciate the knowing looks Wayne gave him when he came to take their orders. He and Cherry were just friends. Obviously nothing could happen between them.

"How would you know if I've been on there?" Cherry asked, showing once again that she had no idea how the online dating service worked.

"Your profile says how long ago you last signed in," he explained. "It's so people don't waste time messaging someone who hasn't checked in in months. Or maybe so people can use it as proof to their girlfriends, like 'see honey, I haven't logged in since we met' or whatever."

"But why are you checking out my profile at all? Just so you can send me harassing messages? I receive enough of those from strangers, I don't need them from you too."

"Ouch, that was hurtful. I'm not trying to harass you, I like to say hi if you're online, that's all." Okay, and I like teasing you, he admitted privately.

"I haven't been using it because there's a guy who won't leave me alone. I tried blocking him, but he keeps creating new accounts. Wait, it's not you, is it? Is this your way of teaching me a lesson or something? I should have known!"

"Seriously? Of course not. If I was doing something to annoy you and you didn't know it was me, then where's the fun?"

"Oh." She visibly deflated. "I kind of hoped it was you, so I could tell you it's not funny and you'd stop." The vulnerability on her face made him want to take her hand and comfort her, but he wasn't crazy enough to try something like that. She might think he was hitting on her, and nothing could be further from the truth.

"You are a teacher, aren't you?"

"What does that have to do with anything?"

"I know your students don't behave perfectly all the time. How do you manage them in a classroom, but you can't handle some random internet guy?" Seriously, she never stood up for herself. He couldn't imagine how she survived teaching middle school for so long. Kids that age had to be more annoying than anything she dealt with from grown men.

"It's different. In my classroom, the students listen to me because I hold a position of authority over them. But when I try to tell this guy to stop harassing me, he won't. He just tells me that we need to meet and that once I get to know him, I'll like him. I'm going to end up having to meet him just to get rid of him." That set off warning bells in Matteo's head. She was going to get herself killed. He'd have to step in and handle this for her. Again.

"Tell you what, come over to my house later and bring your laptop. I'll get rid of the guy." That brought back her smile. Simple kindnesses pleased her more than they should. Poor woman. She liked to pretend to be so happy, but he knew she wasn't that strong. She couldn't handle the rough world of online dating. He figured she probably couldn't handle in-person dating either. Where would she find someone (other than him, of course,) who would tolerate her annoying optimism and false cheer all the time?

# Chapter Forty-Eight

The dogs went wild when Cherry knocked on the door. She heard them scratching and barking and imagined them jumping in circles.

"Jeez, kids. Calm down," Matteo's voice was hard to hear over the dogs' enthusiasm. He opened the door, while trying to block them with his leg. "They really like you for some reason. Come on in."

"I like them too," she replied, "Much better than their master."

Matteo laughed. "I'm the one who has to clean up their shit. So, obviously, I'm not their master, I'm their servant. Come in. Tristan, down!"

"Aww, he's fine. Aren't you, you good boy." She bent to scratch the corgi's head. Tristan was her favorite. A deep longing for the companionship of a dog welled up in her. Someday, when she could afford a proper house, then she would adopt one.

Matteo led her to the kitchen table, where he had set up his own tablet. "Want a beer?" he offered. "I have a couple of Tim and Sam's latest experiments. They're not bad. Or I can open a fine wine."

"Stop teasing me about my profile. I changed it anyway." Goodness, he was intentionally annoying. She felt silly enough putting herself out there, and his teasing made it worse. She should not be in this situation. This was not the life she planned.

"Beer it is." He set down a bottle in front of her. "I hope you like porters."

"Fine, thanks." She opened her laptop. "What's your Wi-Fi password?"

He grinned with an obnoxious twinkle in his eye. "Matteo is a sex god, all one word."

"No, it isn't!"

"Sure is. I changed it right before you came over. You want my help, you have to tell your computer about my sexual prowess. And don't look so horrified, my initial instinct was making the password a description of my naughty bits."

She inhaled and exhaled slowly. He always acted like such a crude jerk, but she needed to let it go. "Computer," she announced. "Fair warning: I am about to type a terrible and preposterous lie."

She logged in and discovered Lyle had sent her dozens of messages in the days she'd been avoiding the service. As she was about to turn her screen to show Matteo, a new one popped up. *Finally! I've missed you! So when are we getting together?*

"It's him, and he's already messaging me." She held back tears. As an optimist, she always looked for the good in people, so when Lyle first started contacting her, she chatted with him, thinking he was just lonely. He took her interactions for much more than they were, and had repeatedly asked her out. She'd been polite at first. But he wouldn't go away. He tracked her down on social media as well, and kept messaging her there. He even tried to connect to her real-life friends.

Matteo scooted his chair next to hers and read over her shoulder. "Wow. This guy can't take a hint, or a direct statement. 'You'd like me if you met me,' 'I won't take no for an answer.' He sounds like a real rapist."

"That's not funny."

"I'm not joking. Don't worry though, I got this. Ready?" He started typing. *Hey Lyle, fantabulous news, my friend is free tomorrow evening.*

*What friend?*

*Didn't I mention it? I told my friend all about you, and now I'm going to hook you two up!*

*No, I want to take you out. Drinks? Or do you want me to come over to your place? I'm ready to ravage you!*

*No thank you. I'd rather introduce you to my friend. His name is Matteo.*

"Oh my goodness, what are you doing?"

"Just watch." He rubbed his hands together maliciously. "This is going to be fun."

*R U trying to set me up with a dude? Wtf?*

*I think you'll really like him.*

*I'm not gay!*

*I get it. Neither is he. *wink**

*Why would U set me up with a dude?*

*Why not? Have you tried it?*

*NO, I M NOT GAY!*

*Right, he isn't either, it's cool. He just wants to date you. Maybe you can exchange bro-jobs?*

"Matteo! You can't write things like that! He thinks he's talking to me!" Cherry was scandalized. This was certainly not how she communicated with people, and she didn't want her name and profile attached to such crudity. And she never heard of bro-jobs either, though she had a disgusting guess as to what they were.

"I told you, I'm getting rid of this guy."

*I don't want to date him. I like you.*

*Have you met him?*

*NO!*

*Then how do you know you don't want to date him?*

"Are you seriously trying to get a date with Lyle?" Why was Matteo so adamant about wanting to meet him?

"Cherish Fernanda Waites, what is wrong with you? I'm trying to make him leave you alone. I'm using the same language on him that he used on you, only he hasn't caught on yet."

"That's not my middle name!" What an exasperating man! Though she did appreciate him standing up for her and helping her deal with her harasser.

*I don't want to go out with a dude!*

*You use the word dude a lot. You must be into dudes.*

*No!*

*You never know until you try.*

*STOP! I like v-slit and only v-slit!*

"What does that even mean?" Cherry asked, and Matteo snorted.

"Really, Cherry? He's talking about the female you-know-what."

"That's so crude! Who says such things?" This was not a vocabulary lesson she was interested in learning. It made her want to wash her eyes with bleach.

"People on MidWestSinglz. Oh, and straight guys everywhere. I mean, I'm with him on that one."

"Now you're being crude. Please stop."

"He's the one who used that expression, not me. But I'll talk to him like you would."

*Heavens to Betsy, Mr. Naughtypants! You know I don't like that sort of foul language. Don't be such a potty-mouth, Lyle. And I don't understand what the issue is. You meet with Matteo, see if you hit it off, take things slow.*

"Better, Miss Waites?" Matteo acted so proud of himself. She rolled her eyes and waited for Lyle's next message.

*It is a big deal bc I M not gay. Why R U being so weird?*

*I'm not being weird, you silly billy. I told you before I wasn't interested in you, but you persisted. And then I told my dear sweet attractive friend about you and he said he liked a guy who can't take no for an answer, so I thought that you'd suit each other. Or maybe un-suit each other. Get it? Un-suit? Take off your suits? Tee-hee.*

"Do you honestly think I talk like that? I don't say tee-hee." She wanted to smack him, the way Matteo was smirking so proudly. It didn't help that he read the words aloud in a prim saccharine voice as he typed.

"You don't like that I said 'tee-hee' but you aren't objecting to describing me as attractive? Why, Cherry Blossom, I'm flattered."

*I don't understand why you aren't interested. We were chatting, everything was going so well. You'd like me if you met me.*

*You'd like Matteo if you met him.*

*No I wouldn't.*

*You don't know that for sure.*

"This guy is not getting it, is he?" Matteo reached over and grabbed his tablet. "Hang on, I'll try another method."

Cherry watched as Matteo logged into his own Mid-WestSinglz account. There were an awful lot of messages in his inbox. How? Why? Who would want someone as insufferable as him? And some of those girls were very pretty, much prettier than Cherry. Oh, and that one had a profile picture with a dog. Matteo probably liked her the most. Gosh, he was so aggravating!

*Hello, sexy! R U Cherry's friend? When r we going 2 meet?*

"Did you send that to Lyle?" Cherry asked. Matteo was bold, she'd give him that. Lyle's response came quickly: *Leave me alone.*

*It's cool, bro, no homo.* Matteo typed back, and then glanced at Cherry. "You may want to go into another room for a minute."

"Why? What are you going to do?"

"I'm going to send him a picture you won't approve of and then ask if he wants more. But I'm doing you the courtesy of inviting you to leave before I undo my pants. Unless you want to stay, that is. I mean, you can participate. We can use your hand for scale."

"Matteo! That's horrible! Don't you dare!"

"I said I'd help you. If I have to fight dirty, I fight dirty. Now, why don't you take Beverly into the mudroom and check her water bowl, while I take care of business."

She left the room, fuming. He was so gross. Why did he act like that? She wasn't sure who was worse, Matteo or Lyle. Beverly whined, and Cherry absentmindedly petted her head. The contact calmed her, and she started to think more positively—Matteo was doing something obscene, but at least he was doing it to help her. He might be rude and crude and gross, but he wasn't directing at Cherry.

"Okay, you can come back now," Matteo called out.

When she returned, his tablet lay face down on the table.

"I figured you didn't want to see what I sent him. His response was great though, before he blocked me. Apparently, he's not interested. And I don't think he likes you very much anymore. Check out the end of your convo."

She looked at her own account to find a complaint from Lyle about her gay friend sending dick pics, and Matteo — as Cherry—responded: *Was it big?*

*Was what big?*

*Don't be obtuse. His you-know-what. Was it huge? Do you want it in you?*

*WTF? What is wrong with you? I thought you were such a nice girl, but you're just a slut.*

*No, I'm not. I told you to leave me alone, and I kindly offered you a rather well-endowed alternative, which you are rejecting. I don't understand. If you want me, why wouldn't you want my friend, too? I mean, I don't want a threesome or anything, but I'm happy to watch while he, to put it politely, tears you a new one.*

*Bitch. I'm blocking you. Don't ever contact me again!*

"See, it worked. He blocked you. And he's going to be too scared to contact you again. Also, it's entirely possible that I may set up some fake accounts and send him some other messages in the future, I haven't decided yet."

"Matteo, you're ... you're ..."

"Awesome? I assume that's what you're trying to say. Now grab your beer and let's go into the living room. There's a documentary on famous dogs throughout history that my babies and I have been wanting to watch. You'll appreciate it."

He did his usual, walking off without waiting for her to agree. But watching a documentary while cuddling Tristan sounded way better than going home alone, so she followed him. It was nice to have a real friend again.

# Chapter Forty-Nine

Matteo poured himself a glass of sherry and pulled out his tablet. He planned to do a little research on ways to make Martha feel better, then he was going to probably open up one of his throwaway accounts and harass that guy Lyle, just for fun. And because he could tell Cherry about it later and she might laugh, or she might get annoyed, which was admittedly a cuter look for her. He liked the way the corners of her eyes crinkled and her cheeks turned pink.

But before he could do anything, his video messaging app dinged. His mother. He hesitated before answering, but as always, his anxiety wouldn't let him deny a call. What if something was wrong?

"Hi Mom." He squinted at the screen to examine the background, so he could see what her life was like now. She visited him once a year, usually in the late spring, but obviously he had never gone down to Florida to visit her. He'd even attended her wedding by video rather than in person.

"Matty, how are you?" she asked, in her warm and reassuring voice. Good, that tone meant she wasn't about to deliver terrible news. Tension drained from his body.

"Getting by, same as always. How are the steps?"

"Doing well. Zoe is filling out her college admission applications, and Troy made the basketball team."

"Yeah, I saw his post about that. I'm happy for both of them." He and his step-siblings shared a friendly virtual relationship, though he'd never met them in person. His mom's new husband had joint custody, but they had yet to schedule their island trips to coincide with his parenting time.

"I'm not calling to talk about them. How are you doing? Your father told me you've been depressed lately." She seemed concerned, as well she should be since depression was not one of his diagnoses.

"I'm not depressed, dad's reading too much into it. Why are you talking to him anyway?"

"You may be over thirty, but you're still our child, and we still share parenting talks," she told him, and he put his face close to the camera to make sure she saw his dramatic eye roll. He didn't need parenting anymore, he was a grown man. "He told me you were saying things like you wish you'd never been born."

"That's not what I said, mom. I said I wouldn't have kids at the risk of spreading my illnesses to yet another generation. Admit it, if you knew about dad's craziness, you never would have bred with him."

"Bred with him?" his mother laughed. "You're hysterical. What do you think I am, one of your dogs? You weren't bred. You know you were a happy accident. And, if early on in my pregnancy, your father had told me about his agoraphobia —if we even understood such things back then—I still would have had you. You were my choice, Matteo. Never forget that."

"Yeah, but if you could go back in time, you never would have gotten pregnant in the first place, right?" After his mother's freshman year of college, she took a summer job at the Whispering Pines laundromat. And that's where she met Monty Capen, a twenty-six-year-old fisherman. Supposedly, the laundromat was also where she conceived Matteo, though he never tried to verify that rumor. Within a week of discovering her pregnancy, her parents withdrew her from college, forced an engagement ring on her finger, and she found herself settling into Monty's tiny apartment. It was not the life she had pictured or wanted, but, as she always said, 'that's how things were done.'

"Matty, even if it were possible to time travel to before I met your father, I wouldn't change a thing, because it got me you. Now, after getting pregnant, there were some things I would have changed. I was just nineteen and I wasn't prepared. But you're my son, and I love you and I'd do anything for you."

"Yeah, I know." He ducked his head to avoid seeing the emotions on her face. Her love made him uncomfortable. He didn't deserve it, he didn't live up to her expectations.

"I don't want you to think you have to punish yourself because of your illnesses. You didn't do anything wrong."

"I never said I did!"

"But you told your dad you have no hope for your future, that you'll never be a husband or a father."

"Of course not! What woman would ever want me in the long term? Who wants to be stuck as my world gets smaller and smaller until they become my caretaker? Nobody would choose that life. Nobody."

"If someone loves you enough, they might."

"Like you loved dad?" He'd overheard all their fights as a teenager, he was fully aware of the acrimonious nature of their relationship.

"Don't be sarcastic. You know things between your father and I happened because we were forced into marriage too young, before we knew each other. We didn't belong together. But keep in mind, I stayed on that tiny island for nineteen years for you. Love for you, son. And some day there will be another woman who loves you that much too."

"But I wouldn't let her. I wouldn't ever let someone fall for me, because I am not going to trap them, so they turn bitter and angry at all they've given up."

"Is that what you think I am? Bitter and angry? No, Matteo, I'm not. Staying for you was my choice. You need to acknowledge that women have autonomy. If a woman decides to love you and marry you and have your babies, it will be her choice. You can't push her away."

"But I can stop her before she gets to the point of wanting to do any of that."

"Sure, you can drive everyone away. And you can shut yourself up in your house with your dogs, and never interact with the outside world, if that's what you want. Or you can reach down inside, find some bravery, and put yourself out there. Now, your father tells me there's a particular woman who was the source of this whole conversation?"

"Sorry, gotta run. Tristan needs to go out. I'll call you next week!" He disconnected before she could say anything else. Then he sat back, feeling defeated. Was the problem really just inside of himself? No, it wasn't. He shut down that line of thinking. He was strong, strong enough to keep anyone from making his mother's mistakes.

# Chapter Fifty

Matteo sat waiting by his phone. Cherry had gone on yet another MidWestSinglz date, as though she hadn't learned from the others. She was so determined to meet someone and have more life experiences that she wasn't being cautious. She even got upset with him when he asked if she had a mobile phone.

"I canceled my cell contract when I moved here, since the island doesn't have service. I'll be fine. We're going out to dinner in Ferry's Landing, and I'll be back on the nine o'clock ferry. Stop treating me like a child." But he couldn't help himself. She was like a child. She had no idea what dating in the real world was like. That's why he went up to the inn and borrowed the prepaid phone Cara used while traveling. Cara lent it willingly, though Cherry wasn't thrilled to accept it.

"Call me if you need help," Matteo told her, though he wasn't sure what he could do. It wasn't like he could come find her, and it really wasn't his responsibility anyway. He just felt strangely protective of her. It was probably because of those cherubic cheeks that made her look so young and naïve. Well, it wasn't just her cheeks that made her seem naïve.

He gave her twenty minutes after the last ferry arrived before calling her house to make sure she got back safely, but her voice mail picked up after six rings. He hung up and waited. Finally, after a half hour of fidgeting and worrying and practicing his deep breathing exercises, his phone rang, and Cara's Texas number showed up on the caller ID.

"Cherry?" he answered, already guessing that she missed the ferry. Good thing his boat was still in the water, he could pick her up at the docks. He reached for his tablet to check the weather conditions.

"Hi, there's a drunk girl here who was trying to call you," an unfamiliar woman's voice told him. Shit.

"Where is she? Can you put her on?" he asked, but only heard the muffled noises of the woman talking to someone else. After a moment she came back.

"She says she needs you to come get her. She's completely out of it."

"Where are you?"

"In the bathroom at Shore Leave."

"Is that a bar?"

"Duh. It's by the lake, obviously."

"Okay, I'm going to have someone pick her up. Can you do me a favor? She was on a date with a creep she met online. Can you keep her with you and take care of her until we can get there?"

"No. She can wait with her date. I don't know her, and if she got too drunk, that's not my fault." The woman sounded annoyed, and he couldn't blame her. He wouldn't want to let a drunken stranger ruin his night either.

"Listen, do you have a boyfriend?"

"Yes."

"Great, are you familiar with Whispering Pines Island?"

"Yeah, so?"

"So let's barter. You keep Cherry safe until we can get her, which will be in about a half hour, and you and your man can have a free romantic weekend getaway on the island. You can stay two nights at Cama Cabanas, and I'll throw in a fancy dinner at the inn. Deal?"

"Can you even offer that?" Aha! He'd piqued her interest.

"Sure can. I own the Cabanas, and my business partner also co-owns the inn. We'll hook you up if you protect our girl." He waited, fingers crossed, willing her to accept. Should he throw in a free ski rental?

"Then you've got a deal."

🌲 🌲 🌲 🌲 🌲

He ran down to The Digs, where he found Tyrell and Sam having an after-work drink. "Hey, I need help," he told them. "Have you heard of Shore Leave? Cherry went on a MidWestSinglz date, and she's stuck there, and kinda incapacitated. We can take my boat, but I need you to go in and rescue her."

"No way," Tyrell said. "Walk into a bar and carry out a drunk white girl? How many bullets do you think the cops would put in me? Or would I be shot by someone else first? Forget it. I'm not interested in dying tonight."

"Why would ... oh. Yeah, okay. Sam, please?" Matteo's heart raced and panic rose. He fought it down. There wasn't time to deal with anxiety now.

"Sure," Sam shrugged. "I can rescue a damsel in distress. But how big is the guy? Maybe I need back up."

"Hang on," Tyrell walked around the counter to say a few quiet words to his husband, then tied on an apron. Tim handed over a set of keys and went out the back door, returning with his coat.

"Alright," Tim said to Matteo. "Your boat? Let's go."

🌲 🌲 🌲 🌲 🌲

Matteo sat in his boat by the docks impatiently waiting. Why was it taking so long? He wished he could call them and find out what was going on, but he didn't have a phone anyway. It was only half a mile to the bar, surely he could go there. How hard could it be to walk a half mile? He stood and tried to force himself to take that first step, to put his feet on the wooden planks. He had to, he could do this ... no, he couldn't. The encroaching dread-darkness caused panic to rise, and he sat back down, full of self-loathing.

Just as his anxiety started to overwhelm him, he saw shapes moving in the distance. As they approached he made out Tim with a purse dangling from his wrist, and Sam holding Cherry in his arms. He waited, rubbing his worry stone, until they got close enough for Sam to pass him Cherry's unconscious body. Matteo set her down gently on the bench and checked to make sure she was still breathing.

"How much did she drink?" he asked. He had expected a call because her date annoyed her too much or she miscalculated the time, not that she would drink enough to pass out.

"When she was awake, she said she just had two drinks," Tim said. "I've served her more than that, and she's never been like this, so I wonder if there was something else in them. Her date did not want to let her go." He rubbed his knuckles, smearing streaks of blood around.

"Sorry if you had to get in a fight." Matteo put a life jacket on Cherry before he started the engine. He didn't want her falling overboard and drowning.

"Don't apologize. I love punching people who deserve it," Tim said. "Besides, this has been a great trip. I got to look at the pictures on Cara's phone."

"I told you, I didn't know she was taking those," Sam said defensively.

"Bullshit, Sammy. You were posing."

"What are you guys talking about?"

"Oh, we got stopped by a policeman," Tim explained. Apparently, carrying an intoxicated woman down the street raised suspicions, though fortunately they were far enough away from Shore Leave that they weren't in trouble for Cherry's date's freshly broken nose. "Turns out Ty was right. He would have been arrested at the very least. The cop demanded proof that we knew her, but neither of us even had ID on us, much less anything to connect ourselves to Cherry, and then Sam said 'oh wait, I can show you. I'm the background picture on her phone.' Quick thinking, by the way."

"Yeah, I pulled the phone out of her purse and unlocked it, but then I was dumb enough to open up the gallery."

"And that's where the nudes are." Tim laughed. "No judgment, you looked good."

"Shut up," Sam muttered.

# Chapter Fifty-One

Cherry woke up at home with a pounding headache. How had she gotten here? She still wore her clothing from the night before, but she was tucked into bed, and a full glass of water sat next to her on the bedside table. She didn't recall coming back to the island. She couldn't remember much, actually. Dinner, and going out for drinks afterward, but then ... mostly blank spaces. Had she been laying on a bathroom floor? Had she gone to a party? She had a vague recollection of sitting at a table with a group of strange women, feeling confused.

When she sat up, she felt worse. Her head somehow both throbbed and spun at the same time. This was the worst hangover ever! She stumbled into the bathroom, and when she came out she tried to crawl back into bed, but missed.

"Hey, you're awake," Matteo's arms suddenly came around her and helped her up.

"What are you doing? How did you get here?"

"You couldn't have forgotten our passionate lovemaking, you said it was the best you ever had. You got back from your date and called begging me to come over," he told her as he gently placed her back on the bed and handed her the water glass.

"What? Never!" she desperately tried to think back. She wouldn't do that, would she? Not with Matteo, he was too insufferable.

"Never, really? You're breaking my heart, Cherry Blossom." He gave her his patented mocking look. "Good thing I'm kidding. You tried to call me, but you were so drunk some other woman did the talking, and now I owe her a free weekend up at my cabins. Sam and Tim rescued you, we all brought you back on my boat, and I slept on your couch to keep an eye on you. By the way, I stand by my earlier statements. That is the most uncomfortable couch ever. Next time I'll sleep on the floor."

Cherry closed her eyes and tried to focus her thoughts. She had a brief and unclear memory being carried in Sam's arms. And there was someone else, a police officer maybe? "I don't remember," she told him, rubbing her temples.

"You told Tim you only had two drinks," Matteo informed her. "Did your date buy them?"

"Yes, there wasn't table service, so he bought them at the bar. They must have been extra strong. I can usually handle my alcohol better than that."

"Oh, Cherry," Matteo sighed heavily and sat on the edge of her bed. "I know you can. I think he slipped something in your drink. I should have taken you to the medical center and made them draw your blood, but at the time I was trying to save you the embarrassment. I didn't want word to spread that the teacher went out and got hammered on the mainland. Sam and Tim wouldn't tell anyone, except their partners, of course."

"No, he wouldn't have drugged me. He was such a nice guy," Cherry told him. He was, he was so polite and he opened doors for her and paid for her meal and kept complimenting her. It had to have been someone else. Perhaps the bartender? Maybe she drank something meant for a different girl?

"Cherry, you always search for the best in people, but I think you're mistaken. 'Nice' in the context of 'I'm a nice guy' doesn't mean what you think it does. Shall we check and see if he's sent you a post-date message?"

"Bring my laptop over here." Matteo was wrong. She would stake money on it. Josh must have been really concerned, especially if two large men carried her out of the bar. He probably sent her lots of messages, trying to find out what happened to her last night.

She logged into MidWestSinglz and found Josh's name right at the top of her inbox. See, he was worried about her.

"So click on it and let's read what he has to say," Matteo suggested, still with that smug expression on his face.

*BITCH! How dare you lead me on like that! Your dumb boyfriend broke my nose! I can't believe I wasted all that money and time on you when you're so ugly anyway. You look like a fat chipmunk. You stupid slut. Never contact me on here again, and you owe me $42 for your share of dinner and drinks.*

"Well, that's all over the place. How can you pay him if you aren't allowed to contact him again? Where's the logic?"

Tears leaked from her eyes and she didn't bother to hide them. Why did Gary do this to her? She should be safe at home, either pregnant or holding a newborn, happy with the only man she ever dated. Why did she have to get thrust into this sick world? This wasn't how it was supposed to be.

"Hey, hey, I'm sorry. I was trying to make a joke," Matteo looked as if he'd never dealt with a crying woman before.

"I just ... I just ... it's all too much," she found herself sobbing, and after a moment, Matteo's arms came around her, and he gently patted her back.

"It'll be okay. You'll find someone, I promise. Give yourself time."

# Chapter Fifty-Two

"Thank you for calling the Inn at..."

"It's just me, you don't have to go through the whole spiel," Matteo interrupted.

"Good morning, Matty." Cara always sounded so professional when he called her at work.

"Did Sam tell you what happened yesterday?"

"He told me there was a heroic rescue, a bar brawl, a near-arrest, and that I need to password protect the photos on my phone."

"Yeah, and he took your phone back. I wanted to look through it later."

"Just so you know, he asked me to take those."

"Sure, whatever you say. So, ask me where I slept last night."

"Or we could skip the games and you could tell me."

"You're never any fun while you're working. I spent the night on Cherry's couch." He waited for her reaction.

"Are you serious? Did you actually get any sleep?"

"I did. I slept like a baby."

"According to Margaux, babies sleep no more than two hours at a time, and they crap themselves. Is that really what you want to brag about? I hope you cleaned the couch afterward."

"Cara!" She wasn't appreciating his big news as much as he expected.

"Relax, I'm joking. Actually, I'm impressed. When was the last time you slept anywhere other than your own bed?"

He tightened his grip on the receiver for a moment. The last time was also the last time he went to the mainland, for Cara's former fiancé's funeral. The entire journey was a nightmare, and he didn't want to relive it. "Chicago, two years ago," he finally said.

"Oh. Then."

"Yeah. So. Anyway, I slept on her couch and I woke up okay. Of course, then I had to run home and feed my babies. I think Beverly was worried about me. She hasn't gotten out of arm's reach."

"I thought she only got like that when you were on the verge of a breakdown."

"I hope not." He hadn't thought of that. Sometimes, the keeshond anticipated his panic attacks and tried to stave them off before they started. He put a hand to his chest. Was his heart starting to beat faster? Oh, no.

"Matty, take care of yourself. A guest needs me, I have to go. I'll come by later to check on you."

With a click, Cara was gone, and Matteo had to think. He had been feeling triumphant, almost empowered. He thought of spending the night at Cherry's as a momentous achievement, but what if the high led to a crash?

# Chapter Fifty-Three

Dear Gary,

I hope Megan dumps you and shatters your heart, and you can't handle being alone and you have to resort to online dating. I hope the women you try to talk to ignore you, and you only get messages from people twice your age and they are only looking for a sugar daddy, and they immediately realize you won't qualify.

I've gone on a couple of dates now, and they were all horrible. One man wouldn't stop talking about himself. He asked me questions, but before I could respond he'd tell me his own answer, and that would remind him of a story and then blah, blah, blah. Another guy tried to order my food for me, and spent the whole time negging me. Do you know what negging is? It's when you tear down a person's self-esteem with insulting false compliments. "My friends don't think you're pretty, but I sure do." Or "I'm glad I met you, I'm so tired of smart girls." Why do people do those kinds of things? Why can't I just meet a decent guy?

And the worst date, I woke up the next morning with an awful headache and no memory of the night before. I think I was roofied. Fortunately, I've made a friend on the island, and he came out with a boat and rescued me from the mainland bar. An amazing local chef brought me a thermos of soup that he called a hangover cure, and his fiancée checked in on me several times. It's comforting to feel like I have friends, but it's not pleasant to be in the situation of needing to be taken care of after having been drugged on a date.

And what can I do about it? If I don't want to be alone for the rest of my life, I have to put myself out there, don't I? It's not like I'm going to magically bump into someone, and we'll fall in love and get married. That doesn't really happen does it? Not more than once in a lifetime.

And that's what worries me. Were you, Gary, my once-in-a-lifetime? There was a cute boy I sat near in my history class sophomore year, and we used to joke around a lot. We ran into each other the cafeteria and had dinner together once, and I felt so guilty about it, even though I never thought of it as anything remotely date-like. But what if he was my actual soulmate? What if he was the one who would have loved me and wanted to be with me forever, but I never gave him the chance because I was too busy throwing my life away with you? Once, on a ladies night out, I met a charming man with dimples in his cheeks and such a friendly laugh. He offered to buy me a cocktail and I wouldn't let him because I was taken. What if it should have been him? What if, in the romantic comedy version of my life, my true love sat next to me in a bar and tried to buy me a drink, and I turned him down? I turned him down because of you, and you turned out to be nothing but a no-good cheater.

Did I throw away all my chances at love? Did I waste everything on you?

How could I have been so stupid?

Your foolish ex-wife,

Cherry

# Chapter Fifty-Four

"Buy you a drink beautiful?"

Cherry looked up as Matteo seated himself on the barstool next to her. She made a face at him. "No thanks, I obviously already have one." She picked up her glass and took a slow deliberate sip.

"What are you so annoyed about? You don't like free drinks?"

"No, I'm not interested in letting you buy me anything, because you're doing your sleazy pretending to hit on me bit, and I've told you I'm tired of it."

"Ooh, feisty. I like it when you stand up to me."

"You're doing it again." Pathetically though, she kind of liked it. She was becoming disillusioned with the men she met online. The only interesting person she'd encountered at all was Matteo, and she certainly had no intentions of dating him.

"Sorry." Matteo waved Tim over and ordered a beer. "Cheers, to me not hitting on you, bro."

"Now I'm bro?"

"Sure, why not?" He grinned and his eyes sparkled. Why did he have to be so cute? She had never liked men with facial hair before, but now she sometimes wondered what that beard would feel like when she kissed him. No! Not when! *If!* If she kissed him, she corrected herself. Which she wouldn't do anyway.

"Alright, cheers, sport." She clinked her glass against his bottle.

"So, any dates lined up this weekend?" he asked, even though she was pretty certain she'd previously told him her rather unexciting plans, which involved restructuring some of the elementary curriculum and deep-cleaning her kitchen.

"No. I've been talking to a guy, but he's giving off some red flags," she admitted. This one was named Ethan, and he managed a sporting goods store. His initial messages had been friendly enough, but she was starting to think he was too pushy in asking to meet before she was ready. He'd repeatedly offered to come to the island that weekend, but she kept putting him off.

"Tell you what, we should come up with a signal," Matteo said. "If you're on a terrible date, and you run into me—which I think you do intentionally, by the way—then you can indicate if you need a rescue, and I will swoop in like a white knight."

"You swoop more like a vulture," she replied, but she appreciated his offer. Some women had friends who would call part way through a date, so they could make an excuse and leave if necessary, but on an island without cell phones, she couldn't fake something like that. "Actually, though, that's a fantastic idea. Maybe I can scratch my nose or something like that?"

"Or flash your boobs?"

"Matteo! You promised you'd stop doing that!"

"Hey, it was worth a try." He always looked so amused with himself. She kind of wanted to push him off his barstool. "Alright, scratch the side of your nose. But with your middle finger, so I know it's not just an itch."

"You're so funny." She started to say something else, but someone tapped her on the shoulder.

"Excuse me, are you Cherry?"

She turned, and saw a face from MidWestSinglz. Ethan. What was he doing here?

"Ummm . . ." she hesitated. It wasn't as if she could lie and say that wasn't her name, he'd seen her picture. Of course, she posted more honest pictures than him. Ethan was much older and far larger than expected. She shot a horrified glance at Matteo, whose eyebrows were lifted in amusement. Quickly, she raised her middle finger and scratched her nose.

"Yeah, she's Cherry, who the hell are you?" Matteo asked. He rotated on his stool and squared his shoulders to appear tougher.

"I'm Ethan, we've been talking online. Who the hell are you?" But Matteo didn't answer, he roared with laughter.

"Are you kidding me? This, again?" Matteo turned to Cherry. "Snookums dearest, your mother is insane!"

"My mother?" she didn't understand. What did her mother have to do with this?

"Yeah, your mother. Who else would do it? This isn't the first time she's set up fake dating profiles for you. So, Ethan, where'd she find you? All the Fish? LoveMatch? MidWestSinglz?"

"I don't know anything about her mother. I've been chatting with Cherry on MidWestSinglz. We've been making plans to hook up sometime."

"Hook up? Are you kidding? You plan to hook up with my girlfriend?" Matteo snickered.

"Girlfriend? What the hell is this?" Blood vessels started to pulse on Ethan's forehead. "Cherry, we've been talking for weeks. Are you telling me you've had a boyfriend this entire time?"

"Entire time? And then some. Yes, she's had a boyfriend the whole time her mom was catfishing you." Matteo took back control of the conversation. "For the past three years, she's had a boyfriend and— if I may be so bold as to say it— a tender yet masterful lover, right sweet cheeks? But Cherry's mom doesn't think I'm good enough for her daughter. We live together, we have three dogs together, but apparently that's not sufficient commitment for her. Cherish, I swear to god, I want to marry you, but I don't want to keep putting up with this crap. You're going to give me the mother-in-law from hell."

"Wait, that wasn't you I was talking to? All that stuff about being single and lonely wasn't true?" Ethan's face tightened with anger, and he clenched his fists. The fists were another red flag, she was afraid he might punch somebody, probably her fake boyfriend.

"I . . ." Cherry looked to Matteo, who was enjoying this far too much. She lacked the capability of lying well herself, but he didn't seem to have a problem with it.

"Oh, buddy, you fell for it. Come on, I know her mother. Didn't you think there was something prudish and old-fashioned in the way she talked? Did she even flirt at all? Did she type out words like oh my goodness, instead of using text-speak? You couldn't tell it was a seventy-something-year-old?"

"Well, now that you mention it, she did sound kind of old. She referred to nudes as pictures without clothing, for fuck's sake."

Cherry wanted to chastise Ethan for his language, but refrained. Matteo could tell she was holding back. His lips twitched as he waited for her to say something.

"Pictures without clothing? Did she send any?" Matteo finally asked, sounding far too interested.

"Matteo! You want ... nudes ... of my mother?" She wasn't a prude, no matter what Matteo said, but she still didn't think talking about nudity was appropriate outside of a committed relationship. And, incidentally, despite Ethan's repeated requests (great big waving red flag!), she hadn't sent any.

"Well, honeybunch, she was pretending to be you. I just wondered if she had stolen any of the one's that I took."

"Oh, screw this. I can't believe I wasted time coming out here. I thought I was gonna get laid. You tell your mom to stop messaging me." Ethan left in a huff, slamming the door behind him.

"That was much easier than I thought," Matteo observed. "But we may want to get out of here before he realizes he's trapped until the next ferry. I can't think of anywhere a guy like that would wait other than the bar."

"You saved me again," Cherry said quietly. He kept telling her she needed to stand up for herself, but he was always there to step in when she needed him. In a way, it made her feel special. It was nice to have someone who actually cared, and she almost felt like part of a team again. That's what she missed about her marriage—the sense of connection, of partnership.

"Yeah, I did. I guess you owe me," Matteo finished his beer, then took her drink and polished that off as well. "And now we're even. Let's go. Come over to my place, we can play with my babies and watch a movie. I'll even let you pick it out this time."

She grabbed her coat and followed him. Honestly, an evening with Matteo and his dogs sounded far more enjoyable than anything else she could come up with.

# Chapter Fifty-Five

"You look stressed," Matteo said as Cherry slid into the booth across from him. Actually, more than stressed. Her eyes were red, like she'd been crying, and she trembled nervously, continuously looking over her shoulder as though she thought she was being followed.

"I think someone hates me," she whispered in a cracked little voice that triggered his protective instinct and made him want to hug her.

"Nobody hates you," he assured her. "We might think you're a little . . ." he trailed off. He had been about to make a joke, but this was not the time, not when she looked fragile enough to shatter. "Okay, tell Uncle Matty what happened so I can fix it." That brought a brief smile.

"Uncle Matty? Really? Nobody calls you that."

"Would you rather call me daddy?" Oh, no, he lost it, the smile turned to annoyance. "Sorry, just kidding. Trying to lighten the mood. Seriously, Cherry, what's wrong?"

"Do you think that guy, the one that drugged me, do you think he would come here? Do you think he wants revenge for Tim breaking his nose?"

"I'm sure he does, but I'm also sure he wouldn't dare set foot on this island. The two men who retrieved you are not the biggest guys here. If he saw the ferry brothers, he'd turn around and run home. Hell, so would I. Duncan is scary."

"Are you sure? Because someone . . ." she paused to wipe away a tear. "Someone left a dead fish at my door. I'm scared, Matteo. Who would do something like that?"

"Wait, this is about a dead fish?"

"Yes, it's just like the horse head in the Godfather movie. Someone is threatening me."

"No, Cherry, that's not . . . you think that was a threat?"

"What else could it be? Why else would someone leave a great big dead fish in front of my apartment? I didn't know what to do, so I kicked it under some snow on the balcony. Will you come with me to make a police report?"

He laughed. She was terrified and possibly traumatized, but he couldn't help himself. "Oh, no, no, Cherry," he tried to get the words out. She glared at him, somehow managing to appear both mad and heartbreakingly vulnerable.

"It's not funny!"

"It kind of is. I put the fish there."

"What? Why would you do that to me?"

"I told you I was going ice-fishing with Timmy this morning. And we had a lot of luck, and caught a few coho salmon, so I brought you one. But I didn't want to just come in and put it in your kitchen and freak you out, so I left it in the ice by your door."

"Seriously? You did that?"

"Yes, as a treat, not a threat. Jeez, Miss Waites. I didn't realize you'd take it so badly."

She stared for a moment, then started to laugh, a relieved giggle making her sound like a child. "Oh my goodness, Matteo. What am I supposed to do with that thing? And why didn't you leave a note or something? Or bring it over after I got home? What's wrong with you?"

"You were at school. How long do you expect me to carry a dead fish around? Don't worry, I already gutted it. I'll teach you how to break down the rest. You'll eat like a queen for a couple of weeks."

"But I'm leaving soon, you know that." Oh, that's right. Winter vacation. There were only a few days of school left and then she was taking off to visit her parents for two long weeks.

"Fish freezes. And won't your folks be proud of you when you show up with some delicious salmon you filleted by yourself? They'll be impressed with your self-sufficiency and ability to thrive in the desolate wastelands."

"I doubt it," she said, but she smiled again, which was his goal. His heart twisted in his chest. He would miss her while she was gone. And worry, too. But he shoved those thoughts away before he could begin the downward spiral.

# Chapter Fifty-Six

Dear Gary,

Merry Christmas! Not really, I hope you're miserable. I hope you went to visit your folks, and everybody there is asking about me and telling you I was the best thing that ever happened to you. I hope they all tell you that, if given a choice as to who they got to keep in the divorce, they would have chosen me.

I'm at my parents, sleeping in the queen bed they bought when you and I got married. Remember how they fixed up the guest room for us, so we'd always feel like we had somewhere to go? All those Christmases, all those vacations when we came down here. Remember summer evenings, you and my dad sitting out on the back patio with a beer? The barbecues? The time you 'helped' dad trim a tree and knocked a branch onto our car? Do you remember all the laughter, all the happiness? It's all gone now.

I drove here, on my own, all the way from Minnesota. I went through a snowstorm. I had to stay in a hotel by myself at the halfway point, and eat gas station food because I checked in so late the restaurant was closed. You would have laughed, and made everything better. You would have attempted to make a gourmet meal out of it, and it would have become one of those fun stories we told. But I was alone, and not laughing.

When I finally arrived, tired and drained, my parents offered to let me sleep in the 'other' room, because it wouldn't hold so many memories of us. The room my mom refers to as her craft room, but we all know she intended it to be a room for her grandchildren, the ones she'll never have. She didn't put pressure on us, of course, but did you know she and I had some long talks about it? She was so open about all of her fertility issues, because she wanted me to be prepared, if we ever tried for kids.

Their fifteen-year attempt was the reason I went for all those exams before we started trying, and my doctor assured me my eggs were healthy and my uterus was welcoming, and I should have been able to conceive easily. I should have, but the intended father of my children proved he wasn't worthy. You were aware of all I went through, right? The blood draws, the invasive ultrasounds? Maybe you didn't know, because you were too busy paying attention to what was going on (or preferably not going on) with someone else's uterus at the time.

So here I am. My parents kind of miss you. They loved having you around, they loved you, though not as much as I did. My mom is angry that the last time you visited was in late January, and she cooked us a delicious meal, and hugged us goodbye, and she never got the opportunity to see you one last time after it all came out, she never got the chance to slap you across the face and scream at you, but also say a final goodbye, because you were part of her family, too. You divorced all of us. You cheated on all of us. My dad is so hurt, he saw you as a son, and you betrayed him when you betrayed me. Did you think about that at all? About our tiny little family? About my parents, who knew you for over a decade, who loved you, who welcomed you with open arms?

Our Christmas traditions are muted this year, sad. My mom is treating me as though I'm fragile. She didn't make pecan pie, because that was your favorite, and she didn't want to remind me of you. We decorated the tree, and when we got out the box of ornaments, I noticed she already removed the ones with your name or your picture, and the ones made by your students. You were gone from the box. Your stocking didn't hang next to mine. You didn't hold my hand in the backseat of the car as my dad drove us around to look at all the holiday lights.

Where are you, Gary? Are you alone? Are you sad? Are you thinking of me and everything we had and wishing you had made different choices in your life?

Wistfully no longer yours,

Cherry

# Chapter Fifty-Seven

"Cherish, dear, you have a phone call," her mother yelled. Cherry came into the kitchen, confused.

"For me, really?" She'd talked to Katie earlier, and there was no one else she wanted to have contact with.

Her mother covered the mouthpiece with her hand. "It's a man!" She looked so happy that Cherry couldn't bear to tell her it was probably a telemarketer—though she had no idea how they got this number. She took the cordless phone and walked away.

"Hello?" she asked, ready for a sales spiel.

"Hey, Cherry. It's Matteo."

"Matteo? Why are you calling me?"

"That was rude. It's Wednesday night. Why wouldn't I call you? My dogs miss you."

"It's Christmas Eve. Shouldn't you be out celebrating?"

"I did that already. Vivian hosts a big open house. Her son Duncan dressed up as Santa. He was taking pictures with kids and Sato's little boy started crying and pooped and his diaper exploded all over Duncan's costume. It was hilarious."

"That does sound funny." She curled up in a chair. Odd how comforting it was to hear his voice. "So you didn't go to the diner for dinner tonight?"

"No, it's closed this week. Just about everything is closed, even the bar. Tim and Tyrell left to visit family yesterday morning. I'm going to be wandering around like a ghost, pounding on doors and crying out."

"Oh, stop. No you aren't."

"Nah, you're right. I'm taking my babies over to my dad's tomorrow, and we're cooking a very small turkey. Well, I told him it's a miniature turkey. It's actually one of those little game hens. But it's just the two of us, so who cares, right? But enough about me, how are you?"

"I'm fine, I'm good. I like seeing my folks." As she said it, she knew it wasn't true. She wasn't fine, she wasn't good. She was lonely and miserable and her future stretched out before her, vast and empty and loveless.

"You don't sound fine. Look, Cherry Blossom, this is your first Christmas single in a long time. You may need to mourn for a bit, and find some new traditions to replace the old ones."

"Like what?" She couldn't think of anything.

"You could dress up as a sexy Mrs. Claus and send me some pics. That might be a fun tradition."

"Stop!" she wasn't as annoyed as she sounded. He'd at least managed to make her laugh.

"Yeah, I'm kidding. Or maybe not. What are you wearing?"

"Pajama pants and a sweatshirt," she told him. "And I'm not getting into any weird talk with you."

"Funny coincidence, I'm wearing the same thing. And I'm sitting in my living room with Beverly on my lap and the other two dozing on the floor beside me. I'm drinking a glass of port and when I get off the phone with you, I'm going to watch a documentary on sledding in the Yukon."

"Your evening sounds rather pleasant, actually."

"Yeah, it does. Life is what you make of it. I have my hard times too, but I've learned to work around them. We don't get to choose life's curveballs, but we do choose what we do when they're thrown at us. Remember that."

"Matteo, I've never heard you talk like that before."

"I'm feeling maudlin. And I'm reaching out to you because this is the night we usually see each other, so I wanted to hear your voice. I know you're going through tough times yourself. But remember Cherry, you create your own happiness."

"Thanks, Matteo. I needed to hear that tonight."

When she hung up the call, she sat hugging her knees in the chair for a long time, staring at the receiver and thinking. Maybe he was right. She could create her own happiness. Wasn't that what she was trying to do when she left everything behind?

# Chapter Fifty-Eight

Dear Gary,

If I ever get married again, I'm not changing my last name. I will be Cherish Waites forever. It almost sounds like the title of something, doesn't it? Maybe a sad poem about a widow, or perhaps a song about loss. Cherish waits forever . . .

She's who I was before I met you, and she's who I am now, and I have to focus on remembering that. I have to take the time to see myself, to learn who I am without you. Because I realize now that while we were married, I lost my identity. I wasn't me, I was an extension of you.

I built my entire career as Mrs. Dryden. That was my name on everything—my classroom signs, the letters I sent home to parents, the signatures on report cards. I was always Mrs. D. Do you have any idea how badly it hurt me during my final semester in Parsons every time a student called me by name? It made my heart ache, because I knew Mrs. Dryden couldn't be me ever again.

But this loss of my identity was worse in social engagements. I was yours, that's how everyone defined me. Every week, we would go to your rec league basketball game, then out for drinks. And I always went as your wife. "Gary and his wife are here!" "Look, there's Gary and his wife!" We went out with those people every single Friday, and they knew me as the woman who came with you. How many of them contacted me after the truth about your infidelity came out? None. They all chose you.

It makes sense that they would; you were on the team. You were one of the guys, and I was nothing more than the accessory you brought to the bar afterwards. I imagine Megan slipped into her new role fairly easily. Did the men congratulate you on the upgrade? Does she like being your girlfriend rather than having her own identity? Or is she pretty enough, outgoing enough, fun enough, that she has her own name? "Gary and Megan are here, hurray!"

Maybe this divorce was good for me. It certainly showed me that I gave up too much of myself. What were my hobbies while we were together? I used to go to your games. I used to watch sports on TV with you. When I socialized, it was with 'our' friends. Even on my ladies' nights, I was out with the other wives, or female coworkers, and even then they still viewed me as yours. I had nothing of my own.

I'm not yours anymore.

And you know something? It feels good to finally acknowledge that, and to finally understand that the change is a good thing. I am my own person now, I can do what I like, and I can find out who I am without you.

I like the woman I'm finding inside me. I'm creating my own happiness, and it's starting to work.

Heck, Gary, someday I might even forgive you. Not today, not yet, but someday.

Things are getting better.

Slowly healing,

Cherry

# Chapter Fifty-Nine

*Whispering Pines Island, January 2015*

*New year, new you,* Cherry told herself over and over. She was trying again, getting back out there and going on another date, though she promised Matteo she'd stay on the island.

She took extra precautions this time. She conversed with Paul via the app for two weeks and then on the phone as well, just to be completely sure he was neither foul-mouthed nor foul-tempered. He listened when she spoke, he seemed sweet, and she found no hidden insults in his words.

Dinner with him was fine. Not exciting, but not terrible either. They were able to chat about inconsequential matters, and if the conversation was a bit dull and lagged occasionally, so what? Sparks could come later, right? There was nothing off-putting about him, at least. And they managed to make it through a meal at Harbor Snax without Matteo coming in and ruining everything, so that was something.

It was dark outside when they left the restaurant, and Paul offered to walk her home instead of suggesting they go out for a drink. She felt a brief twinge of disappointment. Not because she was especially enjoying herself, but because the rest of her evening stretched out ahead of her, and she wasn't looking forward to another night alone.

"Would it be alright if I came up? No pressure, you can say no," Paul asked when they reached the foot of Cherry's stairs. She hesitated. But then she thought to herself, why not? She had to take that next step sometime. She was an adult, she was allowed to have some fun. And she needed some life experience. Besides, the temperature outside had fallen well below freezing, and he had to wait for the ferry somewhere. So she let him in.

He admired her apartment, and they sat on the couch and made small talk. Conversation started to wane, and Cherry thought it was time to head to the docks, but Paul unexpectedly asked, "Cherry, this night has been magical. I feel so deeply connected to you. May I please give you a kiss?"

She took a moment to consider, and almost said no. But her second first kiss would happen sooner or later, so why not get it over with now? Paul wasn't a bad guy, and this might help her move on from Gary. "Of course," she replied, and he placed his hands on her face and drew their lips together.

Cherry knew how to kiss, that was easy. She thought she was kind of good at it, too, despite only ever having done it with one man. But apparently, every man used a different technique. Paul's tongue forced itself past her lips, which she expected, except he seemed to want to lick her back molars. She tried to tilt her head, to adjust her own tongue, to figure out if his methods were weird or if maybe she only thought so due to her own lack of proficiency. Paul explored her mouth, even licking the roof of it, and she finally recoiled enough that he withdrew.

"That was amazing," Paul whispered, "Can I kiss your neck?"

Okay, the asking was odd, but at least his tongue was out of her mouth now. She consented, and he treated her to sloppy wet lips moving over her skin. The moisture left behind as he moved his mouth made her shiver with cold. He misinterpreted that as a sign of pleasure. "Mmmmm, Cherry, you taste so good. May I please kiss your shoulder?"

She let him, sitting frozen as he slid the collar of her shirt down enough to expose the top of one shoulder. A trail of saliva led from the side of her face all the way down, and she wanted to shower it away. And what was she supposed to do now? Kiss him back? Ask permission to kiss his neck? She sat awkwardly, desperately wondering what to do. This wasn't how it worked on television, and she had limited personal experience to draw from.

"Oh, Cherry, you are so beautiful. May I please touch your breasts over your shirt?" At least he wasn't trying to kiss her anymore.

"Okay, I guess," she mumbled. Oh no, he groped her like he'd never touched a woman before. This didn't turn her on at all. Quite the opposite. Was this strange massage intentional? And why did he have to moan like that?

"Yes, oh, yes, Cherry, I want you so badly. May I please touch your breasts under your shirt?"

This would be a good time to put a stop to this, before he got his hands, or worse, his slimy mouth, all over her torso. She needed to stand up for herself before this got even grosser.

"Ummm, I'm actually starting to get uncomfortable with this," she told him, bracing for a reaction. If he was anything like her previous dates, he'd immediately call her an ugly slut. She looked around in case she needed a weapon, but of course, she had nothing. Where was Matteo when she needed him?

Paul leaned back, breathing heavily. "I understand. I don't want to do anything without your consent."

"Really?" She was more surprised than she should have been. Perhaps she was becoming jaded, her innate optimism being whittled away by the onslaught of not-so-nice men in the dating world.

"Cherry, I respect you. This is only our first date—of many, I hope—so I don't mind taking things slowly. Our physical relationship will grow over time, when you're ready." He reached out and stroked her face, and she tried not to recoil. "I'm so glad we've found each other."

"Oh, yes, me too," she lied and then looked at the clock, and her heart dropped. It was too late. The last ferry had already left. His eyes followed hers.

"I've missed the ferry, haven't I? I don't want to impose, but maybe I can stay here? I promise, I won't do anything you don't want me to. But perhaps by the end of the night, you'll feel more comfortable with taking our relationship to the next level?" His smile made her cringe. This date had been a huge mistake. But wait . . . she had one last hope.

"Just a minute, let me make a call." She picked up her phone list and pretended she had to look up the number. *Please pick up, please pick up*, she willed him.

"Somebody's lonely," Matteo commented, instead of saying 'hello' like a normal person when he answered. He was infuriating, but she was relieved to hear his voice.

"Hello, Matteo, this is Cherry Waites," she responded in a casual tone. "I was wondering if you still run your water taxi service for people who missed the ferry." Paul could hear every word, and she hoped Matteo understood the intent behind her question. Luckily, he caught on quickly.

"My taxi service? Ha! Yes, I sure do. I don't have any scheduled runs tonight, but if you've got a fare for me, I can probably set something up. Hang on, let me check the weather and ice reports."

She held the receiver tightly and gave Paul a strained smile. If Matteo couldn't cross the lake, she'd be trapped here with him. Could she convince him to take a room by himself at the hotel? Or at one of Matteo's cabins?

"Everything looks good, should be clear enough. You think you can be at my launch in ten minutes?"

Sweet relief coursed through her veins.

"Perfect, thank you." She hung up the phone. "Did you hear that? We can head down now."

"I'm glad it's still running, though I can promise you, if you let me stay, I wouldn't try anything. I respect you too much for that." Paul reached out and tucked a lock of hair behind Cherry's ear, and she somehow kept from cringing.

"I understand, and I appreciate it, but I'm not comfortable having a man spend the night, especially on the first date." This went better than expected. She had honestly been afraid of what would happen when she kicked him out.

They walked down to meet Matteo together. He was standing on his boat, checking something on the steering column. Someday she should ask him to teach her how to drive it. Or captain it? Maybe she also needed to learn the correct nautical terms.

"Twenty bucks for a one-way trip," he said by way of greeting.

"I'll take care of it." Paul pulled out his wallet, which was not as magnanimous as he made it sound, considering the ride was for him.

"Alright, hop in, both of you," Matteo said. Cherry had hoped to say her goodbyes on land, but Matteo apparently did not read the situation the way she wanted him to.

"A late night voyage on a boat, this is kind of romantic," Paul told her when they sat down. Matteo made them put on life jackets and then tossed them a thick blanket.

"Keep warm, it's a cold crossing."

Paul eagerly spread the blanket over their laps.

"May I put my hand on your leg?" he whispered to her.

"Sure," Cherry replied, hoping the small concession would keep him satisfied. This was so awkward.

Fortunately, the bone-chilling cold and the wind made conversation difficult, and they crossed the lake without Paul trying to put his hand anywhere else. When they arrived at the docks, Paul turned to her. "I had a wonderful time tonight. May I please see you again? And may I please kiss you goodnight?"

"That would be lovely," Cherry lied about seeing him again. She hoped he'd offer a peck on the cheek, but no, here came that big tongue forcing its way into her mouth. She was fairly certain she heard Matteo snicker.

"We've arrived, so both of you, out," Matteo's voice interrupted them.

"Out? Aren't you taking me back to the island?"

"That'll be another twenty."

"Are you kidding me? You're going right back there!" She didn't bring her purse and she couldn't believe he would do this to her. He was supposed to be her friend!

"That's how taxis work, miss. Have to pay your way." Matteo wore an ostentatious white captain hat with gold leaf on the brim over his knit beanie, and he put two fingers up and tipped the ridiculous thing at her. Gosh, he was annoying.

"Don't worry sweetheart, it's on me. Please call me when you get home, so I know you made it back safely." Paul handed Matteo another bill and finally, finally walked away.

When Paul was out of earshot, Matteo turned to Cherry. "Quite a show you two put on. Maybe I should be paying you."

"Don't talk about it."

"Why not? Hey, you can vent over drinks at The Digs. I'm buying. Your lover there just gave me an extra twenty."

"You weren't actually going to charge me for passage back, were you?"

"Of course not. But I did want to make him pay as an apology for having to witness that tongue action. God, Cherry, it was like a thick slimy snake or something. Gross, I didn't think that's what you'd be into."

"Please don't remind me, Matteo. Why is it so hard?"

"It's not, after what I just saw. In fact, I think it crawled back inside."

"Stop being so obscene! You're a horrible person! I hate you!" And that was it. She couldn't take anymore and she burst into tears. Why did everything have to be so difficult? Why couldn't she meet a decent man? Why did Gary leave her, thrusting her back into the dating world, when all she wanted was stability and security, and someone who didn't make her skin crawl when he touched her?

"Don't do that, Cherry, I'm sorry. For real, I'm sorry. Please stop crying!" He didn't come near her, just stared from behind the safety of his center console. "It was a joke, I was teasing."

"You always say that, but it's not funny. Why are men so terrible? Why are they so disgusting? Why can't I meet someone who wants to get to know me and spend time with me and doesn't kiss like a desperate lizard?"

"Not all men. You just have a shallow pool to choose from, and all the good ones are taken. I could have warned you long before you moved here. Now, wipe your tears before they freeze and have a seat, so we can head back. And then we'll go to the bar, order some warm drinks, and you can tell me all about your awful date, and eventually, you'll even laugh about it. And I promise, I will make no creepy remarks, and I won't hit on you at all."

# Chapter Sixty

Cherry slept so deeply it took four rings before the telephone fully woke her up. She squinted at the clock. Who would call her at 2:00 a.m.? Fear struck—had something happened to one of her parents? They were so old, and her father had already had one heart attack.

"Hello?" she asked, breathless. Was it a hospital? The police?

"Hey, put on your warmest clothes. I'll pick you up in five minutes."

"Who is this?"

"Who do you think? It's Matteo. Get dressed as warmly as possible. It's freezing out."

"What happened? What's wrong?" She tried to think of what kind of emergency there could be. Was it his dogs? "Did something happen to Tristan? Oh no, is it Martha?"

"No, they're fine, and so am I. Don't ask any more questions, just get dressed. Unless you already are. Do you sleep in full winter gear?"

"Matteo, it's two in the morning," she protested. She was wide awake now, and quite annoyed.

"I'm going to be at your door in about five minutes. And I'm hoping to see you in a nightie. Or in snow pants and your big coat, your decision. Bye." He hung up before she could argue any more.

She did manage to pull on multiple layers, as well as a hat and gloves, before he arrived. He looked disappointed when she opened the door.

"Darn it and consarn it, I was hoping for something sexier. I pictured something silky and red, and super low cut."

"Stop being a jerk, I'm too tired to put up with you. What's this all about?"

"Come with me, you'll see." At the bottom of the stairs, he stopped her. "But not yet, it's a surprise. I need you to wear a blindfold."

"I'm not letting you blindfold me."

"Cherish Bonita Waites, you have to learn to start trusting people. I promise, nothing bad is going to happen. It's only a cool surprise if you don't see it before we get where we're going."

"That's not my name, and I'm not walking around in the middle of the night with a blindfold on."

"Of course not, I brought the box bike. You can ride with Tristan. I'll settle you in all nice and snug."

"Where are we going?"

"Do you not understand the word surprise? You're no fun sometimes. Trust me, I'd never do anything to hurt you. At least, not in front of Tristan. He likes you for some reason. He'd probably bite me."

She finally acquiesced. She let him blindfold her, though for a moment she wondered where he'd gotten it. No, she didn't want to know its history. He helped her into the box and wrapped a blanket around her. Tristan sat at her feet to start, but he jumped up on her lap. When she tried to smooth his fur, her gloved hands encountered strange ridges. "Is he wearing a sweater?"

"Of course he is, it's cold out. And he likes it. But don't peek, and that's not the surprise anyway. Now hang onto his collar. I don't want him jumping off while I pedal."

"Are you sure this is safe?" she shouted as he started the bike. Riding with a blindfold, after such a strange awakening, and not knowing where she was going made her uncomfortable. She wanted to be more adventurous, but not necessarily like this.

"This one has studded tires, stop worrying. Relax, and enjoy the ride," he shouted back. She didn't have much choice in the matter, so she did. Well, the relaxing part, not so much the enjoyment.

Her face had gone numb from the wind when they finally stopped. "Can I take this blindfold off now?" she asked.

"Just a minute." His voice was closer than she expected. "Here, I've got you. Let me help you out." His hands carefully guided her. "Right this way, easy steps, now, here." He walked her a few feet away from the bike.

"Now?"

"Yes, now. Take your blindfold off."

She did, and the sight took her breath away. Green fire danced across the entire world, filling the sky, and reflecting off the thin ice of the lake. "Matteo, this is, this is . . ." she was at a loss for words.

"Spectacular, isn't it?" He sounded proud of himself. "Have a seat." That's when she realized where they were, at the overlook on the north side of the island.

Cold radiated from the bench, even through her many layers of clothing, and she shivered a bit, but she didn't care. She couldn't take her eyes off the aurora. "I've never seen the Northern Lights before. This is incredible!"

"I figured you hadn't, since you've never been farther north than Ohio. We get some amazing shows up here, but not as often as I'd like. The best ones are in the middle of winter. The reflections on the lake ice contribute something special."

They sat together in silence, staring at the sky. A shooting star streaked through the green and purple veils.

"Ohhh!" she gasped at the same time he said "Make a wish!"

"I wish for more moments like these," she said honestly.

"You can't say it out loud, or it won't come true. Surely you know that by now, Cherry Blossom." She looked over and realized he was staring at her with a tender look on his face. Then, of course, he had to spoil the moment. "I bet my wish was naughtier than yours."

"Why are you like that all the time?"

"Like what?"

"Over-the-top flirting, when you know it isn't getting you anywhere. You're trying to make me uncomfortable. Why do you have to ruin things?"

"How do you know I'm not actually flirting? I could be madly in love with you."

"Very funny. You just like to tease."

"True, true." He remained silent for a long moment. "Look, Cherry, I don't mean to make you uncomfortable. I do like making you blush and I do like the face you make when you're thinking about slapping me, but I don't want to annoy you so much that you stop talking to me. I like being friends with you. I like our Wednesday night dinners. I like that you trust me enough to put on a blindfold in the middle of the night."

"And I like spending time with your dogs, so I'm willing to tolerate you too." She meant it as a light-hearted joke, but realized it sounded mean. "No, I'm kidding. I like spending time with you. You're my favorite person to watch movies with. I also enjoy arguing with you about books, even though your taste is abysmal. And I know I've probably never said this, but I do appreciate how you've come to my rescue so many times. And yes, I like that I feel safe enough with you—despite your constant coming on to me—that I know a middle of the night invitation will be something worthwhile."

"I have lots of middle of the night invitations for you," Matteo teased.

"You did it again, already. What is wrong with you?"

"Haven't we been over this? There's so much wrong with me that I don't even know where to start."

"Shush, you aren't that bad." She leaned back against the bench, stared up at the sky, and felt more content than she had in a long time.

# Chapter Sixty-One

Dear Gary,

My letters to you are evolving. If I ever actually sent them, you would notice. You'd see the change. I'm moving on. I'm getting over you.

Well, not entirely over you, but over the romance of you.

I think about you sometimes, but I don't miss our relationship. I miss some elements of it, but I realize I miss you as a friend. I don't miss you as a lover, even though you were the only one of those I've ever had. I don't think of you that way anymore. I don't miss your body, I don't miss sharing a bed. I don't miss your hands, I don't miss your kisses, and I don't miss our lovemaking. That's all gone and dried up and blown away in the wind.

I've developed a crush on someone else. It's not going to go anywhere. He's not my type. He's not someone who 'does relationships,' in his words, and you know me. I want to skip all the dating and move straight to the real stuff, the relaxed 'I don't have to do my make-up let's spend the evening in sweatpants on the couch' kind of thing. Where we know each other well enough that we don't have to pretend or hide. That's what I miss most about you. But sometimes I look at this other man, and I imagine the two of us reading in bed next to each other, or taking our dogs for walks, or arguing over whose turn it is to do the dishes. Mundane fantasies, I know. But those little things are what's special about having a life partner. All the minor inconsequential moments that I guess I took for granted.

I never wanted an exciting life. I wasn't interested in world travel or adventures or finding myself. I wanted a nice quiet life, in a nice quiet house, with someone I cared about. I wanted to raise a family and celebrate holidays and take long evening walks and grow old with the love of my life. I wanted to one day sit on a porch in my rocking chair and look back on everything I'd done with a sense of contentment and peace.

I used to think you were going to be the one in the other rocking chair.

But it won't be you.

And now, I accept that.

Moving on,

Cherry

# Chapter Sixty-Two

Cherry woke up in a dark room, huddled under all her blankets, but still shivering. She looked at the clock, but it was off. And what was that loud pounding sound? Oh, the door. She started to get up to answer it, when it flew open hard enough to slam into the wall and someone called her name.

"Cherry? Cherry, where are you? Are you okay?" Matteo came charging through her apartment, uninvited, all the way to her bedroom.

"You have your boots on!" she cried out when he appeared in her door way.

"Oh, yeah, sorry about that, I tracked snow in, didn't I?" He looked down at his feet, but despite his words he didn't seem to be at all apologetic.

"Why are you here? Why are you breaking in at . . . what time is it?"

"It's almost nine o'clock. Why are you still in bed?"

"Nine? Oh no, my alarm didn't go off! I'm late for work!"

"Cherry, the school is closed. Maybe you haven't noticed, but the electricity is out."

"It is?" She was not a morning person, so she hadn't actually processed why her clock was off until he pointed it out. No wonder she could see her breath; the apartment had electric heat.

"All of Whispering Pines lost power early this morning. We don't know what's going on, yet. The phones are down too. Vivian has been trying to sort it out with the mainland. The lines under the lake may have ruptured, which means it could be days until they can be repaired. And, apparently, you also missed the massive blizzard." That explained why there wasn't much light coming in through the curtains. A storm had been in the forecast, but when she went to bed the night before, it had been merely flurrying.

"If school is canceled, I'm not late, so why are you here?" she repeated, keeping her comforter wrapped tightly around herself. She couldn't help having a sour mood, triggered by the abrupt awakening, and made worse because now, thanks to Matteo, her carpet was wet, and she couldn't plug in her hairdryer to dry the soggy footprints.

"There's a snowstorm accompanied by a power outage, nobody had seen you, and you hadn't checked in. I'm here to make sure you're still alive. I'm kind of a hero, if you think about it."

"What exactly is heroic about breaking into my apartment and getting snow all over the place?"

"Look, Cherry, you're new here, and you aren't particularly self-sufficient. You've never shown yourself to be knowledgeable about the basics, so as far as anyone knew, you could have killed yourself by now."

"I'm not suicidal!" Cherry was horrified. "Yes, my marriage ended terribly, but that's not grounds for killing myself. Why would anybody think that I would?" She tried so hard to convey that she was alright and she thought she was pulling it off.

"Okay, you're misunderstanding me. Do you know what an exceedingly common cause of death is during power outages? Not here, but in general? Carbon monoxide poisoning, from people foolish enough to use gas generators or coal stoves indoors. So in dangerous times like these, we, the valiant longtime community members, go around and do house checks, verify everyone on the island is alive. And we always start with the newest residents first, because they're the most likely to screw something up. Tim, Sato, and the ferry brothers are going around the outlying neighborhoods now. And I, your dashing superhero, came here first, to rescue you."

She found herself laughing at the idea of Matteo being a superhero. "Where's your cape?"

"Oh, I'll show you my costume some other time. You'll appreciate my tights." And there, he had to do it again. Why did he say things like that? And why didn't she mind as much as she used to?

# Chapter Sixty-Three

Matteo waited in the living room while Cherry got dressed and gathered her things. "Don't forget your toothbrush!" he yelled to her.

"I've packed overnight bags before," she informed him.

"Oh yeah? For naughty getaways? Tell me some stories, Cherry Blossom." He dropped down onto her couch. It was too upright to be comfortable. Why didn't she have any throw pillows? He thought about ordering some for her, but talked himself out of it. He didn't need to be buying her gifts, even if he could imagine the smile on her face and maybe the hug that she would give him in thanks.

"How long will the power be out?"

"I said I'm a superhero, I didn't say I'm psychic too," he responded. How long would it be out? How were his dogs? He needed to check on them again soon. What if they were getting into trouble? They knew not to get up on the hearth when the fire was burning, and they weren't stupid, they should be fine, right? But what if... he tried to stop the invasive thoughts. *Focus on Cherry*, he reminded himself. *Focus. One thing at a time. Finish this task first.* His worry stone was in his inner pocket, where he couldn't access it, so he rubbed his thumb against his palm instead. When he got control of himself, he continued.

"It may be a couple of days, it's happened before. I think almost all of your third graders are blizzard babies."

"No, oddly enough, they all have November birthdays. We ate cupcakes every day for a week straight. Snowstorms don't hit that early, do they?"

Matteo laughed. "No, they don't. Blizzard babies come nine months after the storm. They're quite common here."

"That makes sense." Cherry emerged from her bedroom, fully dressed in multiple layers and carrying a small suitcase. "So why don't people go to the mainland during power outages?"

"Are you kidding? Nobody's crossing the water in these conditions. The ferry's trapped over there and won't be back until the Coast Guard ice cutters come through. We could be stuck for a week. That's why it's important to keep track of people."

"I've never been in anything like this before." Were Cherry's eyes wide with excitement or fear? He couldn't tell. "Do we all stay at the community center the entire time?"

"Not everyone. Some people just huddle around their fireplaces and shelter in place. But any family with elderly people or small children will be there—it's the only place with a big generator, so it's the only warm building. I, personally, will be in and out all day, depending on where I'm needed, but then I'm going home. I can't leave my babies alone."

"You can't bring them to the center?"

"Only if I put them in cages, and I'm not doing that. We'll be fine at my house."

"*We'll* be fine?" The look on her face made him feel as though he'd overstepped his bounds.

"Me and the dogs. Though you're welcome to stay with us, if the idea of sleeping in a room with a hundred people, full of babies crying and loud snoring doesn't appeal to you." He hoped she would say yes. He worried about her sometimes, and it would help his anxiety if she was with him. Then he wouldn't have to worry about her accidentally poisoning herself, or going out in the blizzard and getting lost, or any of the other things newcomers to the island tended to do.

"I don't know if I trust you enough," she replied, and that stung a little.

"Cherish Bartholomew Waites, how dare you? I slept on your couch when you were roofied. What do you think I'm going to do to you?"

"That's not my middle name. And you're always hitting on me, so I don't know how seriously I can take your invitation."

"And you're always rejecting me, and I always take no for an answer. We're friends, Cherry. Jeez, lighten up. The offer stands, if you want it. But for now, we head to the center. You can eat breakfast there."

🌲 🌲 🌲 🌲 🌲

Matteo led Cherry through the snowstorm. The whiteout limited visibility to mere feet, and voices couldn't be heard over the howling wind. Fortunately, Cherry's apartment was just a few short blocks away, and they were able to get there safely by trailing one hand along the walls of the buildings. They finally stumbled through the entry way.

"I have never experienced anything like that!" Cherry told him as she unwound her scarf from her face. Her cheeks glowed pink from the cold, and he wished he could put his hands over them to warm them up. Of course, that wouldn't work, not only would she probably slap him if he tried, his fingers were like icicles.

"That wasn't even that bad," he said. "Don't worry, it's supposed to clear up a bit later this afternoon. We might get some sunlight. Hang up your coat and everything in here. Now, where's your suitcase?" He could tell by her expression exactly where it was: safe in her apartment, or maybe at the foot of her stairs. Great, he was going to have to go back out in this weather.

"Are you kidding me, Cherish?"

"I can't believe I didn't bring it!"

"Don't worry. I'll go back for it later. For now, we need to check in and get some grub. That's the nice thing about storms like this—they provide all the food. Sam and Wayne always try to one-up each other, and we all benefit. The outage during last year's polar vortex netted me some of the best meals of my life."

He led her to the registration desk, where Cara was seated with a hot cup of coffee and a stack of binders. "Morning, sunshine," he said to her. "Look, I found the teacher."

"Does it count as finding someone if they weren't actually missing?" Cara asked, and he heard Cherry snort with laughter. Of course they'd team up against him.

"Whatever, I'm a hero."

"I'm not sure that word means what you think it does," Cara replied. For someone who was supposed to be his best friend, she sure was a terrible wing-woman.

# Chapter Sixty-Four

Cherry managed to keep herself occupied. Most of her students were in the community center, so she gathered the youngest ones up to play games. She took a break, after a particularly long game of Duck Duck Grey Duck, and went to look for some coffee. Margaux had set up a table with a massive urn and an assortment of pastries. A donation cup sat next to the display, but Cherry's wallet was in her left-behind suitcase. She hesitated for a moment, wondering what to do.

"If you didn't bring money, you can kick in some cash later," Cara came up behind her. "Or write an IOU and stick it in there if it makes you feel better. Nobody cares. We all know who the freeloaders are, and you aren't one of them."

"Thanks," Cherry said, finally helping herself to a cup. "This is really well organized."

"It's happened before. Lots of times. You get used to it," Cara said. "We had a power outage for a week once when I was a kid. Matty and I were so stir crazy by the end of it." Funny to think about Matteo as a child. She could picture him, a little tow-headed hellion running around with a pack of dogs.

"I hope this one doesn't last that long."

"It probably won't. Viv is hounding the electric company. She happened to be on the mainland, so her sons have been radioing her and she's dealing with everything in person.

She thinks we'll have the power back soon, if only because they want to get rid of her. Hey, do you mind if I give you some advice?"

"Sure." Cherry was open to it. She'd never imagined going through anything remotely like this before.

"Find somewhere else to sleep tonight."

"Why?"

"Oh my god, you have no idea what it's like here. I made the mistake of staying the first night during the big blackout last February. Grandma Leske walks around muttering to herself all night, there are a lot of men who snore loud enough to shake the rafters, babies cry constantly, and we don't have enough earplugs for everybody. I've already told Sam, the weather is supposed to clear for a bit around three this afternoon, and we are putting on our snowshoes and getting the hell back home. Some of the cooks who live in town can take over the dinner."

Cherry thought about it. Matteo sort of invited her over, but she wasn't sure how valid the invitation was. She sometimes couldn't tell if he was serious or teasing. "Well, maybe I could sleep at Matteo's? I think he has heat."

"He has a big fireplace, and he doesn't snore," Cara confirmed. "If Matty says you can stay there, take him up on the offer. He keeps a well-stocked pantry and a full bar too. He's kind of a survivalist."

"How do you know he doesn't snore?" Cherry asked, though she suspected she knew the answer. Cara laughed.

"I've passed out drunk there enough times. His house is very convenient and he always serves my favorite tequila."

"But what about the dogs? Aren't you allergic?" That's what Matteo said, wasn't it? The one woman he ever loved was allergic to his dogs?

"No, I love them all, especially Beverly. I'd adopt one myself if my neat-freak fiancé didn't subscribe to the awful belief that animals don't belong in houses. I don't think it's something I'll ever talk him into."

"My ex didn't like dogs either, but we had a cat for a while." Cherry's mind raced. She always assumed Cara was Matteo's one-that-got-away. She fit the profile. Matteo had known her for a long time, she was a seasonal worker for years, and it was just last summer when she began dating Sam. Had she guessed wrong? Was there someone else who Matteo was in love with? Not that Cherry needed to know. It wasn't like she was competing for his affection or anything. But who was his secret crush?

"Hey, Sam's gesturing at me. I need to see what's going on. But before I walk away, listen, I know you and Matteo are just friends, but he's a decent man, and you're safe with him. Obviously, if you decide to hook up, that's your business, but I want you to know that he is a guy who will take no for an answer. Like, if you spend the night with him, there won't be any obligations on your part. Oh god, Sam is going crazy. I better deal with him." With that nugget of wisdom, Cara walked away, leaving Cherry staring after her.

Of course there wouldn't be any obligation, she thought to herself. Not that Matteo ever meant it when he hit on her anyway. He liked to tease, that was all.

# Chapter Sixty-Five

When the storm lightened up sufficiently, Matteo skied to his father's house towing a sled full of logs, enough to last a couple of days, hopefully. His dad was coping just fine. That was one thing about being housebound, blizzards didn't change the routine at all. Then he headed back to his own place to check on his dogs and stoke his fire before returning to town.

Nobody else was out in the cold, and he couldn't blame them. The windchill was biting and painful, especially on the tiny strip of exposed skin between the bottom of his goggles and the top of his scarf. Still, he had to admit, he enjoyed this kind of storm; he liked the adventure of it, and, while usually changes to his routine threw him off, this was one he welcomed. When he could help during emergencies, he felt valued and confident, and that helped him cast aside some of his anxieties.

The lobby of the community center was crowded with outerwear, and Matteo stepped in a puddle of melted snow almost as soon as he pried his boots off. Great. Now his socks were wet. He hoped somebody had a dry pair he could borrow. He'd have to ask around, but he had something more important to do first.

The main room bustled with activity. "Hey, you made it back," Cara greeted him at the door. She checked his name off on her clipboard. "How's your dad?"

"Good, he's actually enjoying himself," Matteo said, but he wasn't paying attention to her. He scanned the room with his eyes. Ah, there she was. Cherry sat on a stool surrounded by young children, reading them a book. She seemed really into it too. From this distance, he couldn't identify the title, but the story evidently involved rabbits, because she kept making bunny ears behind her head and then encouraged all the kids to hop in a circle. A sharp pang of regret stabbed at his heart. She would be such a good mother, and that was why he had to stay away from her.

"Jesus, make a move already." Cara elbowed him unnecessarily hard in the ribs.

"Shut up, Cara," he told her crossly. "I don't like her like that. Besides, she's not my type."

"Because she's not a slutty tourist?"

"Because she's not into the casual thing, and I'm not into relationships. We're fundamentally incompatible."

"You could be into relationships. You could try one sometime, you know. Some people enjoy them."

"I'm not taking relationship advice from you. I've met your fiancé. Your taste levels are suspect. I have no idea what you see in him."

"You mean Sam, that gorgeous man who cooks, cleans, and worships the ground I walk on? The one who takes care of me and makes me feel safe?"

"Yeah, that sounds like it sucks, Cara. I'm not looking for that."

She laughed at him. "You're right, it does suck. Don't worry, I'll make sure you never have anything of the sort. I'm going to go tell Cherry some stories from your past."

"Go ahead. She's my friend—and only my friend—so she won't care." He didn't want to have this discussion. He'd already come to terms with the fact that Cherry was not meant for him. She was just a temporary visitor to their island, an ephemeral bright spot. She wouldn't stay forever, she'd move on to bigger and better things, and those could never include him.

"Friends, whatever. I told her she should crash at your place tonight, even though you're an asshole. You're welcome."

"I'm walking away now." And he did, but he could feel Cara smirking behind his back. She didn't know everything. Fortunately, it was easy to find distractions.

🌲 🌲 🌲 🌲 🌲

"There you are!" Cherry's voice came from behind him as he perused the pastry selection, and he turned and smiled.

"Here I am!" he replied, trying to match her cheerful tone. He couldn't, he sounded too sarcastic. The little frown she responded with was so adorable it made him ache inside. He took a bite of a croissant to chase the pain away.

"I've been thinking about tonight," she began, and he braced himself. She was going to sleep on a cot here, and although it was ridiculous, he would spend the entire night worrying about her. It was so stupid. He wished he could stop, but his anxiety didn't release so easily, and something bad would happen and she would get hurt or injured, and . . .

"What about it?" he asked lightly. He wanted to make a joke, but it would just drive her further away.

"If your offer to let me sleep over tonight still stands, I'd like to take you up on it. I mean, I've been warned that there's a lot of snoring here and I don't want to wear earplugs."

"That sounds good for you, but what's in it for me?"

"Probably nothing, but I know Tristan wants me there." She smiled, and as always, it made him want to smile back.

"Yeah, fine, you can stay with me. But only for Tristan's sake. He tends to worry." Some of his perpetual burden lifted from his shoulders. He'd be able to keep Cherry safe tonight.

# Chapter Sixty-Six

For the second morning in a row, a loud pounding on the door woke Cherry up, pulling her from a deep sleep in cozy warmth. She tried to ignore it, burrowing in under the blankets, snuggling closer to her pillow, a pillow that was warm and firm and breathing softly.

"I can't answer the door until you get off me." Matteo's voice jolted her back into reality. He was the pillow. She lay spooned up against his back, her arm wrapped over him, face pressed into his body. "But then we can get right back to it. Maybe I'll roll over and you can drape yourself on my front instead."

She pulled back in embarrassment and horror, but wasn't fast enough—the door already opened. She wished she had time to run from the room and hide, so that whoever came in wouldn't make the wrong assumptions.

"Matteo, you okay? You here?" Timmy entered through the front door, bringing the cold and ice and howling wind with him. "Oh, good, there you are. And you too, Cherry."

"It's not what you think," Cherry said, but her face turned bright red, making her look like a liar. She knew exactly what he must think, walking in and seeing them together on a mattress in front of the fireplace. She should have slept on the couch.

*No Longer Yours*

"None of my business." Tim closed the door behind him. "I'm just checking on people, and you weren't responding to any calls."

"Oh, oops. The battery probably died." Matteo got up and crossed the room to shake the radio. "I think I've got some others. Hey, how's my dad? Has he checked in yet?"

"Someone's on their way to his place. Let me call you in, and I'll ask," Tim pulled out his own radio. "Hawkeye to base, come in base."

There was a crackling sound and Tyrell's voice came through. "Baby, stop calling yourself Hawkeye, it's not going to stick."

"Yeah, we'll all keeping using Baby as your nickname," Matteo snickered.

"Shut up." Tim hit the button again. "Matteo and Cherry are safe, just needed to change their radio batteries. Anyone talked to Monty Capen yet?"

"Yeah, Johnny Mills called in a few minutes ago. Tell Matteo that his dad is fine, but is a bit grumpy, since he ran out of cream for his coffee. And we got an updated forecast. Word is the storm is going to blast us all day, but should let up overnight."

"I'll take my dad some creamer later," Matteo promised, and Tim relayed the information. After turning down an invitation to stay for breakfast, Tim turned to go. "This was my last stop. I'm heading back to the center. Come by later when it clears, there's going to be a feast. Until then, keep warm." He winked before pulling his goggles back down, and Cherry wanted to sink into the ground. Everyone was going to think she made love to Matteo last night.

But nothing had happened, they dragged Matteo's mattress out in front of the fire, that was all. They'd eaten cold cheese and crackers, drank a little wine, and spent hours debating the merits of various authors. It had been fun, and non-flirty, and certainly non-sexual. She'd noticed that Matteo had been careful to not even joke about anything, which was almost disappointing.

No, not disappointing. Appropriate. He behaved appropriately, and it was silly for her to feel let down. Nothing was going to happen between them anyway.

# Chapter Sixty-Seven

Matteo watched through the window until Tim passed out of sight. The snowfall wasn't too bad at the moment, but hunkering down in place was the best idea. He looked back at Cherry, still sitting on the mattress with the blanket wrapped around her shoulders. She was clearly not the kind of person who could just get up and go. Her hair was a mess, all matted on one side. She'd need a shower and a hairbrush, and he only had one of those things on offer. Well, two, if she didn't mind ice-cold water.

"Well, Miss Waites, you appear to be stuck with me a while longer."

"I should go home," she told him as though that were even an option in this weather.

"No, your apartment isn't going to be warm enough. And it's snowing again. When it clears, I'll take you back to the community center, and, hopefully, there will be a hot meal waiting. But for now, we're far safer sheltering here. If you want, I can come back to bed, and we can cuddle some more. But will you let me be the big spoon this time?"

"Don't say that, I'm already embarrassed." She covered her cheeks with her palms as though she thought that would prevent him from seeing how pink they had become. He thought about what he'd like to do, go over to her, shove her hands away, and kiss her, kiss her and fall back and just ... nothing. He'd like to do nothing. He wasn't going to even try. *Quit being an asshole,* he reminded himself. *She deserves better.*

"Don't worry, nobody in town thinks you'd stoop so low. They all know you like my dogs better than me. Speaking of the dogs, I need to go shovel a path to their private bathroom. Would you mind starting breakfast?"

"How? The power is still off."

He stared at her a moment. Sometimes he forgot how utterly lacking in self-sufficiency she was. "With the cast iron pans, same way we made cookies last night. Look, there's a fireplace five feet away from you. No, never mind. You don't know where anything is here anyway. Tell you what, go back to sleep. When I get back, I'll make food for both of us." He went to the mudroom where he pulled on his snow pants and coat, and struggled into his boots. The shovel waited for him outside the door, frozen to the wall. He kicked the handle to loosen the ice and then pried it away.

Years ago, when Martha was a tiny reluctant puppy, he had gotten smart about winter elimination. One would think that a husky would have no problems, but the snow confused her, and she tried to do her business inside instead. When he inherited this house from his grandparents, he built a small walled shelter near the porch, with a plastic door he could slide aside easily. It gave the dogs a snow-free space and kept his house cleaner. Unfortunately, a storm like this meant that the path he had cleared just ten hours ago was already covered over.

He took longer than planned to clean it off again, but when he finally got it clear enough he opened his back door and whistled. Tristan and Beverly came running eagerly, Martha less so.

"Stop whining, you were bred for this weather." He resorted to picking her up and carrying her to the sheltered spot. "Hurry up, pack, it's freezing," he told them, stomping his feet to keep the blood flowing.

They finally finished, and he led them back inside, carrying Martha, who seemed a bit shaky. The other two wanted to stay out and frolic in the snow, but they could wait until later, when the temperature climbed above zero and the blizzard calmed down. He pried off his boots and shook the icy crystals off his clothing. There was going to be a puddle in the mudroom that he'd have to mop—or maybe not as Beverly started busily licking the melting drips from the floor.

"Hey, what's that smell?" he asked as he entered the living room. Cherry knelt by the fireplace, where she'd raked the coals over to one side and was using them to fry bacon and scramble eggs, and there was even slightly burned toast on skewers. Perhaps she wasn't so incompetent after all.

"Surprised?" She grinned proudly. "You shouldn't be. I told you I taught sixth grade."

"More grateful than surprised. And also confused. I didn't realize cooking over a fire was included in the curriculum. Ohio sure has some weird home-ec classes."

"You don't do Sixth Grade Camp here? It's a big thing. Every school district in Ohio does it. I guess I assumed it was everywhere."

"I have no idea what you're talking about. But remember, I went to school on a rural island. I wouldn't say I've had the universal experience," he told her, sinking down onto the couch. He watched her cook for a moment. *This is what life would be like if I could have a relationship*, he thought. *Waking up together, making breakfast, showering* together afterwards ... no, stop thinking like that. And anyway, no showers today. He fought down the bitterness that sometimes rose up in him. If it weren't for his crippling panic attacks, this could be his real life.

# Chapter Sixty-Eight

Lunch at the community center was amazing, though there was no way Matteo would tell Sam that. His ego was big enough already.

"Did you try the burgers?" he asked Cherry, when she finally took a break from playing with children. "They're venison. I'm pretty sure Tyrell contributed the meat because he's sick of eating Timmy's kills. He told me once he's thinking about going vegetarian, just so his husband stops bringing home dead animals."

"I thought they tasted odd. I mean, not odd, but different." Cherry smiled, but it didn't quite reach her eyes.

"New things, right?"

"Yeah. Speaking of new things, I was thinking perhaps I should sleep at the community center tonight. I've never done it before, it may be fun." Again, she gave him that strained smile.

"I can tell that's not the real reason. Is it because my house smells like wet dog? You get used to it." He tried to make a joke to quell the panic rising in his chest. His heart was already racing. Why did this woman set him off so easily?

"It's because people are starting to talk. You know, after this morning..."

Yes, after this morning, when he had laid awake for twenty minutes, listening to her breathe, feeling her soft breasts pressed against his back, pretending he deserved to feel so comfortable with another person, pretending it was something he'd one day be allowed to have. After that? Of course she'd have a problem with it.

"After Tim barged in and found us in a compromising position? If people are already gossiping we may as well just do it for real."

"Matteo!" There, he got her. Her face turned pink. He loved how easily she blushed.

"What? I don't mind. And if your reputation is in tatters anyway..."

"Stop it!" She actually stomped her foot in anger. God, she was adorable. "It's not just my reputation. Did you know people think you've been intimate with every woman on the island, and I'm your latest conquest?"

"That rumor is completely false. There are plenty of women I don't have carnal knowledge of." He scanned the room. "Cara; Margaux—she's my second cousin, you know; anyone under eighteen, obviously ... actually, scratch that, anyone under twenty-five, I think. Yeah, Nessie's twenty-six. Ummm..." he kept scanning. "Anyone over forty-five too. And there aren't that many women left. So there."

"That's still a lot." She didn't look happy with him, not that it was any of her business who he slept with before he met her. Or after he met her for that matter. They weren't in a relationship.

"A little experience is not a bad thing," he tried to defend himself.

"A little?" she asked skeptically.

"Little?" he replied, deliberately misunderstanding her. "No, I guarantee that's not the word you want to use to describe me. Want to see?"

"I most certainly do not! Matteo, you aren't funny. I'm staying here tonight."

Well, that was disappointing. He had been looking forward to another evening in front of the fire, arguing about books and talking, and feeling so relaxed in her company. Now he'd be stuck worrying about her instead.

"Fine, do what you want. I don't care either way, I was only trying to be nice," he lied. And then he walked away. He didn't need her anyway. He could manage just fine without her.

🌲 🌲 🌲 🌲 🌲

The sensation of waking up with someone else in his bed was rare but welcome. Yesterday, Cherry had spooned against his back, today she lay across his chest, a warm heavy weight.

"Mmmmm . . . Cherry, your breath stinks," he murmured in his half-awake state, and she started whining and licking his face. No, not Cherry. It was Beverly, who knew she was supposed to stay off the bed unless he needed her comfort.

"What's wrong girl?" That's when Tristan let out a sharp bark, and he came fully awake. The power had come on sometime in the night, but that wasn't the issue.

Tristan alternated between barking and sniffing at Martha. Martha was curled in her bed, where she had spent most of her time lately, but now she wasn't even reacting to Tristan's nudges. Matteo felt his heart stop. Not Martha, not now. He practically jumped across the room to get to her, put his hands on her body, and found nothing. No breathing, no heartbeat.

Martha was gone.

# Chapter Sixty-Nine

Cherry made it back to her apartment, finally. The sun shined, the electricity functioned, and all was well with the world. Well, not entirely. She had to snowshoe on top of fresh powder while carrying her small suitcase. Next time, she would plan better and pack a backpack. Once she got home, she wanted nothing more than a hot shower and a long nap. Cara had been correct in warning her that she wouldn't get much rest at the community center, and she realized she shouldn't have let worries about her—or Matteo's—reputation keep her from getting a good night's sleep at his house.

But that was in the past. She'd survived the night and now she could change out of her clothes. After two days of wearing the same layer of long underwear, she was starting to smell. Fortunately, she had an on-demand water heater, so she didn't have to wait for an entire tank to warm up before showering. While she luxuriated in the warmth, she heard her phone ringing. Probably Matteo, making sure she arrived home safely. She'd call him when she got out—though she wouldn't put it past him to come running over to check on her. She thought it was kind of sweet that he worried about her, even if he acted like he did it because he thought she was incapable of taking care of herself.

After drying her hair and putting the teapot on to boil, she checked her voicemail. And yes, she was right, it was Matteo. But she was wrong about his reason for calling.

His recorded voice shouted "Cherry, it's Martha. She's dead. Martha's dead ..." then dissolved into incoherent sobbing. Martha, dead? How could this have happened? Sure, Martha had been declining lately, but dead? Oh no, poor Matteo.

It took far too long to reach Matteo's house, since she still wasn't particularly skilled with her snowshoes and kept falling into snowbanks. When she finally got there, she went straight to the side door, then hesitated. There were two pairs of skis she didn't recognize leaning haphazardly against the wall. But no, Matteo called her. She needed to go in.

She followed Matteo's custom and didn't bother knocking. The first person she found was Sam, in the kitchen, scrubbing away at a sink full of dirty dishes.

"What are you doing here?" she asked. She should have expected him though, because of course Matteo would call Cara.

"Just because we had a power outage doesn't mean people can't clean up after themselves," Sam replied. "There are a couple of days' worth of dishes in here. And can you guess the last time Matteo cleaned the underside of his range hood? Because I doubt it was anytime in the past five years. How does anyone live like this?"

"Where's Matteo?"

Sam looked at her for a moment, then, and seemed to remember what was going on. "Oh, yeah, sorry. He and Cara are in the living room. Did you hear about Martha? He's really broken up about it."

Cherry was about to ask why he wasn't out there as well, but Tristan ran in, barked once, and started heading back to the living room. He turned to glance at Cherry as if to say 'why aren't you following me, yet?' so she hurried after him.

That's where she found Matteo, curled up in the fetal position on the couch, with Cara kneeling on the floor, rubbing his back. "Cherry?" Cara asked in confusion. "How did you know?"

"Matteo called me. Is he okay?" He didn't look like it. Her heart broke for him, losing a beloved pet like this.

"He called you? Interesting," Cara said. She crossed the room and asked in a whisper, "Can you take over here? I don't want him to be alone right now and I need to call the ferry brothers to come pick up the body."

Cherry took Cara's place on the floor and gently touched Matteo's arm. "What can I do?" He sat up to look at her, grief evident on his face. She'd never seen a grown man crying before, or at least not like this. Gary always cried when his favorite sports team lost, but this was different. This was real and raw, and she had no idea how to make it better.

"You weren't here," Matteo said, and his tone made it sound like he was accusing her of something. What? Did he blame her? Martha was old and had been weak for a very long time.

"I came over as soon as I heard," she protested.

"Yes, but you weren't here! You weren't here when she died! My baby is dead!"

"Matteo, I'm not a veterinarian. There's nothing I could have done for her."

Tears still streamed down his face. "But you're better than me! You would have made her last night special. Her last meal was dry dog food, for fuck's sake. I know you sneak her bits of meat. She would have had that. And you like to stay up late talking. You talk so goddamn much we still would have been awake to hear her last breaths, I would have been able to hold her and soothe her. Instead, she died alone, *because you weren't here!*" His voice rose until he was yelling.

"You're being irrational," Cherry said, trying to keep from shouting back. She didn't want to fight, not while he was in the throes of such terrible grief, but he was wrong.

"No I'm not! You weren't here! You're supposed to be my friend. You should have been here!"

"Please stop yelling at me. I know you're hurting right now." She reached a tentative hand out, wanting to pat his arm, or touch his shoulder, or maybe give him the great big hug that he so clearly needed, but he recoiled.

"I don't want you here, Cherry. Go home. You couldn't be here for Martha, so I don't need you now."

"But Matteo, I didn't know..."

"Doesn't matter. You were so concerned about your reputation that you couldn't come over, and my dog died alone. Get out of my house. I don't want to deal with you right now."

His words hurt. She had been overly worried about what people were saying and she would have much preferred to stay with him last night, but that had nothing to do with Martha's passing.

"Martha wasn't alone. She was surrounded by her family." Before he could yell any more she walked away, pushing past Cara in the doorway to the kitchen and hurrying to the mudroom for her coat. She tried to put her outdoor gear on as quickly as possible, so she could leave before breaking down.

When she was outside and strapping on her snowshoes she allowed her own tears to flow. They stung her cheeks and froze to her scarf.

"Cherry, wait," a male voice called as she set off. She paused, taking a second to collect herself before twisting around carefully to look at Sam.

"It's fine, I'm going home."

"You know he didn't mean any of what he said, right? He gets like this sometimes."

"I know."

"You're crying," Sam pointed out. He looked helpless, yet another man incapacitated by a woman's tears. "Ummm, don't cry, Matteo's an ass, and his dog just died . . ." he trailed off and shoved his gloveless hands into his pants pockets. He had come after her in such a hurry he wasn't even wearing a coat.

"I'm not crying about Matteo, I'm crying about Martha. I know he's not really mad at me. I'm giving him space. Seriously, Sam, go back in before you freeze. Matteo knows where I'll be when he's ready to talk." She gave him a tremulous smile, and slowly snowshoed the rest of the way home, where she could curl up in front of her own fire, and mourn Martha alone.

# Chapter Seventy

It had been ten long, sorrowful days since Martha's death, days Matteo spent lying on the couch, one hand in Beverly's fur, staring at the ceiling and wishing he could go back in time. This was different than his panic attacks. This was pure grief. He couldn't face the world without her in it. When he had been at his lowest point, dropping out of college and realizing that he'd have the same confined miserable life as his father, that tiny ball of fluff was the only thing that kept him going.

A knock on the door startled him, but he didn't answer. Probably Cara, come to tell him off again. He'd left his rental shop closed over the weekend and missed meeting two of their cabana guests, and she had been livid. He didn't bother defending himself while she chewed him out, and he hadn't called her since, though he did plan to open his shop on Friday. He didn't want to risk another tongue lashing.

The door opened, and a face peered around it. "Matteo, are you here?"

Great, the other woman he didn't want to see.

"No, I'm not. Go away."

Cherry ignored him and entered anyway, with a box of pizza and a bottle of wine. "Here, hold these so I can take off my coat."

He didn't move, so she waited a moment before giving up and setting them on the ground. Then she hung up her coat, removed her shoes, and managed to grab the pizza box again before Tristan could pounce on it.

"Matteo, you can't just lay there. I brought food. You need to eat."

"I don't *need* to do anything." He kept his hands on Beverly and his eyes on the ceiling, willing her to leave him alone to wallow in his pain.

She put the pizza on the coffee table and took a deep breath. "I know it's Wednesday, and we usually go to the diner, but I didn't think you'd be up for it. So I'm going to grab a plate and a glass for you, and when I come back, I'm going to sit here and make sure you eat. And then I'll leave." And she had the nerve to walk into the kitchen, Tristan happily bounding at her feet as though she had the right, as though she wasn't trespassing and annoying him.

"Are you here to tell me to man up and get over it?" he asked when she returned.

The question startled her. "Why would I say that?"

"That's what everyone says. Martha was just a dog." Even though he was only repeating it, the words hurt. She wasn't just a dog, she was his baby, his companion, his partner.

"Martha was so much more than a dog. We both know that. You aren't supposed to get over her like she didn't matter to you."

Cherry was the first person to offer such comfort to him, and he felt tears threaten. He forced them away. He'd already humiliated himself by sobbing in front of her before, he didn't want to do it again.

"It's been over a week, I need to move on," he told her as firmly as possible, even though he didn't believe his own words.

"No you don't. Everyone's mourning period is different. You need to take your time. Did you know Gary and I were together for thirteen years?"

"Yeah, I don't care." His response was intentionally rude. He didn't need to listen to her dredge up stories about her failed marriage.

She sighed deeply and repeated herself. "Gary and I were together for thirteen years. I imagine that around the time I met him, you were adopting a fluffy little puppy and naming her Martha. Thirteen years is a very long time to have someone special, someone you love in your life. And when they're gone, they leave a massive hole behind. And you can't easily close up that hole, no matter how hard you try or how badly you want to. It's been almost a year for me since I found out Gary was a cheating liar, and it still hurts. I'm still in mourning for all the good parts of our relationship."

"Martha was better than Gary." He couldn't help being belligerent, but he appreciated her attempt at making him feel better.

"Believe me, I agree. I only knew Martha for a short time, but I loved her too. So, Matteo, take your time to mourn. But you also need to take care of yourself, so you can be the best possible dog-dad to Tristan and Beverly. They need you. Now sit up, have some pizza, don't drink too much wine, and you can revel in your misery some more later." She placed a slice on the plate, and he found himself obeying her, shooing Bev off the couch, and accepting it. The first bite reminded him he hadn't eaten all day, and he was suddenly ravenous.

"Why aren't you eating?" he asked eventually, when he'd shoved the last of the crust in his mouth and reached for a second piece.

"I wasn't sure if you wanted me to join you. Last week ..." she trailed off. Oh, that. First he kicked her out of his house when she came over to be supportive, then last Wednesday, he left a rather rude message on her voicemail informing her he would not be joining her for dinner and she was not to bother him. Apparently, she decided there was an expiration on that admonition.

"I'm not eating an entire pizza. And you need some wine, too. I don't like to drink alone." *I don't like to suffer by myself,* he thought. And for once in his life, looking at her tiny smile and bright eyes, he didn't have to.

# Chapter Seventy-One

Dear Gary,

I've been thinking about sex a lot lately. Is that a weird to say in a letter? It's not something I ever felt comfortable talking about. It's such a private thing, the idea of desire, and bodies coming together, and the faces people make. That's an odd turn of phrase, I know. But I've always felt sex is so personal, and putting it into words trivializes the importance, turns something that should be special into a 'thing' everybody does, even animals. The value and meaning are stripped away.

But I've been having these dreams of a man, and he touches me so intimately, and I wake up sweating, with the sheets twisted around my legs, and with an aching sense of loss when I realize he's not here. I want to be touched again. I've been so alone.

Do you remember when we lost our virginity to each other? That was such a momentous occasion for me. I remember discussing it with you a week beforehand. We'd been dating about six weeks, and making out as often as possible. The first time you put your hand up my shirt I almost cried from nervousness, and you looked both scared and awed. Neither of us knew what we were doing, we just knew we liked it.

Then one day, you told me your roommate wasn't going to be home. You were so adorably timid, but you tried to be so casual. "Keith is visiting his parents this weekend," you said, while barely able to make eye contact. "So I guess I'll have the room to myself." I instantly knew what you wanted to say. It was the first thing that popped into my mind, too: privacy. We could finally 'do it.'

And we discussed the logistics in detail, because we were trying so hard to be mature adults. You agreed to be the one to buy condoms. (Honestly, I was afraid to, not only because of what the cashiers might say, but what if I got the wrong kind, what if they were too small, or worse, too big?) And then we planned our special night.

We had dinner at Easy Street Cafe, because that was the nicest restaurant we could afford. It wasn't a chain, which, at the time, seemed extravagant—where you grew up, Burger King was fancy. On the walk there, I made a lame joke about the name and you thinking taking me to Easy Street meant I was easy, and you laughed. You said, "Cherry, you aren't easy. You are astonishing, and beautiful, and I think I'm falling in love with you." My heart melted, melted I tell you. I kind of gasped out that I thought I loved you, too, and we kissed, and you said you couldn't wait for later.

All through dinner, we were both jittery with nerves. I kept giggling like a little girl, and you dropped your fork three or four times. But we survived the meal, and we went back to your room. Your floormates were around. I'm sure they planned to go out, but it was only eight o'clock, and freshman had to wait until the upperclassman got drunk enough to let them into their parties. So all those guys who were pre-gaming in the room two doors down from you cheered when we walked by, and I'm sure my blush extended all the way to my toes.

But then, there we were, in your room and so very nervous. I wanted candles and rose petals, and all the things you see in the movies, but candles weren't allowed in the dorms, and I didn't expect you to get roses just to tear them apart. You did have a bouquet of daisies waiting for me though. Sure you bought them at a discount from the grocery store, but to me they were the most beautiful flowers I'd ever seen. (Is it any wonder that I hate the sight of daisies now?)

I didn't know how to start, and neither did you, so we finally turned off the lights, laid down on the bed, and started kissing. And then you got excited and took off all of your clothes. I'd touched your private parts before, but that was the first time I'd seen you naked. Yours was the first and only one I ever saw (except for the homeless man who urinated in front of us in Toledo) until all those horrible men sent me pictures when I started trying to date again. You were the first (and still only!) man to see me in the nude as well. I felt so uncomfortable taking off my clothes, so afraid of being judged. But you were so sweet, you told me my body was beautiful, and I actually believed you.

The sex was not great, you know that. I remember lying there and wondering if I was doing everything right, if that was how I was supposed to feel. I expected sex to be transcendent. I expected to scream and moan and shake and sweat. Instead, I lay on my back, trying to figure out where to put my hands, while you rocked on top of me, then you gasped and grunted and lay still. "That was amazing," you said, and I agreed, but in reality I wondered if that was all there was to it.

Things got better between us, with practice. You definitely started lasting longer. And the act started to be fun for me as well. I never achieved an out of body experience or anything, but I enjoyed myself. I enjoyed the physical closeness.

Sometimes I wonder what your first time with Megan was like for you. Were you nervous? Was it awkward? Did you make corny jokes like you did with me? Or was everything amazing and special and mind-blowing? Was she better than me? Did she make you feel like a real man? Did she roll her eyes back in her head and scream? Or was it all the same, but different?

Someday, I am going to do those same things with some other man. I wonder what that will be like? In my dreams, the ones I've been having lately, we writhe and grab at each other, but I awake with a sense of lacking, an emptiness.

But it's going to happen for me, right? Someday I will make love to someone else. Will I enjoy it? Will I feel open and adventurous and beautiful? Or will it be something shameful and disappointing, something I do just to get it over with, to terminate my connection to you and make it so you are no longer the only man I've ever been with?

I wish you and I had talked about sex more openly. I wish I'd talked about it more with Katie or my other girlfriends.

Maybe then I would be more comfortable discussing it now. I once had a conversation with some women here on the island, and they were so open. They joked around about how sex is helpful for 'keeping warm in the winter' and they made suggestions as to which of the single men here I should take to warm my bed. Men they'd already slept with, with no shame, and no jealousy. I wish I could be like that. I wish I could be that brave, or that free, or that empowered.

But I'm not. Yet.

Who knows what the future holds?

Cherry

# Chapter Seventy-Two

*Whispering Pines Island, February 2015*

After half-dialing and hanging up numerous times, Matteo worked up the nerve to complete the phone call.

"Thank you for calling the Inn at Whispering Pines..."

"Check your caller ID. You don't have to go through your whole spiel, Cara. Just say hi."

"This is the reception desk, so I'm always going to answer professionally. You never know who is listening."

"Are your calls bugged?"

Her responding sigh was less professional that it could have been. "Matty, what do you want?"

"I have my measurements for you. For the tuxedo rental." He read off the numbers to her.

"Finally. I needed these yesterday."

"I couldn't leave my house to get measured yesterday. Sorry. You should have let me wear my own tux." He didn't like using his mental illness as an excuse, but he had no choice. The previous day every time he touched the doorknob he developed an overpowering sense of dread. The panic set in, even when he merely opened the door to let his dogs out, so he ended up spending most of the day sitting in his living room, hands in Beverly's fur, trying to take deep breaths and keep from having a heart attack. Not that he'd ever had a heart attack, but that's what it felt like coming on every time.

"I've told you a thousand times, you can't wear that awful shiny 1970s era monstrosity to my wedding. And I'm sorry, Matty. I should call and check on you more often." She actually sounded sorry. Cara had always been the one who helped him through his worst times, and things had been difficult since Martha's death. How much would their friendship change after her marriage? "Though I should point out that I've been asking for these for months."

"Weeks, not months. And it's okay that you can't be bothered to check up on your oldest and dearest friend. I totally understand, for real. I don't feel neglected at all. You were busy wedding planning. Hey, listen, since we're talking about your wedding, can I bring a date?"

"A date? It's in two weeks, and you want to add someone to my guest list?"

"Is that a 'no'?"

"I'm teasing you, Matty. I don't care. It's a small wedding, there's plenty of room for one more. Besides, I own part of the inn, I can do whatever I want. But I do need a name for the place cards."

"I was planning on asking Cherry."

"Really?" The silence stretched long after Cara asked that question. Matteo recognized this psychological technique, her use of silence to make him babble, but he wanted to wait her out, make her ask something else. But he gave up first.

"Yeah, really," he finally said. "I thought it would be fun to bring her." Cara still didn't respond.

"I like spending time with her, that's all."

Silence.

"Look, we're friends, so it's no big deal. I thought she might enjoy the party."

Still nothing.

"Damn it, Cara. You know, don't you? You know I like her."

"Ha! Of course I knew. I've been trying to get you to admit it for months. I'm glad, I like her too."

"How could you tell?"

"Because sometimes when you look at her, you clench your jaw tightly, like you're in pain, and you stick your hand in your pocket to rub your worry stone. Or at least, I hope it's your worry stone. If I'm wrong about that, I don't want to know."

"Yes, it's my worry stone, you pervert. You really noticed that?"

"I notice everything." He could hear her smiling through the phone. "Matty, you two would be a fantastic couple. I hope it works out for you. But find out if she wants beef, fish, or vegetarian, and tell me soon. Sam's obsessed over the food enough as it is."

"Yeah, I will. You did put me down for one of each, right? I want to bring leftovers home."

"I have a guest. Goodbye, Matty." She disconnected, and he stood staring at his phone for a moment. Great, he'd scored the invitation. And now he had to go through with it. Could he handle this? The little mouse scrabbled its claws against his heart, and he took a deep breath to chase it away. Yes, he was ready.

🌲 🌲 🌲 🌲 🌲

Matteo clipped a leash to Tristan and took him out the door. Surely Cherry would be receptive to the idea of a date with him, if he brought her favorite dog when he asked.

He headed toward the school. The kids would be out in about a half hour, which gave him time to sit on the patio and get his head into the right space. But as he passed the drugstore, he looked up at Cherry's apartment—as he always automatically did—and spotted someone moving in the window. Why wasn't she at school? Had something happened? Was she ill? Why didn't she call him? No, this worrying didn't help anything.

"Come on, Tristan. Let's go see to your girl," he said, and the corgi recognized their destination and eagerly trotted up the stairs, tail already wagging. Matteo opened the door after a perfunctory knock.

"Cherry Blossom?" he asked, looking into the living room. But it wasn't her; it was a strange man. Tristan let out a startled bark.

"Who are you?" the stranger asked.

"Better question. Who are you and what the hell are you doing here?" Tourists weren't usually on the island midweek. They didn't belong wandering around people's personal residences anyway.

"Oh, sorry, I just realized what this looks like. I'm Gary Dryden. I came to visit my wife, well, my ex-wife, and she wasn't home, but the door was unlocked..."

"So you came in anyway? There are other places to wait for her. Public places that don't involve illegal breaking and entering." Matteo looked around to figure out if anything was out of place. Cherry wasn't the neatest person. She left books and scattered bits of clothing everywhere, so he couldn't tell.

"It's not breaking and entering. We're still friends. She wouldn't mind me waiting here, out of the cold."

"You tracked snow on her carpet, she'd mind that." Matteo and Tristan were respectful enough to stay in the tiled entryway, but Gary had left a trail through the entire apartment, there were even wet footprints leading to the bedroom.

"Who are you, her boyfriend or something?" Gary stood up taller, like he thought his height advantage was intimidating. Oh, was he priming for a fight? That could be fun.

"I'm a concerned citizen who thinks you shouldn't be in a lady's house when she isn't home without her knowledge or permission. If you don't get out of here right now, I will call the police and have you forcibly removed." That was a minor lie. Deputy Mills was on duty, technically, but he had no idea where, and Matteo wasn't carrying a radio. If he needed help, he'd have to use Cherry's phone and ask Tim to come up from the bar and practice his bouncer skills.

"Whoa, no need for police!" Gary held up his hands in supplication. "I'll go wait for her somewhere else." He took it much easier than Matteo expected.

Matteo considered what he was doing for a moment. He had been on his way to ask Cherry to go as his date to his best friend's wedding, and he still planned to do that but ... maybe not. Why was her ex-husband here? Did she expect him? Were they getting back together? *It's up to her*, he decided. *Lady's choice.*

"Listen man, I'm heading in the direction of the school. Class lets out in about a half hour. I can show you where it is, and you can wait outside for her."

"On the school property? No, I'd better not. I can hang out in a restaurant or something."

"Diner's open, but you'll have to order some food, and you'll have to tip well."

"I always tip well."

"Me too, twenty percent."

"Yeah? Because I always tip twenty-five percent at a minimum. More if the service is good," Gary responded, and Matteo tried not to laugh at the absurdity of the situation. Were they really posturing over tipping?

# Chapter Seventy-Three

"Hey, there's my good boy!" Cherry said, when she saw who was waiting for her after school.

"I'd rather be your naughty boy," Matteo responded, and she smacked his arm.

"Clearly, I was talking to Tristan, wasn't I? Oh yes, there's my good boy." She knelt down and started petting him, and the corgi wriggled with pleasure. She really should get a dog. Maybe this summer, when she'd have time to train it. But no, she'd need to move into a house first and she wasn't ready for that kind of transition yet. She liked her cozy little apartment.

Matteo watched her with an odd expression in his eyes and a tightly clenched jaw. She straightened up and brushed the snow off her knees. "Are you here for a reason?"

"What, I can't come by to say hi? Tris and I happened to be in the area, that's all. But I'm willing to be a gentleman and escort you home."

"Only if you carry my bag and I take Tristan."

"Deal."

She ran inside for her bag and her coat. At her old job, she used to stay after school for hours, but here there was less bureaucracy, and nobody to judge how much work she did based on physical presence. She could do her planning and grading at home, stress free. It was a pleasant change.

"Any big plans this weekend?" he asked as they walked.

"Nothing exciting. Reading one of those books I borrowed from you. And I might go to the mainland and do a little shopping. If there's anything you need me to pick up, let me know." She would have asked him to join her, if she thought he could. It would be nice to have a companion for off-island activities.

"That's it?" He stopped walking, right in front of the diner.

"Why? You have something fun in mind?"

"No, I just wasn't sure if you had another MidWestSinglz date or not. Men always seem to be around you." There was an edge behind the question that she couldn't quite figure out.

"You of all people know I haven't been on a date in weeks," she informed him. "But I'm sure if I did, you'd find a way to interrupt it."

"Rescue you, you mean. So did you stop dating because you're interested in someone?"

"Wouldn't that make me start dating?" She hoped he mistook the sudden pinkness of her cheeks for windburn rather than embarrassment. A flash of memory popped up, of waking up with her arm draped over his chest, of his sleepy eyes, of the way he sometimes stared at her with such tenderness when he thought she wasn't looking.

"I thought perhaps you stopped going out with random guys you met online because you were talking to your ex again." He looked away, seemingly fixated on something in the diner window, his reflection, probably.

"I haven't spoken to Gary since we signed the divorce papers," Cherry replied. She had no desire whatsoever to talk to him. The day after the divorce was finalized, he emailed her some chatty nonsense, as though they had some sort of salvageable friendship. She sent it straight to the trash and then blocked all future correspondence from him. It was over.

"Yeah? But don't you want to see him, maybe catch up a little?"

"After everything that happened? Are you crazy? Oh, no, sorry, I didn't mean that . . ." She'd messed up again.

"Two things. One, yes, I am crazy. Two, if you don't want to see him again, start running now. I'll provide defense."

"Matteo, you aren't making any sense!"

"Cherry!" The familiar voice made her freeze. No, that couldn't be him, could it? She didn't turn around yet, just kept her horrified eyes locked on Matteo's face. He shrugged.

"It's not too late to run."

## Chapter Seventy-Four

"I can't believe you're here." She stared across the table at him. Why did she agree to come sit down in the diner and talk? Why, why, why?

"Is that a good 'can't believe it' or a bad one?"

"What do you think?" She studied Gary's face, a face somehow both familiar and strange. The man she once loved was still there, but with more lines in the corners of his eyes than before. He'd lost weight as well, and not in a healthy way—Gary always had a hard time motivating himself to eat when stressed. A tiny part of her wanted to reach out and embrace him, feel those old feelings of contentment and love, but most of her was still so very angry.

"I owe you an apology," he told her, and she wanted to slap him. Those words were a full year too late. "I was being so selfish before, about everything."

It took her a moment before she could respond. Instinctively, she wanted to be nice, to accept his apology even though he clearly didn't mean it, and it certainly wasn't enough. But like Matteo always told her, she needed to stand up for herself. This was her battle to fight, and she needed to make Gary understand exactly how terrible his actions had been.

"Selfish?" she finally managed to say. "That's what you want to apologize for? Your selfishness? I had to get tested for STDs. My entire family and all of my friends know my husband was cheating on me. Our co-workers kept your secret and laughed behind my back about it for a full year. My middle school students made fun of me—they learned all the sordid details from the news. The humiliation was so great I had to leave town. That's what you did to me. Now you trivialize everything by saying you were merely selfish?"

"I wasn't thinking."

"You were thinking, just not with your brain."

Gary ducked his head and looked at her from under his lashes in the same endearing way that once made her fall in love with him. It brought her back to when they were teenagers and the world was at their feet. How had things gone so wrong since then?

"I think things were just too perfect with you, with us. You know me. You're the optimist, and I'm the pessimist. I kept waiting for things to go bad. And then when we started talking about having a baby, it kind of hit me that I had lived a life that wasn't meant for me. I didn't deserve such happiness, to have it all, a steady job, a nice house, a beautiful wife and a child ... it was too much. Hooking up with Megan made me feel bad, deep down inside. I felt rotten. And I deserved to feel rotten. I needed awfulness in my life, to counterbalance all the things I wasn't worthy of. I understand it all better now, I started seeing a shrink and I've learned a lot about myself and my actions."

"You have a lot of nerve blaming your cheating on our happiness. You lied to me for a full year. You were having relations with another woman behind my back. In fact, when *you* brought up having a baby, you were already months into your affair, so don't you dare say that our family planning had anything to do with it. I was happy too and then I ended up having to be the one to move away, to give up my home and everything I owned and start over with nothing."

"Hey, wait, you made that decision. You could have taken the house and the furniture and everything. You forced me to buy you out. I was willing to walk away. I could have moved into Megan's apartment with her."

"Yes, Gary. Blame me. It's my fault I couldn't stand to look at everything we bought together, everything we built, and continue seeing it every day with your betrayal hanging over me." She folded her arms across her chest and glared at him. She had imagined this confrontation so many times, but in her fantasies he was much more contrite.

"Cherry, babe, I'm so sorry. I've never been sorrier about anything in my life." Well, that was closer to what she wanted to hear, but it still wasn't enough.

"Did you tell Megan you were coming here?"

"No." His shook his head and frowned. "We broke up." Somehow, his words still had the power to wound her. He didn't come to see her because he was sorry, he came because he was single.

"Oh, so that's the real reason. Megan dumped you, and you're afraid to be alone? You haven't been single since you were eighteen, so you can't figure out what to do with yourself? Go home, Gary." She couldn't help feeling a bit of *schadenfreude*. Now she didn't have to keep imagining him doing the things Tyler Rivera showed her in those awful marriage-destroying photos.

"Cherry, I don't have a home."

"You sold our house?" That was a fresh horror. Her heart broke when she signed the papers, taking herself off the title and mortgage. Their home had been a symbol of their dream life, and she still thought about it wistfully. She had loved every brick, every tile, every quirk of that little house, until the moment Gary tainted it all with betrayal.

"I didn't want to, but I had to pay my lawyer bills. I told you in my emails."

"I blocked you, Gary. I never read your emails. What bills? They can't be from the divorce, you paid for that up front."

"No, from my criminal defense case. You really hadn't heard? Shit. Oh, sorry, excuse my language. Cherry, things went bad for me. Really bad." He went on to tell her of his life the past eight months, of the publicity surrounding Megan's acrimonious divorce from her wealthy husband, and how the cheating came to light. And how a second grade girl saw their picture in the paper and asked her parents, "Is that why Mrs. Rivera was kissing Mr. Dryden's private parts?" Apparently, two children were given a hall pass during the class' weekly music lesson, and witnessed an act of fellatio in the back of his classroom. Unfortunately for Gary, the enraged parents of those students filed a complaint with the police and he was convicted of aggravated indecent exposure, landing him on the sex offender registry, and resulting in the loss of his teaching license, and of course, his job.

Cherry instinctively reached across the table and took his hands. "Gary, I'm sorry that happened. But you need to stop making it sound like you're the victim here."

"I am the victim! You know me, you know I would never hurt a child. My behavior was irresponsible, but not criminal."

"What part of 'I had my private parts exposed in front of children' isn't criminal? You were on school grounds, during the school day. There's a time and a place for cheating on your wife, and that's not it."

"You sound like you're still upset with me. I'm suffering, babe. I'm on probation and I have to see a court-ordered therapist, and I'm not allowed near children. I had to move back to Indiana, but I can't even visit my parents because my nieces and nephews are there. It's killing me Cherry." Tears started leaking from his eyes.

She hated him, but she didn't like seeing him in such pain, and those tears were real. She couldn't let him get to her though. This was her moment to stand strong. "Is that why you're here? To tell me your sob story?"

"Actually, I came because neither Katie nor your parents would give me your phone number, and you didn't respond to my emails. I miss you, babe. I wanted to see if you were ready to give me another chance. I don't expect you to jump in and marry me immediately or try and get pregnant right away or anything. I just want to know if I will ever be able to work my way back into your heart and show you that I can be the man you deserve and that we can rebuild our lives together. What do you say?" He looked at her, so full of hope, saying the words she would have killed to hear months ago. But it was too late.

She took a deep breath. She was happy here. She was rebuilding her own life, one that no longer had room for him.

"Gary, no. I'm sorry. Too much has happened that I can't forgive. I'm moving on, I'm healing, and I'm starting over on my own."

His face crumbled. But then he smiled, his old familiar smile that used to melt her heart. "I understand it will take you some time to trust me again. I'll give you all the time you need. I know we have to start from scratch. Will you at least unblock my email address?"

"I can do that," she told him. That was an easy gesture to make on her part. Unblocking him wasn't the same as welcoming him back in to her life.

# Chapter Seventy-Five

Dear Gary,

I sometimes wondered what I would feel if I ever saw you again. Would I be hateful and slap you and scream in your face? Would I embrace you and bury my head in your chest and long to kiss you? Would I still be angry, would I be happy, would I face you with a sort of wistful nostalgia?

It was none of those things, and all of them, all at the same time.

But when you left yesterday, when I watched you walk out the door of the diner, hands in pockets, heading down to the docks, all I felt was empty. Drained.

The truth is, our conversation made me realize something very important, something I should have seen from the beginning. It wasn't about me, was it? It was never about me.

All this time, I asked myself what did I do wrong, why wasn't I enough, how could I have been better, how could I have changed things? What could I have done to keep you from cheating?

But it really was all you. You were selfish, Gary. You were selfish, and you were wrong.

You tried to blame me, for being too happy. For making you too happy. That's bull-pucky, and you know it.

None of this was my fault. I deserve better.

You were an enormous part of my life for such a long time. You held such significance. And even after you shattered my heart into dust and ground it under your heel, you still took up too much space in my mind.

That's all over now.

I am not going to allow myself to mourn you anymore.

I'm creating a new life for myself. Here in this cold snowy place, I've found a sense of peace. I'm getting to know myself better. I'm taking more time to think about the rhythms of my life. I'm meeting new people, and learning that I don't have to be surrounded by a crowd to be happy.

With less bitterness than before,

Cherry

*No Longer Yours*

# Chapter Seventy-Six

Cherry sat in the coffee shop, reading student essays. Her high schoolers had turned in their research papers on Friday, and she hoped to return them for revisions on Monday. With so few students in the different grades, it was easy to have a swift turnaround. It wasn't like the old days of trying to wade through a hundred and fifty book reports, often by students who clearly hadn't read anything.

Cara interrupted her with a cheerful greeting. "Oh good, Cherry, I'm so glad I ran into you. Matty never told me, do you want the fish or the beef?"

"Fish or beef what?" Cherry blinked up at her, confused.

Cara waved her hand dismissively. "Who knows? Sam has changed his mind a thousand times. His old roommate from culinary school offered to do the catering, and they're on the phone arguing over things every single night. All I know is one dish will be fish, one will be beef, or, of course, there's a vegetarian option."

"But I mean, for what?" Cara's explanation did not alleviate her confusion.

"For my wedding next weekend. Sorry, I should blame Matteo. He said he was bringing you as his date, but he never got back to me on your meal preference. Not that it really matters. I'm sure Sam is going to over order, so everybody will probably be able to eat one of each. I swear, that man is going crazy trying to give me the perfect night."

"I . . . um . . . fish, I guess?" Why did Matteo tell Cara that Cherry was his wedding date? And why didn't he ask her first? They'd had dinner together on Wednesday, and though the subject of the impending nuptials came up, he never once mentioned that he'd added Cherry to the guest list.

Fortunately, Cherry was still grading an hour later when Matteo himself came wandering in for coffee. It must have been his lunch break—he wore what she had come to recognize as his 'shop clothes', jeans and a big cable-knit sweater with a matching hat. He nodded at her without saying anything as he entered, but as soon as he had his drink he came and joined her, uninvited, as always.

"Busy day for me. Lots of tourists renting cross-country skis for the weekend. Have you had a chance to hit the trails recently? Though it looks like you're pretty busy too."

"These are my high school students' research papers. They got to choose their topics, so I'm actually learning a lot of interesting things. I might need to verify some of the 'facts' that Jack included in his hockey versus bandy analysis though."

"I hope he came to the correct conclusion. If he picked hockey, deduct thirty points from his grade," Matteo said. He was warming his hands on his mug, and she couldn't help but look at them. Those are a working man's hands, she thought to herself, firm and callused and so strong. He probably gave great massages. But she didn't need to think about such things. It caused too strange a sensation inside her body.

"I saw Cara today," she ventured, and watched as Matteo tensed slightly.

"Yeah?" he asked, raising an eyebrow. "That's interesting."

"She wanted to know my meal choice for her wedding. Someone gave her the impression that I was going as your date."

"What did you tell her?"

"Fish."

"So you want to go?"

"I'd rather have been asked. What's going on?"

"I was planning to invite you, not like as a 'go on a date with me' thing, but more like 'you're my friend, let's drink on someone else's tab.' But I didn't, because I thought you'd have better things to do."

"What better things? I think it would be fun," she told him. She hid her disappointment that he made it so clear he wasn't asking her out. She knew he wasn't the relationship type, but sometimes she wondered if maybe something true hid behind the teasing and the over-the-top flirtations. If he ever asked her on a real date, she would accept.

# Chapter Seventy-Seven

"I hope this isn't going to be weird for you, but we have a free room at the inn for the wedding," Matteo told Cherry the day before the event. He watched as her face turned pink. She was adorable when she was uncomfortable.

"I thought we were just going as friends. This isn't a date, Matteo."

"You think I don't know that?" he asked in as mocking a tone as he could muster. "It's going to be cold and snowing. Do you want to walk or ski up there in your fancy dress and heels? Wait, you are wearing a fancy dress and heels, right? I'm in the bridal party, I need my companion to look good."

"I bought a new dress, but I hadn't thought about the logistics."

"The room is for us to get dressed in, and also, to crash in if we don't want to stumble home in the snowy dark. Don't worry, it's got two beds, and I won't touch you at all. Unless you want me to, then it's game on, sweetheart." He winked salaciously, and earned himself the rolled eyes and annoyed response that he wanted.

"Don't act like that. You're lucky I said I'd go at all, since you didn't actually invite me." Oh yes, that again. He would have, and he would have made it clear that it was a more-than-friends invitation, and brought flowers and chocolates and whatever else people were supposed to do on real dates, if he hadn't run into Gary. Somehow knowing she was going back to her ex made him boil with jealousy. He had just started to let his guard down, just started to think that maybe he found someone who could handle his craziness, and *bam*. Her husband shows up. He'd decided not to ask her after all, and hadn't told Cara yet before she ruined it by asking Cherry her meal choices.

"The inn is gorgeous. We can sit around in the lobby and drink spiked hot chocolate all afternoon. Well, you can. As the bridesman, I have to help Cara get ready." The wedding party was small, with just him and Cara's cousin Amy standing up for the bride. Sam's side consisted of Sam's older brother and Timmy; Matteo still wasn't sure how the whole walking-down-the-aisle thing was supposed to work.

"What are you going to do? I know you're not helping her get dressed."

"No, apparently Sam doesn't approve of me doing that. My job is to distract her stepmother and keep her from driving Cara and Amy crazy. Also, I've been told that if her stepmother is wearing white, I am to spill a glass of red wine on her. I've been practicing my moves. Though, in all honestly, Sam should do it. He's so clumsy it would seem more realistic."

"Who's Amy?"

"The maid of honor. I think I might have mentioned her before, Cara's cousin? The one who used to work at the inn in the summer?" He stopped, realizing he said too much. While he tended to avoid using Amy's name, he had told Cherry about her one night months ago, but didn't want her to make that connection. Cherry didn't need to know that Amy was the one he had once been so in love with. It didn't matter now anyway. Amy had a husband, and Matteo, well, his heart had moved on. Too bad it moved on to someone else unobtainable.

"Anyway, Miss Waites, I'll be happy to take you there tomorrow. Pack an overnight bag, and I'll pick you up with the box bike. But don't bring pajamas, I'm pretty sure the inn has a nude-sleeping-only policy."

"Very funny. If I'm sharing a room with you, I'm wearing a chastity belt for my own protection."

"Perfect. So, like I said, I'll come by tomorrow, with a box bike and a lock-pick set." He raised his eyebrows suggestively, and she blushed again. God, she was endearing. She was the pinkest person he had ever met. If only ... no. He reached for his worry stone to focus his thoughts. He was going to survive this wedding.

# Chapter Seventy-Eight

"Well, what do you think?" Matteo came out of the bathroom dressed in a tuxedo. The clothing wasn't the shocking thing though.

"My goodness, what happened to your beard?" It had been so long since she'd seen the face under the hair she almost didn't recognize him. Matteo scratched his chin and frowned.

"Cara told me she didn't care about any stupid island contests. If I was going to be in her wedding pictures, I had to shave. You know this means Timmy is going to win, again. I kind of think he set me up. I should ask how much he paid her."

"Isn't Tim a groomsman? I'm sure he shaved too. And you look good, really." He did, oh, he looked good. The beard made him rugged and manly, but his smooth skin made him downright handsome, and she had to fight the urge to run her fingers through his messy blond hair. The tuxedo fit him well, showing off his body in a way that bulky sweaters never did. He bowed elaborately at her complement and then grinned.

"Alright, your turn to fancy yourself up. I'm going to go find the bride and ask what she needs me to do, so the room's all yours. I'll be back in an hour or two. I'm not going to knock though. I'm hoping to catch a glimpse of you in a state of undress." He winked as he left.

As soon as the door closed behind him, she hurried to the bathroom. If he was going to be gone for a couple of hours, she planned to take advantage of the huge bathtub and all the goodies that accompanied it. She filled the tub with steaming water and bath oils, and allowed herself to sink in and relax ... until she heard the room door open.

"Sorry, forgot something!" Matteo's voice called out.

"Don't come in here!" she shrieked, furious.

"I'm not, jeez. I'm not a pervert. I only want to see what you are enthusiastically willing to show me. I'm leaving now, so you're safe."

*Jerk*, she thought to herself. What would she have done if he came in while she was bathing? She sort of wondered if maybe it would have started something. No. He liked to flirt with her for the sake of making her uncomfortable, not because he was interested at all. It didn't matter that her feelings for him were changing when he made it clear that his never would.

She took her time getting ready. It had been months since she'd done anything different to her hair other than running a brush through it, so she wasn't as practiced with the curling iron as she used to be. It had been awhile since she'd put on any makeup as well. She'd stopped after the first week of school when she noticed nobody else on the island bothered. But she wanted to look pretty tonight.

When she finally emerged from the bathroom, she spotted a box on one of the beds. Chocolates, from the local shop, with a note: *Sweets for my sweet ... ha ha, just kidding. Thought you'd like these though.*

So Matteo returned to the room to drop off a gift? What did this mean?

🌲 🌲 🌲 🌲 🌲

"Wowsers, Cherry Blossom, you clean up well." Matteo looked her up and down appreciatively when he came back to escort her to the ceremony. "Had I known, I would have invited you someplace fancy a long time ago." Her skin burned hot with a blush.

"You sure know how to ruin a compliment."

"What? No, you're always adorable. Just now there's something sophisticated about you too. And I like your lipstick. It's going to be a pain to wash off my neck later though." She almost wished she could believe he was serious.

"Don't get your hopes up."

"It's not my hopes that are ... sorry. I'll stop. You ready for this?" He opened the door, then held out his hand to take hers. She smiled, accepted, and let him lead her out. This was going to be a fun wedding; she was sure of it. And maybe, maybe the open bar would give her the courage to tell Matteo what she'd been thinking about him ...

# Chapter Seventy-Nine

Cherry hadn't paid much attention to the marriage ceremony itself, though she was sure it was lovely. Instead, she leaned back in her seat and tried not to stare at Matteo. It was a universal truth that all men looked attractive in tuxedos, but he looked especially good. Without the beard, his face was boyish and charming, and his lips were so inviting. But she shouldn't let herself have such thoughts when he didn't reciprocate them.

When the ceremony ended, she found herself somewhat at a loss. Matteo went off to get pictures taken with the rest of the bridal party, and the other people she knew were occupied. Tim was in the pictures too, and Tyrell, who worked at the inn, was acting as event coordinator. Most of the guests were Cara's relatives, or so she assumed based on how they all shared a facial structure and spoke with varying degrees of the same Texas drawl.

"Hello, I believe I have been looking for you." Cherry turned at the sound of the voice. The speaker was tall and lean, with green eyes that crinkled in the corners. He sounded European, an unusual accent in this sea of Texans.

"I think you're mistaking me for someone else," she told him politely.

"You are Cherish, no? Matteo suggested I find you," he said. Oh, that was it. Matteo was sending her men now. Could he make it any more clear that he wasn't interested?

"Sorry, I don't know what Matteo told you..."

"He tell me, find my Cherish and keep her company, please. That is what he said. He and my wife are occupied with photography, which may take a long time."

She took another look, and now she noticed the ring on his finger. "Oh, you're Fabio, right? The maid of honor's husband? It's nice to meet you."

"And you are the girlfriend of Matteo?"

"No, we're just friends. Or frenemies, maybe."

"I don't know what that is, but here, I have brought you champagne. Cheers!"

"To the happy couple." Cherry touched her glass to his and took a sip. It was just as amazing as she expected. The inn was a gorgeous venue, and she already knew how particular Sam was about all manner of consumables, so obviously everything would be elegant and delicious. This was far nicer than her own wedding, and she hoped this marriage would turn out happier.

🌲 🌲 🌲 🌲 🌲

Fabio managed to keep her entertained throughout the cocktail hour until everyone was seated at the reception, and the bride and groom, accompanied by the wedding party, made their grand entrance. Matteo sat next to her, and immediately leaned over to touch her back. As he reached for her, she was momentarily stunned. Was he trying to put his arm around her? Was he actually making a move?

No. No, he certainly wasn't.

"Oh my goodness, you awful man. Your hands are freezing! Don't touch me!" She tried not to shriek too loudly.

He laughed and rubbed his hands together. "Can you believe they made us do pictures by the gazebo outside? I thought Amy and Cara would freeze to death. At least us guys had jackets on. I'm sure they'll turn out beautiful, but shit, it sucked being out there."

"That explains why they started so early," Cherry replied, refraining from pointing out his language. She had wondered why the wedding took place at 4:30, but given the sunset times it made sense. The photographs were probably spectacular, with the snowy backdrop. Her own wedding had been in the summer, and it rained, so her pictures were taken indoors. She had still loved them though, until she watched the album burn in a cathartic post-divorce bonfire.

"Did you notice she made Tim shave his beard too? I bet Ty bribed her." He seemed gleeful. "I don't mind losing the contest as long as he loses too."

"Sounds selfish."

"No, selfish is me eating your entire appetizer." The plates arrived, and he grabbed hers and moved it over. She laughed and took her plate back.

"Nice try. I've been looking forward to this food. You know it's the only reason I accepted your invitation."

"Really? I thought it was my dashing good looks that convinced you." He winked and then held up his glass in a toast. "To you, Miss Cherish Alonso Waites, date of the best looking man in the room."

"Wrong on all counts," she replied, but she clinked her glass against his anyway.

# Chapter Eighty

After dinner ended, it was time. Time to do something very foolish.

"You have to dance with me, come on." Matteo took the glass from Cherry's hand and set it down on the table, then tried to lead her to the dance floor.

"Are you a good dancer? You aren't going to break my toes or anything, are you?" She looked up at him with those bright eyes, and he clenched his jaw. Do not try to kiss this woman.

"I'm a horrible dancer, but it doesn't matter, this is a slow song. We just have to sway, and anyone can do that." He tugged on her hand, and she did come with him this time, and maybe that was a terrible mistake. He was playing with fire now. He knew she wasn't going to stick around, he knew she was going back to Gary, he should never have let himself get his hopes up, but still. Here she was, with him. Here she was in a low cut dress making him think all kinds of inappropriate thoughts. Here she was, letting him hold her.

He slid his hands around her waist. "What is this dress made out of? I like it." And he did like it, so smooth, so slick, he could envision his hands sliding all over this fabric, sliding down further, cupping her ass cheeks, or better, sliding up, sliding up to the straps and slowly slipping them down, pulling her dress down, and she would look at him and her cheeks would turn pink. Was she one of those women whose blushes spread to their cleavage? Oh, he would like to find out. With a great deal of mental effort he forced the impossible fantasies away.

"Some kind of satin, I think," she murmured. Her head rested against his shoulder. He had expected her to be stiff and uncomfortable, holding him at arm's length and reminding him about what was appropriate, but no, she pressed right up against him, possibly too close, because, soon, she'd definitely be able to feel the direction his thoughts were going.

Matteo tried to think of other things. He surveyed the room. Everybody was dancing. Cara was holding tight to her new husband, who had his eyes closed and a dreamy expression on his face. There were Tim and Tyrell, in a corner, locked in an embrace. And of course, there were Amy and Fabio. She wasn't like most of the women, swaying gently against her lover. No, she was never like that. Amy was whispering in Fabio's ear, and giggling, and Matteo could imagine the string of dirty words coming out of her mouth. He once had such a crush on her. Funny how childish that seemed now. What was it he saw in Amy, anyway? She was pretty and fun, and had a crass sense of humor, and for a long time that had been all he wanted in a woman. He changed, he supposed. Matured, maybe. Or maybe finally met the right one. Too bad she wasn't sticking around either.

He closed his eyes and breathed carefully, slowly. It didn't help. It didn't distract him from Cherry's body touching his, from the way the fabric slid so smoothly under his fingers. *Focus on something else*, he told himself, *stop thinking about what you want. Deep breath. Remember looking through the window at the diner, at Cherry reaching out and taking Gary's hand? Focus on that. Focus on the way they stared at each other, the history between them. Focus on how Gary gets what you want.*

"Ouch," Cherry's voice broke through his spiraling thoughts. "Matteo, you're hurting me."

He realized he had been pressing his fingertips into her back, digging in tightly. "Sorry," he said. "I really didn't mean to hurt you. I was distracted . . ."

"Distracted by what?" She tipped her head back, and her eyes met his, and he drew in a sharp breath. She was so close to his face. He gazed deeply into her eyes and felt his heart rate increase, and that familiar tightening in his chest. As he watched, her little tongue came out, so briefly, as she licked her lips. Did she even know what she did? Did she have any idea how she made him feel?

"Just, you know, everything," he said, being as vague as possible. *By you, by the curve of your neck, by the way your breasts are touching my chest, the way your dress slides so easily under my fingertips.*

"Matteo," his name came out in a whisper, and he knew from the way she looked at him that she was begging him to kiss her, she had to be. Her lips parted, and he started to lower his mouth to hers . . .

"Alright folks, it's time to clear the dance floor so the newlyweds can cut the cake," Tyrell's voice on the microphone startled Matteo, and he took a step back. Damn it. He lost the moment.

"Oh, goody. Cake. That's exactly what I wanted right now," he said, and he hoped he saw the same disappointment reflected in Cherry's eyes. It was for the best though. Tyrell just prevented him from making a terrible mistake.

# Chapter Eighty-One

"Would you like a shot?" Cherry turned at the sound of Fabio's voice.

"Sorry, what?"

"Tequila shot. It was supposed to be for my wife, but she is in more photographs, and I do not wish to keep holding the glass."

"You should drink it," Cherry said. She had no desire to do shots right now, and she couldn't understand why everybody on this island seemed to drink tequila all the time. It tasted awful!

"No, I am not a tequila man. Too harsh for me. Here." He held it out again, and this time she accepted. Why not? She was at a party, her date was busy, and she needed to do something to mute the surge of feelings rising up in her. There had been a moment when she and Matteo were dancing when she had such an urge ... she downed the shot to avoid that line of thinking.

"Do all American weddings take so many pictures?" Fabio asked, and she was glad for something to talk about.

"Mine didn't, but I got married before social media became a big thing. Nowadays, everything has to be picture perfect. Didn't you have a wedding?"

"Ah, not as such. It was rather quickly thrown together in my in-laws backyard, so that my beloved's great-grandmother could attend. I know she would prefer something like this." He gestured expansively around the room. "But in the end, there is the bride and groom and their love and nothing else matters, no? That is what is important."

"And cake!" Matteo interrupted the conversation to hand a plate to Cherry. "You'll love this. Margaux made it. Shall we sit and enjoy?" Something slightly sarcastic colored his tone, and he pulled out a chair for her in an overly dramatic manner.

"What's gotten into you?" Cherry asked.

Matteo just grinned. "Nothing, I'm having a great time. Hey Fabio, Amy seems to be having a great time too."

"My wife makes everything fun. It is her special gift."

"Oh, believe me, I'm familiar with her special gift. But you knew that, right?"

"Yes. Her other gift is her perhaps excessive honesty. I'm aware of all of her past ... mistakes. Nothing that happened before we met matters, to either of us. Now, speaking of my lovely wife, I'm going to find her. Cherish, enjoy your ... date." Fabio smiled, nodded at Cherry, and walked away.

"What was that all about?" she asked Matteo, but she had an inkling.

"Nothing. I had a thing for his wife years ago, but it's been over for a long time. Finish your dessert and let's get out of here. I'm tired." He started shoveling his own cake in his mouth. She watched for a moment, then sighed and started eating. It was probably delicious, but she couldn't taste it. At least now she knew who broke his heart. The pretty, vivacious bridesmaid with a perfect figure. Figures she'd be his type. Maybe the only reason he brought Cherry as his date was to pretend to Amy that he was over her.

🌲 🌲 🌲 🌲 🌲

Matteo was silent as they walked down the hallway, and she wondered if he was drunk, or just fixating on Amy, his first love. It was like that moment while they were dancing hadn't happened at all.

"That was a lovely wedding, but I'm so glad I can finally take these heels off," she said as he closed the door. She reached down to remove her shoes, wobbled and almost fell. Matteo's hands caught her from behind and raised her up.

"Somebody's had too much to drink," he teased. She twisted in his arms to face him, and he didn't let go.

"Matteo..." she began, and his grip tightened for a second before he released her and backed away.

"Cherry Blossom," he replied, with such an odd expression on his face, longing and tenderness and something else, something that almost looked like regret. She took a deep breath and thought about the way his fingertips had dug into her waist earlier, the tension and desire that radiated from them. He was the one who kept telling her she needed to stand up for herself, and now she was going to do it. It was time to take charge of her life, time to take what she wanted.

She kissed him.

And it turned out she did know what she was doing, she did remember how to kiss. And he responded so swiftly, so powerfully.

Instinct took over and then something happened, something inside her she had never felt before. There was this need, this deep primal need, to be as close to him as possible. It wasn't enough. She couldn't get close enough. She wanted to draw him into her, to absorb him.

His tongue was in her mouth, his hands wrapped in her hair, but she needed more, needed to be closer. Too many layers of fabric impeded them. Why did they need clothes anyway? What good did clothing ever do but separate people? She needed him so badly...

He suddenly wrenched his face away from hers, one hand locked in the hair on the back of her head, pulling her backward and forcing her farther away. The sudden absence of his mouth on hers left her shaking. He stared into her eyes for a moment, gasping, before releasing her hair and retreating several steps, panting hard. His shirt gaped open, the top three buttons missing. Had she done that? A thin sheen of sweat glistened on his forehead.

"We have to stop," he said, holding up a hand as though to ward her off. "You're drunk, Cherry."

"What? I'm not drunk," she told him. This was not drunkenness, this was something else entirely. A fire burned inside her, he had ignited something new and bold and exciting. Where did this come from? She had never experienced such raw lust before.

"You are. I can taste the tequila and I'm not going to take advantage of that." He backed away slowly, and when he reached the door he fumbled for the knob without looking. He acted afraid to turn his back on her, afraid she might pounce.

"Really, I'm not drunk. I don't know what came over me, but it's not from alcohol," she said, touching her face. Her lips felt bruised and swollen, and ready for more.

"Right. Listen, Cherry, I like you and all, but I'm not going to be your revenge fling or your throwaway fuck, or whatever it is you need before you get back with your husband. I'm going home."

"Matteo, wait!" she called, but the door shut behind him, leaving her cold and alone, and confused. What was he talking about? She wasn't getting back with her ex-husband.

## Chapter Eighty-Two

Matteo managed to avoid Cherry throughout the post-wedding brunch, though she tried to approach him several times. He used the excuse of helping serve the food, even though Cara had hired waiters to do that. Immediately afterward, he made arrangements for Tyrell to bring her back in a cart with some of the other guests, and he took off, claiming he had to take care of his dogs.

After he picked them up from his father's, he went home and took the longest coldest shower he could stand. He needed to erase the smell of Cherry from his skin, he hadn't been able to do so last night, that long night of tossing and turning and battling panic attacks on the couch in the lobby. Luckily, nobody saw him, or, if they had, they were discreet enough not to say anything.

He tried to escape the feeling Cherry's kiss aroused in him, but the cold shower didn't help. Neither did masturbating. He kept thinking about it, about the softness of her skin under his hands, the sleek feel of her dress. And how she clung to him, pulling him in closer, and how good it felt, both to be so desired and to be with someone he desired.

But it was all fake. She wasn't going to stay on the island, she was going to leave and go back to Gary. Her contract was only for one year, and while he knew the council planned to ask her to renew, why would she? Why would she when her husband wanted her to come home? There was nothing for her here.

He was able to stay clear of her for a full week, even though changing his routine set off a panic attack on Wednesday evening. His thoughts spiraled, tormenting him, insisting that if he wasn't at the diner, didn't eat on his usual schedule, something bad might happen. It might be the night the restaurant ceiling collapsed or there was a fire, and since he wasn't around to rescue Cherry, she would die. He recognized the absurdity, but he couldn't break the cycle of thoughts, until he finally got out a bottle of tequila and erased them that way. He usually knew better than to use alcohol to combat the panic, but he had no other choice.

But then, that Saturday, he was in his shop helping tourists pick out cross-country skis, when the bell over the door chimed, and he saw her face again. His guts clenched. She looked so innocent, and so sweet, and so much too good for him.

"I'll be with you in a moment, ma'am," he said, more for the benefit of the tourists than for her. He tried to drag out the rental process, hoping someone else would come in and provide an additional distraction, but no such luck.

"They're gone. Can you please talk to me now?" Cherry begged as soon as the door shut behind the group.

"Can't," he told her, though he wanted nothing more than to cross the room and take her into his arms and see if she wanted to do the same things sober as she had when drunk. "I've got to fix a bike." He walked into the back room, half-hoping she'd follow. She did.

"Matteo, can we talk about what happened after the wedding?"

"You mean when you got drunk and sexually assaulted me?"

"What? When I what? Is that what you think happened?"

"All I know is I was taking a woman who—when sober—has made it very clear she wants nothing to do with me back to her room, and she attacked me, and forced herself upon me. Which would have been fine, again, had she been sober, and had I any hope that there was something behind it."

"Matteo, maybe there is something behind it. Maybe I just wanted you. Maybe you're the one who's been there all along, and I started to see that we could have something."

"And maybe you wanted a revenge fuck on your husband. Got to get it out of your system, right? Well, you've got three months until your contract is up, I'm sure you can find someone in that time."

"Why are you always so nasty? You're a horrible person. I don't understand why I'm attracted to you at all."

Her words made his heart stop. "Cherish Renée Waites, are you saying you're attracted to me?"

"You still haven't guessed my middle name correctly. And I was."

"How about now?"

"I might be. Sometimes when I look at you I think . . ."

He got as close as he could without touching her, because if he touched her, he'd never be able to stop. "You think what?"

And then the bell, the fucking bell, rang and some tourist called out, "Helloooo, anyone here?"

"I think you have a customer."

"I hate customers. I close for lunch in an hour."

"Come over to my apartment and we can . . . talk."

"I'd like that. I'd like to . . . talk."

# Chapter Eighty-Three

Cherry took time to change into a nice skirt and her favorite shirt, and applied a little bit of makeup. Then she felt silly and washed her face. And then she reminded herself that he had complimented her lipstick the night of the wedding, so she put some of that back on, just in case.

Her apartment was a mess. She ran around frantically, gathering dirty clothes and shoes, and attempting to corral her books into some semblance of order. In the bedroom, she paused and looked down at the rumpled sheets and solitary, lonely pillow. Should she make her bed? Would it be more inviting if she didn't?

And was she seriously thinking about doing *that*? Of taking that gigantic leap forward with a man who didn't want a relationship with her? The delicious sliver of anticipation deep down inside confirmed that she was.

His footsteps bounding up the stairs startled her—he was early. That ended her debate on what to do about the bed as she rushed through the apartment, getting to the door just as he opened it. Would that man ever learn manners?

"Hey," he said as though this were an ordinary visit. He didn't break eye contact as he removed his coat and boots and then stood in the entryway, staring at her.

She realized he was waiting for her response. "Hey," she said back.

Matteo shook his head and took a step closer, onto the carpet. "I thought you wanted to talk. Is that really all you have to say?" Before she could answer, his hands—still ice cold from outside—cupped her cheeks and drew her in for a kiss.

There was the magic, again. There was the fire, the passion, everything that'd always been outside of her grasp. When he drew back, she saw sadness in his eyes.

"You know I'm not what you need, right Cherry? No matter how good this feels, I'm not right for you. I can't be."

"Why not?"

"You know why not. I'm too needy, too weak. I'm crazy, and sometimes housebound, and I require too much care. And I'm an asshole about it too. You can't hitch yourself to my wagon. I'll drag you off a cliff."

"Will you ever accept that this island isn't a prison? I'm here by choice."

"But for how long? You always say you need a commitment before you touch anyone's you-know-what, and I don't know that I can offer you that."

"I didn't say I needed a commitment, I said I needed an emotional connection before intimacy, and I thought we had that. I do, at least."

He smiled so tenderly it made her heart twist. He gently traced one finger down the side of her face. "Cherish Estelle Waites, you know I do too."

She gasped. He did it. He really did it! That had to be a sign! "Oh my goodness, Matteo. You guessed my middle name!"

"I was on the hiring committee," he reminded her, amusement glinting in his eyes. "You put it on your résumé. I've known all along."

"You are incorrigible," she informed him. "But I don't care." Now she was again standing up for herself, and taking what she wanted. She planted her mouth on his, and nothing else mattered. This was different, so different than it had ever been with ... who was she with before? She couldn't even remember his name. There was nothing but this moment and the feel of his lips, and the way they were tearing at each other's clothing.

Somehow, his shirt came off, and she was momentarily startled by his pelt of chest hair. It was softer than she imagined, far softer than the stubble that scratched her lips, her face, her neck. She wrapped her fingers in it to pull him closer, closer, but still not close enough.

"Fuck, Cherry, you feel so good," he whispered into her ear, and she didn't even care about the foul language, she only cared about his hot mouth, and his hands, oh his hands, and how they reached under her skirt, and suddenly, her panties were around her ankles and she was stepping out of them as they continued stumbling through the living room.

Bedroom! Her mind screamed, because she needed him now, and she steered their frantic groping toward her doorway. He didn't even glance at the unmade bed before he shoved her down and stood above her for a moment, panting. "You sure about this?" he asked in a voice raw with desire.

She lay back, stretched her arms over her head and closed her eyes. Yes, she was sure, she had never been so sure about anything in her life. This was it—this moment, this man—this was what she had been waiting for. Nothing existed, nothing mattered, other than the heat rising within her, the way her body was bursting with possibilities and desire. This, this was how she was supposed to feel.

"Yes, more than I've ever been sure about anything. Please tell me you brought a condom," she said, startling herself with her own audacity. This was what everyone talked about, this was what she had been missing for so long, possibly forever. There was nothing more than his hands on her legs, his mouth, his tongue working its way slowly, so tantalizingly up her inner thighs, all the way up to her...

"Whoa, hey, wait, what are you doing?"

He stopped and drew back, confusion conflicting with the lust in his eyes. "What? Are we not doing this? You literally just said ... am I misunderstanding something? You dragged me into your bedroom..."

"Yes, I know, but I meant what specifically are you doing right now?" She propped herself up on her elbows so she could see him better. He tilted his head and studied her before his eyes widened in revelation.

"Cherry, are you serious? You were married for almost ten years. Didn't your husband ever go down on you?"

"Well, ummm ... no. I mean, once in college. But it was awkward, and he didn't like it, so we never tried again."

Matteo stared at her incredulously. "Cherry Blossom, that's absurd. You just relax, lady. You are in for a real treat." And he ducked his head again.

Relax, he had said, and she tried, but how could she? How could she relax when her whole body was vibrating, when every molecule quivered at such a high frequency that she might shatter into a million pieces. And then a violent uncontrollable shudder ran through her, and she cried out, she couldn't help herself. She screamed and shook, and opened her eyes, and, "Gary?"

"What did you just call me?" Matteo pulled back abruptly and then turned in the direction she was looking.

"What the hell are you doing with my wife?" Gary stood in the doorway, flowers in one hand, a suitcase in the other, shock mixed with fury on his face.

Matteo stood up, turned toward Gary and deliberately antagonizingly slowly licked his lips. "Well, I do believe I just delivered her very first orgasm, and if you'd kindly leave the room, I'm going to give her a second and third, and maybe take one for myself."

Cherry was never sure afterward who threw the first punch.

# Chapter Eighty-Four

Restraint, restraint. That had been what was going through his head when he went over to Cherry's. They were just going to talk, and he would explain that no matter how badly he wanted her, how he craved her, how he couldn't imagine going one more day without her, they could never be together. He was going to tell her all of that, and leave. That was the plan.

But the second he touched her he couldn't stop. He tried. Oh, how he tried, but it all felt so right, and she was so eager and hot and willing, and her body was so soft, so inviting. And though he tried, all the careful control evaporated and nothing existed but her, until she said that name. Gary.

And there he stood, smug bastard. The only man who had come before him, holding flowers and a suitcase. And then all the restraint was really gone, and the next thing Matteo knew, he was lying on his back in the snow at the bottom of the stairs, surrounded by shattered wood, and Cherry screamed, and people came running.

Matteo was hazy on the details, but somehow now he was in the medical center, and Tim stood over him, arms crossed. "You're going to have to help me with the repairs," he said.

"I didn't ... what happened?" He remembered punching Gary, multiple times. According to the pain in Matteo's face,

Gary must have gotten one or two good ones in himself. He tried to move but his arm hurt.

"You and some guy completely destroyed Cherry's stairwell. You were brawling and took out the railing and the siding, and fell about half a story. You were lucky that you landed in a snowbank. And you were lucky Tyrell happened to see you. Actually, no. Cherry was lucky."

"Was she hurt? I think I heard her screaming..." The panic started rising inside him. Was she okay? He'd hate himself if she had gotten hurt because of him.

"No, she's fine. I think what she screamed was something like 'stop fighting, you idiots.' I meant she was lucky Ty came along because he had on his long coat and lent it to her rather quickly before anyone else got there. She was crouched over you trying to stop the bleeding from your arm and uh... she wasn't wearing much clothing and um... putting his coat over her meant he was the only one who saw her... ummm... you know, she was wearing a short skirt... and ummm..."

"Timothy, you are a grown man. You can say vulva."

"Shut up, Matteo, or I'll poke you in the wound."

"How did I get here?" Matteo couldn't remember. He must have hit his head. That would also explain the ringing in his ears.

"A big, strong, sexy bear of a man carried you. You're welcome, by the way. You have a concussion and you were fighting the nurse, so they drugged you so they could stitch you up. Your wounds are all from the wood. One piece passed all the way through your arm. I think they gave you a tetanus shot too."

"Awesome. Where's Cherry?"

Tim shrugged. "I heard her voice earlier. I think she's in the exam room with the other guy. He's in much worse shape than you. But I'm sure she'll be in to yell at you soon."

"I hope so." He leaned back on the pillows. He was so tired and achy, and the panic that had begun when he briefly thought Cherry was hurt had not yet dispersed.

🌲 🌲 🌲 🌲 🌲

Soon after Tim left with a promise to check on Matteo's shop, the door opened again. The island medical center was small, so it was no surprise that the nurse who ran it came in, drew the curtain around Matteo's bed, and wheeled in another patient. He couldn't see the person on the other side, but he could make a pretty good guess.

"Gary, I'm sorry this happened." That was Cherry's voice. Yep, he was right. It was Gary in the other bed, as if this whole thing couldn't be made worse. He was injured fighting for her, and yet she chose her ex-husband, the man who cheated on her for months.

"I still can't believe I walked in on that, Cherry. I thought we were getting back together. I told you, I've changed."

"We've both changed, Gary."

"But we still love each other, right? I mean, I know I messed up. I lost everything. You, our house, my job, my retirement, it's all gone. But if I can win you back, we can rebuild. We can make up for lost time. We can have a baby, or two, or three. I can stay at home and raise them, and we'll have the best life, the life you deserve. We can have it all again."

"Gary, you lost the house and all your money because you had to pay your criminal defense attorney, which had nothing to do with me. You were fired because you had relations with Megan in your classroom, and a child saw you. That's not my fault either. You got yourself on the sex offender registry and you lost your teaching license. All of that was preventable by not cheating on me. Don't try and make me feel bad for you." Cherry's tone sharpened, and Matteo was proud of her. He kept himself from shouting encouragement though. He didn't think she knew he was listening.

"But Cherry, we can build a life together again."

"So I can work and pay your bills? You get to stay home with the kids? I can take care of everything, because in your selfishness you lost it all? Gary, think about what you're asking of me."

"Cherry, I know you inside and out. I've known you since you were an awkward teenager who'd never even kissed a boy before. And I was just some dumb kid from Indiana trying to figure out how to escape my trashy family. We did everything together, we became who we are together. I realize I fucked up . . ."

"Language, Gary!"

"See, I did it again. I know you don't like cussing. I messed it all up, but I already explained everything to you and I thought you understood that I got scared. Our lives were too perfect, and I couldn't handle it. But I'm not scared anymore. We belong together. If you can forgive me for cheating on you with Megan, I can forgive you for cheating on me with that guy who attacked me."

"Gary, we're divorced. I did not cheat on you!"

"But we had been talking about getting back together, and when I came up here all ready to move in, you've got his head up your skirt? That is cheating, but it's okay. You wanted to punish me and make me jealous, and that's fine.

I mean, it's going to annoy me when I see him around town. I'm always going to want to punch him in the teeth, but I can get over it."

"Gary, what I was doing in my bedroom had nothing to do with you. You're the only one who thought we were getting back together. I already told you, you and I are through. I've moved on, for real. I discovered someone else out there for me, someone way better than you. Someone I trust. He might be rude and he might tease me too much, but he'd never ever hurt me the way you did. I've fallen in love with another man, and quite honestly, I need to thank you. If you hadn't cheated on me, I never would have realized how empty my life was, how loveless, and joyless."

"You can't be serious. You're only saying that because you're still angry with me. You know we're meant to be together. We have a history!"

"History is in the past. Listen, I only came here with you to make sure you're okay, and to tell you that I'm going to convince Matteo not to pursue assault charges against you."

"He hit me first! I'm going to be the one to file charges against him!"

"I didn't see that, Gary. Now, if you'll excuse me, I'm going to find out where they put him."

Matteo finally spoke up. "Here, Cherry. On the other side of the curtain."

She pulled it back, and he noticed how pink her lovely chipmunk cheeks had turned. "Did you hear all of that?"

"Only the part about you falling in love with another man. I'd very much like to meet him. He sounds sexy."

# Chapter Eighty-Five

Cherry took in the sight of Matteo sitting up in a hospital bed. He was still shirtless, and his right arm and chest were wrapped in gauze and medical tape. One eye had swollen shut, and his lip was bruised. But his smile was still broad, and, unlike Gary, he still had all his teeth. Gary's voice called out from behind her, "Hey, they can't put both of us in the same room! He attacked me!"

"Sorry, friend-o. This is the only room in the center. You're lucky you got a bed at all," Matteo said.

"Friend-o?" Cherry raised her eyebrows.

"You don't like it when I swear, so you'd really not like what I want to call him." Matteo held her gaze, and the blush rose in her cheeks again. She went to his bedside and gently touched his chest, running a finger along the bandages.

"How badly were you hurt?" There was blood still, she could see that.

"Pretty badly. They tell me I might be dying," he told her solemnly. "Do you feel sorry for me?"

"I don't! You assaulted me!" Gary shouted from the other bed. At some point, Cherry feared Gary might notice that he could get up on his own and would attack Matteo while he was one-armed and unable to fight back. She turned and pulled the curtain closed before sitting down on the edge of Matteo's bed.

"You aren't dying."

"Yes I am. Well, not because of this, more of an existential everybody dies type of thing. These wounds, that I got by—dare I say it—heroically defending your honor won't be what kills me. I did have some big splintery pieces of your stair railing go all the way through my arm and I have stitches on my chest that will leave a sexy, manly scar. I expect you'll kiss my wounds later? You'll probably have to bathe me too, in my convalescence." He caught the hand she had been using to trace his injuries and held it tightly to his chest. She felt the steady beat of his heart, and the moment when it suddenly sped up. Panic attack? No, not with that longing on his face.

He winced as he moved his injured arm, and put his right hand on her thigh. "I see you haven't gone back to your place to change yet. Rumor has it you flashed Tyrell, and he gave you his coat to save your dignity." He lifted her skirt to take a peek, and she slapped his hand away.

"I only wanted to see," he protested. "And maybe touch a little."

"Shush. Not here. You know better."

"Actually, I don't know better," he said. "I'm still learning what you'll let me do." He made a face that showed he obviously wasn't contrite. Then he winced again when he tried to move his hand off her leg.

"Matteo, I'm so sorry about all this," she began, but he cut her off.

"Don't apologize. None of this is your fault. Honestly, I was having a great time with you before he interrupted. I'm mostly annoyed that I'm stuck here, sharing a room with him, because I think he'll loudly object to the things I'm going to do to and for you."

"Matteo!"

"Hey, asshole, I can hear you!"

"Hey, buddy, I don't care," Matteo called, then grinned broadly. "See Cherry, I didn't even swear at him. I think you should give me a kiss for good behavior."

"Maybe I should." She leaned in to give him a gentle peck, mindful of his bruised lip. His uninjured arm pulled her closer, and he didn't seem to care so much about his lip as he kissed her back, pressing into her until she was afraid she wouldn't be able to stop if it kept going. She pulled away as much as she could, but his left hand tangled in her hair, keeping her head in place and forcing her to look him in the eyes.

"Oh, Cherry Blossom. I have waited so long to do that. You need to spring me from here so we can go finish what we started earlier."

"I think you're free to go, aren't you? Why are they keeping you? Put on your clothes and I'll take you home."

"I can't. My shirt is somewhere on your floor, remember? And so are my shoes. And your ex-husband's dignity, I think."

"I CAN STILL HEAR YOU!"

"I KNOW!" Matteo shouted back. "Will you take me back to my house and nurse me back to health? My arm is weak and injured, so I'm going to need you to be on top."

"Matteo!"

"I'm just giving suggestions for my care. You do want to help me get better, don't you?"

# Chapter Eighty-Six

While Cherry went back to her apartment to get Matteo's clothes and shoes, Johnny Mills came by to find out what had happened.

"I don't really know much, other than I was attacked," Matteo told him.

"You hit me first!" an outraged Gary shouted from the next bed.

"Come on, Matteo. I have to write up a report and I need to know the truth. We don't allow vigilante justice here as you're well aware." Johnny may have been Matteo's friend, but he also had a job to do—but that didn't mean Matteo had to make it easy for him. "Talk to me, Capen."

"You haven't read me my rights."

"You aren't under arrest! Look, the only witness to the start of the fight swears she didn't see who threw the first punch."

"Even if it was me, that guy was trespassing. He broke into Cherry's home uninvited and then got mad when he found her occupied with me."

"Occupied how?"

"Oh, that's why you're here. You came for the dirty details, which I'm happy to provide." Matteo raised his voice slightly. "You see, officer, she came onto me. She invited me over and practically jumped me in the doorway. We were lucky we made it to the bedroom. That's when I found out her previous lover was completely derelict in his duties, but fortunately, I possess a magic tongue and I . . ."

"THAT'S ENOUGH!" Gary staggered through the curtain. He looked worse than Matteo expected, though it made sense—he'd always been taught to aim for the face. "I'M GOING TO KILL YOU!"

"Officer, this man just threatened to murder me. I would like you to take him into custody immediately." Matteo leaned back against his pillows and smiled.

# Chapter Eighty-Seven

Cherry very carefully guided Matteo home. He leaned on her for support more than she expected, and she worried that his injuries were worse than she thought.

She tucked him into his bed. "Stay with me?" he asked, with hope in his voice as he grabbed her hand.

"I will, but first I'm going to walk Tristan and Beverly and give them some food. And I'm going to Antonio's to pick up a pizza. Pizza makes everything better, right?"

"But you will come back?"

"You are an extremely needy patient. Yes, I'll come back. I'm not going to eat an entire pizza myself."

He tightened his grip on her hand. He was rather strong for a convalescent. "Promise?" he asked again, and that's when she recognized the anxiety building up in him.

"I can let them run around in the backyard, if you like. I'll stay."

"No, take them. They've been cooped up all day. But don't be long."

She leashed the dogs and took them out the door. They were only going to get a short walk today, just into town and back. They'd be disappointed at not getting to frolic in the snow, but she was more concerned about Matteo.

As she passed the docks, she spotted a familiar face. Gary. He was still here. She paused, wondering if she should talk to him, but decided there was nothing more to say. Unfortunately, he had a different opinion.

"Cherry? Hey, Cherry!" he left his lonely bench to come running over to her. "When did you get dogs?"

"They're Matteo's," she replied.

"Oh." For a second, he looked so forlorn she almost pitied him. In their former life, spending the afternoon at the medical center while he was checked over for injuries would have brought them closer together. But that was all gone now, and she realized that, for the first time, she had no regrets.

"Well, Gary, I need to go. I have to pick up dinner."

"So you weren't looking for me, were you? Cherry . . . is this really it for us? Is this the last time we see each other?"

She frowned, considering. A brief flashback, to eighteen-year-old Gary with his crooked grin, wrenched her heart. So much of her life had been given over to this man, so much of her time, and energy, and love. And then he threw it all away.

"This is my home now, Gary. This is my life. You're no longer a part of it."

They stared wordlessly for a moment, then Gary let out a long sigh and broke eye contact. "I'm going to get on that ferry and go back to Indiana. And find a dentist and fix my teeth. And I'm going to mail you a Christmas card every year."

"Someday I might even open the envelope. Goodbye, Gary." He frowned and for a moment he looked like he wanted to say something else, or perhaps hug her one last time, but she tugged on the leashes and walked away without looking back.

# Chapter Eighty-Eight

She did come back. He wasn't certain that she would. A tiny doubt niggled the back of his brain, warning him that things were too good to be true, that he didn't deserve this, that no matter what she said at his medical center bedside, she didn't mean it. She couldn't possibly have any feelings for him. He loathed the doubt, the little mouse on its wheel going around and around, digging its claws in.

But she came back, and the wheel stopped turning for a moment. She stood there, in the doorway of his bedroom, looking uncertain. He felt the same way. What were they to each other now? What could they be?

"You can come in, you know," he finally said, and he hated how harsh his voice sounded, how sarcastic. She flushed, and he regretted it.

"I know," she replied, and something about the solemn way she pronounced those words pierced his heart. Life was changing today.

"What kind of pizza did you get?" he asked, around the lump in his throat.

"Barbecue chicken with extra onions. Your favorite."

"Yes, but are you sure you're going to want to kiss me with onion breath? Maybe we should make out for a while before we eat, just in case."

"You're incorrigible." She set the box down on his nightstand, after clearing off a stack of books. He caught her hand.

"No, I'm serious. I'm an injured man, and I need some loving far more than I need food. My arm hurts, distract me from the pain."

"Didn't the medical center give you pain meds?"

"Not really. They gave me a local injection when they did the stitches, but it's worn off, and I can't take pills. They mess with my head too much. All I can do is ice my injuries and manfully cry." He'd tried pain medication before, and it sent him into such an anxiety spiral he wouldn't even let himself take an aspirin anymore, for fear of how it might affect him.

"I'm sorry, Matteo. I'm sorry all this happened." She carefully joined him on the bed, curling herself against his uninjured side. The warmth of her body was comforting, and he slipped his arm around her. It felt so strange to be able to do something like this, to feel both so comfortable and so insecure at the same time.

"I'm not sorry," he replied. "In fact, I have only one regret about today."

"Oh? What's that?"

"I regret going up the skirt first. Tactical error. I've been waiting a long time to see your boobs, and your meddling ex interrupted us before I could."

"Matteo!" She sounded scandalized, but he suspected she was pretending.

"It's true. What am I supposed to do now, when I can only see out of one eye? Look twice as long, I guess."

"Stop." She sat up and stared intently into his eyes, and he was afraid. Had he taken it a step too far? "Matteo, you've been doing your fake flirting for so long, I don't know when I can take you seriously."

"Cherry, it's not fake, and hasn't been for a long time. Sure, last fall, I was just trying to annoy you, but not anymore. Now I'm saying how I feel."

"Oh." She blushed, that adorable blush that covered her whole face and then, so quickly he couldn't catch more than a glimpse, pulled up her shirt and flashed him. She looked even more embarrassed afterward. He kissed her, a swift little peck on the cheek.

"Thank you for that. I heard every word you said to Gary today. You really have moved on from him, haven't you? You're no longer so bitter."

"I wasn't bitter," she said.

"You were. You tried to hide it behind that wall of optimism, but I saw through you. You were hurt and angry and bitter, and I don't blame you. But I was afraid when he came back, somehow the history you two have would wash all of those negative feelings away. I get what it's like to cling to the past, to cling to safety. Starting over here like you did took a lot of bravery, but I didn't know if you'd be able to sustain it, not with the love of your life begging you to come back."

"He was my first love, not the love of my life. I think our connection was strong because we went through our early adulthood together. Once we got married, I settled into my life and never once reflected on who *I* was or what *I* needed. I'm always going to remember our time together with a bit of wistfulness, but I think since I've been here, I've changed. I've become stronger."

"Yeah? How much stronger? Stronger like you can wrestle me down and take advantage of me? I'm in a weakened state, so you probably can."

"I don't know. You held your own against Gary pretty well."

"Yes, but now I'm injured and entirely at your mercy. Oh well, I surrender."

"And I accept your surrender." Her smile lit up the room, and she kissed him.

# Chapter Eighty-Nine

*September 2015*

Dear Gary,

I moved again back in May, and as I was packing I threw a random assortment of junk into a box. That particular box has sat undisturbed and forgotten for months, until one day my boyfriend decided to use it as a stool to reach something on a high shelf, and his foot went through the lid and he fell. After I doctored his skinned knee, and we made love on the floor, I opened the damaged box, thinking everything in it could probably be thrown out. Most could, but not this. Not this notebook, full of letters I never sent.

You can't imagine the incredible rush of feelings seeing it again brought forth in me. For months, I poured my heart into these letters to you, letters I knew you would never read. It was cathartic, at the time.

Now I look back and I feel a deep sadness for the woman I was. I wish I could reach through these pages and comfort her. I wish I could whisper in her ear 'It gets better.'

Because it does get better. It gets so much better.

After I sat down and read these old letters, I cried, not for you, but for the me I used to be. Then I wiped my tears and took Penelope, Tristan, and Beverly for a walk. We went down by the lake, and I stared out over the cool water, and I felt nothing but contentment. When I started writing, I had just moved here, sad and lonely and afraid, still digesting the fact that the man I was married to had carried on a semi-public year-long adulterous affair. I was still reeling from the betrayal, and I thought I'd never be happy again.

But I am. And I'm happier than I ever thought possible.

I am in love Gary, and now I know how it feels to be loved in return, to be loved so truly, so deeply, that it resonates in my heart and soul. There is nothing complacent and tame in my relationship. There is nothing dull, nothing fragile. There is only great love and intense passion.

I remember one particular night in July, I was at the local bar, waiting for my boyfriend to arrive. I swear, I felt it when he walked in. I wasn't facing the door, but I knew he was there and turned just as he entered. There was a bachelorette party going on, so the bar was packed full of dozens of attractive young women, all with shining hair and perfect figures and alcohol-induced flirtatiousness. And do you know what Matteo did? He maneuvered his way through that crowd, eyes on me, and kissed my cheek. I teased him, saying that I couldn't believe he found me, when there were all these beautiful women in the bar. And he looked confused and said 'What women? You're the only person I saw.'

And that's how our relationship is. I'm the only one he sees. Sometimes, he watches me with an expression of wonder on his face because he cannot believe his luck. And sometimes, in our intimate moments, he looks deep into my eyes, and I see his fierce love burning for me. I hope he sees it reflected back.

I owe you a debt of gratitude. If it hadn't been for you, Gary, I would still be in Parsons, Ohio. I would be teaching the same classes at the same school. I would follow the same routines, day in and day out, year after year. And I would never know what I was missing out on. I would never have fled to this remarkable island. And I would never have found such joy.

I don't know what the future holds, but I am not afraid of it. Matteo and I may never marry. Maybe I'll be able to convince him to have children with me, maybe I won't. But whatever is coming for us, I will embrace it. Matteo once told me that life is what you make of it, and I'm making mine a thing of beauty.

Blissfully, ecstatically, no longer yours,

Cherry

*No Longer Yours*

**For a fun look at Cherry's future, check out**

# Cherry Christmas, Baby!
Available on Kindle

It's been nearly two years since Cherry Waites left her philandering ex-husband. Life is better than ever. Except for one little thing...

Cherry has a secret. An unplanned but desperately wanted and loved secret. But it's also a secret that might destroy her relationship.

Matteo can sense something is amiss with his girlfriend. She's been acting strange lately. He can only come up with one possible explanation: she's planning to break up with him. He'll do anything to change her mind.

When the two of them take a Christmas trip, secrets are spilled, tears are shed, and one of Whispering Pines most beloved couples have to make a decision that will change their lives forever.

**Now available:**

# If This Were a Love Story
## Whispering Pines Island Book 3

She's an alcoholic. He won't touch a drop. Will her struggle with sobriety uncork more trouble, or be the road to true love?

Amanda O'Connell tries to drown her problems with vodka. So when an attempt to lie her way out of a DWI goes wrong, her family intervenes and sets her up with a summer job on remote Whispering Pines Island. Painting the town red on her first night there, she meets a hunky, tattooed drummer... who promptly rejects her drunken advances.

Everett Ryan wishes he could trade his late father's ferryboat for a Coast Guard cutter. And while Amanda brings a breath of fresh air to his boring island life, he's not interested in anyone with the same addiction that killed his dad. But when she's sober, he can't resist their red-hot chemistry.

Determined to win over the man of her dreams, Amanda vows to break up with the bottle. But Everett fears even if she manages to stay on the wagon, their love won't survive the end of the tourist season.

Can Amanda and Everett conquer their demons and chart a course for a beautiful new relationship?

## About the Author

Sara LaFontain is usually in Tucson, but you can find her more easily at www.saralafontain.com or www.facebook.com/saralafontainauthor

## Read the entire Whispering Pines Island Series:

That Last Summer: A Love Story

Say the Words
A Short Story Sequel to That Last Summer

No Longer Yours

Cherry Christmas, Baby!
A Short Story Sequel to No Longer Yours

If This Were a Love Story

## Acknowledgments

No author writes in a vacuum. This book could not have been completed without support.

I love all of my beta readers and the advice they give. Thank you Ryan, Llyana, Tiffany, and Women's Fiction Writer's Association members Joanne Tailele and Amanda Swain

My editor Amanda Slaybaugh does a fantastic job though I suspect she's ready to beat me over the head with a how-to-use-commas-appropriately guide.

Leigh McDonald handles my cover designs and somehow manages to take my rather vague ideas and turn them into something beautiful.

None of this would be possible without the support and encouragement of my friends, especially Llyana, Lori, and Mary. And of course, my husband Ryan, who keeps me supplied with chocolate to fuel my writing sessions.

Thank you all!

CPSIA information can be obtained
at www.ICGtesting.com
Printed in the USA
BVHW031132311021
620381BV00021B/288